CALL AND RESPONSE

CALL
AND
RESPONSE

Stories

•

Gothataone Moeng

VIKING

VIKING
An imprint of Penguin Random House LLC
penguinrandomhouse.com

These stories were previously published in slightly different form in the
following: "Botalaote" as "Botalaote Hill" (*Oxford American*, 2017); "A Good
Girl" (*American Short Fiction*, 2021); "Small Wonders" (*One Story*, 2020);
"Bodies" (*A Public Space*, 2017); "Homing" (*Virginia Quarterly Review*, 2022);
"When Mrs. Kennekae Dreamt of Snakes" (*Ploughshares*, 2022).

LIBRARY OF CONGRESS CATALOGING-IN-PUBLICATION DATA

Names: Moeng, Gothataone, author.
Title: Call and response: stories / Gothataone Moeng.
Description: [New York]: Viking, [2023]
Identifiers: LCCN 2022016236 (print) | LCCN 2022016237 (ebook) |
ISBN 9780593490983 (hardcover) | ISBN 9780593490990 (ebook)
Subjects: LCGFT: Short stories.
Classification: LCC PR9408.B683 M63 2023 (print) |
LCC PR9408.B683 (ebook) | DDC 823/.92—dc23/eng/20220520
LC record available at https://lccn.loc.gov/2022016236
LC ebook record available at https://lccn.loc.gov/2022016237

Printed in the United States of America
1st Printing

Designed by Amanda Dewey

*This book is dedicated to the memory of my grandmother
Ntlale Refakae, and to my mother, Teko Botshameko Moeng*

In my world people plan for themselves and dictate their requirements to me. It is a world full of love, tenderness, happiness and laughter. From it I have developed a love and reverence for people. I foresee a day when I will steal the title of God, the unseen Being in the sky, and offer it to mankind. From then onwards, people, as they pass each other in the street each day, will turn to each other and say: "Good morning, God."

—BESSIE HEAD, "Why Do I Write?"

We complained to our parents, "We never go anywhere!" and they replied, astonished, "Where do you want to go, you've got all you need right here!"

—ANNIE ERNAUX, The Years, translated by Alison L. Strayer

CONTENTS

CALL AND RESPONSE

Botalaote

In the morning, woken by the two gunshots, I heard the rising flurry of ululations that followed and knew immediately that I would go to the wedding, no matter what my mother said or did. I understood that the two cows to be slaughtered for the feast had collapsed upon the swirling red dust, that an old man would be stalking toward them to plunge a knife into the quivering warmth of their necks, that soon the whole yard, only five compounds away, would be swarming with joyous people. My friends would be there, and I wanted to be there too.

In my cousin Tebogo's room, which I shared, I lay in my bed, listening to my mother's feet thumping up and down the passage, forcing the whole household awake. Doors slammed in her wake. In the kitchen, dishes clattered, hot cooking oil splattered, and the aroma of frying potatoes rose. In the bathroom, where my parents conversed, water streamed into the plastic tub my mother used for the patient's bath, her voice weary and my father's distorted by the toothpaste foaming his mouth. Water slapped at the sides of the tub as Mama lugged it into the patient's room—formerly mine—on the other side of the wall I was tapping my foot against. As I did every morning, I imagined I could smell the Dettol disinfectant Mama eddied into the water with her fingers; I imagined the steam fogging up the mirror I had bought for myself and stuck up on the wall, warping my books and posters, my photos and my magazines.

I did not want to think about my mother's hands bathing the patient—her sister, my aunt—so I thought about the wedding. I knew that the men would be draining the cows of their gushing blood, peeling off the skins to reveal the fatty meat underneath, slicing the bellies open and offering up enamel bowls to receive the tumble of glistening intestines. I knew that the men would be kicking away the intrepid dogs slinking toward the meat and at the same time playfully jostling with the women about which cuts would go to the men for the seswaa and which to the women for the beef stew. I knew that a congregation of aproned women would already be working at the fire at the back of the yard, boiling beetroots and potatoes, peeling and slicing and cubing cabbages and carrots for the salads for the coming crowds. I knew that the women would soon break into their songs, celebratory and caustic—*The cakes are delicious, but marriage is difficult; we are leaving, you stay and see for yourself*—and that they would dance and ululate and whirl around the bride—*Come out, come out, come and see, this child is as beautiful as a Coloured*—as she walked on the carpet, which had been laid out so her white dress would not touch the red dust of the yard. I knew that almost all the people in our ward, Botalaote, would be at the wedding, everybody except the very old, the new mothers, the newly grieving, and the sick.

It was three weeks since Tebogo and I had finished our form two exams and a month since the patient had been brought home from the hospital. After completing my exams in October, I dreamt of doing things, of going away while my mother and father were at work, of visiting my friends in their wards and wasting the luxury of the day with our talks about boys and such. But since the patient had arrived, it seemed my mother did not even want me to leave the house.

In my and Tebogo's room, I stayed in bed listening to my father complain about how much time my mother was taking, about *Mma-Boikanyo, the day has begun,* about *Mma-Boikanyo, what will people say?,* about *Mma-Boikanyo, people will think we are scared of work.* Mama was a big woman, with a lot of energy and a miraculous capacity to complete half of her daily chores before the rest of the household awoke. Before the patient came into our house, when Mama woke Tebogo and me up at five thirty a.m.—talking her old stories about a woman needing to be up before the sun—she would already have a pot of soft porridge and a kettle of Five Roses on the stove. On weekends, she left early for funerals, and often by the time Tebogo and I awoke she would be back, her shoes kicked off, sighing over her tea, poring over the funeral program, an addition to the pile she kept in her bedroom. Before, she was just like the other mothers. She shouted orders and called instructions for chores. But since the patient had been brought to stay with us, Mama was different. She still rose early, but sometimes she would put on a pot of water and forget to switch the stove on. Sometimes she forgot the name of the woman she had hired to take care of the patient during weekdays. Sometimes she called home from the furniture shop she worked for and forgot why she had called, or called home when really she wanted to call the district council office to talk to my father. On weekends, when she had to go for a funeral or a wedding, she came into our room, apologetic and full of bribery. I knew she would soon come.

Mama knocked and opened the door.

"Banyana," she called softly. Tebogo started snoring, the sound seesawing, seesawing, and I wanted to laugh. I kept my face to the wall and my eyes closed.

"Girls," Mama said again, her voice invading the room. "Are you awake?"

My bed sunk under her weight as she sat down.

"Boikanyo," she called my name. I turned around. I opened my eyes. I yawned and stretched my body.

"Dumelang," I greeted her. Mama looked all fancy in the dress made from the blue German-print fabric that the married women had chosen as their uniform for the wedding, but her hair was still covered by the brown stockings she wore to protect it overnight. The skin on her forehead was raised and pulled back, so I knew her cornrows were tight and still painful. She reached her hand out to touch my shoulder.

"I am up," I said before she could touch me, and sat up on the bed.

"I made you some fresh chips," she said.

I folded my arms and leaned against the headboard, shivering as its coldness startled the small of my back.

"I put a bit of brown vinegar on them," she said. "Just the way you like. And some chilies."

My mouth watered at the thought of the chips, cut in thick chunks, heaped in a bowl, vinegar-drizzled, speckled with red chili flakes.

"Mma-Boikanyo," Papa called from outside the door, "please, woman."

My mother turned her head to the door. "Everybody knows we have a patient, Rraagwe-Boikanyo." She turned back and smiled at me.

"Ao Mama mma," I said, "I also want to go to the wedding."

"I will come back early," she said. "Then you can go."

She had said this to me before, on a day I wanted to get my hair braided. I considered bringing that up, but, though Mama had changed, I was not yet sure of how much back talk she would tolerate without an instinctive back-of-the-hand slap, without calling in the reinforcement of my father. I had never minded obeying my mother, doing everything she wanted—sweeping the yard, cleaning the house, making tea, watering the peach and mango trees, doing my own laundry, going to the store for fatcakes and paraffin and meat—but since the patient had come, all the buying of forgotten necessities went to Tebogo. It was her pocket now that jingled with change from trips to the shops. She returned popping gum, her pockets full of toffees, and, always, she would toss just one toffee and one piece of chewing gum my way.

"Okay," I said. "But Tebogo can't go either."

"It is you your aunt needs," Mama said. "Now, come on, get up, what kind of woman are you if the sun finds you in bed?"

I got up and watched Mama and Papa leave. Mama switched the stockings on her hair for a headscarf. An apron hid the pleats in the skirt of her dress. Under her arm she carried the pale yellow enamel bowl that she used at every such function; she had her initials—DB—written on the bottom in brown paint. My father, in his dark green overalls and a wide-brimmed khaki hat, looked different than when he went to work. He looked like he was going to dig a ditch.

I went into the kitchen. I uncovered the bowl of chips on the table. I took one and bit into it. The potato was only half-cooked, so I spat it out.

OUTSIDE, the sky was a vast blue dome, steadfast and distant, enshrouding the whole ward, the whole village. Tendrils of white clouds trailed on the sky's surface. The air was already dry, so I knew it was going to be another hot day. From Mma-Tumo's yard several compounds away, where the wedding was being held, the intermittent sounds of car hooters and ululations taunted me. Standing on my tiptoes on our veranda, I could see the green top of the tent where the bridal party would sit to be ogled by everyone. I wanted to see the multicolored balloons that I knew would be strung all around the entrance.

I went to my old room, the patient's room, and cracked open the door. It was November, yet she lay on her mattress on the floor—asleep?—under a sheet and a blanket. Above the blanket, her head poked out. What used to be a full head of hair was now just dust-brown and reddish fibers. She was on her side, facing the wall. Sometimes we lay face-to-face, I realized, with only the wall coming between us. I shut the door and went into the bathroom.

When I walked back into our bedroom from the shower, Tebogo kicked the cover off her body. She stretched and yawned loudly, wide-opening her mouth. I applied lotion to my body in silence and put on my favorite yellow sundress with the spaghetti straps.

"What are you getting dressed up for?" Tebogo asked.

"Mama said you have to stay home," I told her, "to help with the patient."

"You are lying," Tebogo said. "She didn't."

"Yes, she did."

"I wasn't sleeping, ngwanyana, I heard her."

"You have to help me," I said. "Papa said."

"She is your aunt, not mine."

Tebogo was the only daughter of my father's only sister. When her mother found a job in Mahalapye, Tebogo stayed in Serowe with us because her mother lived in a one-room house in a yard full of other one-room houses. We were both fifteen and had only a two-week age difference. I was the older. When we were younger, our mothers would dress us in the same sets of clothes, differing only in color, and in primary school we told everyone that we were twins. We looked too different, though—I was all dark, all skinny, all gangly. She was shades lighter than me, but not light-light, not yellow-light. She was on the girls' football team and had huge muscles in her legs. Whenever she came from football practice she would eat a pile of phaletshe—whether there was beef stew or morogo or not.

"Mama made me some chips," I said. "You can't eat them unless you help me."

"In my own uncle's house?" she said. "You won't give me food in my uncle's house?"

"Mama made them for me."

We raced to the kitchen. I got there first and held the bowl of chips high above my head.

"Okay," she said. "Fine. I will help."

We put the chips back into the pot, which was full of oil, and switched the stove back on. Then we sat at the kitchen table eating the chips with slices of bread, washing them down with cups of tea. Tebogo speculated about what the bridal party was wearing and in the same breath said they were probably not as well dressed as the one she had seen at a wedding in Mahalapye. The previous year, her mother had taken her off Mama's hands for two weeks during the second-term break. Since then, nothing in Serowe was ever as good as anything in Mahalapye. The town was only two hours away, but Tebogo acted as if she had been all the way to Gaborone, or even to Johannesburg. She explained everything on the television and tried to convince me that she had learned new dances up there.

"Ao mma," I said. "Still talking about that wedding?"

"I am telling you," she said. "That bride was beautiful, and the bridesmaids, wena, heish, and the men. I am telling you. Even you, you would say so if you had been there."

The wedding sounds followed us into the kitchen: Brenda Fassie songs and, just before noon, a cacophony of car hooters and a swelling of ululations.

"They must be arriving from the church," Tebogo said. We ran outside, she still in the shorts and T-shirt she wore to bed. Cars inched past our yard, balloons blooming all over their windscreens and their side mirrors. Tebogo ran out through the gate, alongside the cars, without even bathing first or anything.

"You smell!" I yelled at her. My stomach clenched and my chest ached with the frustration of not being there. I sat on the veranda, shouting greetings at all the people who walked past our yard.

I went in to check on the patient. She seemed asleep. My Boom Shaka and Arthur Mafokate posters were still on the wall. I removed a plastic bag with two rolls of toilet paper in it from the magazines I kept stacked by my wardrobe. I wrinkled my nose against the smells of the room: the Dettol disinfectant, the damp towels, the stale urine, the adult diapers. A half-finished bowl of soft porridge and milk sat on a side table far from her, jostling for space against the giant bottle of Dettol and a roll of cotton wool. Her breaths were loud and ragged, taking so much effort that the blankets rose and fell with each one. Sometimes the breaths ended in moans. Her cheeks were so sunken it looked like she was perpetually sucking at a mint hidden in her mouth. Sometimes when I went into the room, she tried to talk to me. I could not look at her then. Her speech, interrupted by coughing, trailed wisp-thin and low, required me to lean in, to look at her disgraced and hideous face. It made me angry, that she required this of me, as if she were still my aunt Lydia.

Before she was the patient, my aunt Lydia never looked like this, pitiful and vulnerable as though she were a newly hatched chicken. Before, she had her own car. A Corolla that she took on drives from

Orapa, where she lived, to Pilikwe to see her and Mama's parents, and then, always, to Serowe to come see Mama. Whenever she came to visit, she would share my room and my bed. At night, I fell asleep to her stories about her and Mama's life when they were younger, way before every household had a landline, about the boys who made bird sounds behind the house as a signal to the girls to come outside. Mama spent a lot of time in the room with us, for Lydia was good with hair. She would often plait Mama's hair first, then mine and Tebogo's. Lydia sat on my bed, and Mama sat on the floor between her legs. They fought over the mirror the way they must have done when they were younger. When Lydia did my hair, she would turn me around so I could face her.

"Look at you," she would say. "You are so beautiful, you are going to give these boys some trouble."

"Lydia, what are you saying to my child?" Mama would say.

"But you know boys are trouble, right?" my aunt Lydia would concede. "You should take care of yourself."

Mama and Lydia giggled at the latter's stories of life in Orapa, a mining town, stories about her friends, all of whom she only called by the cars they drove—Audi, Jetta, Benz, Hyundai, Venture. When Aunt Lydia was at our home, Mama became somebody else— somebody softened into girlishness, who called her sister "girl," whose lips and teeth darkened from sipping red wine, who gently teased Papa into shyness by greeting him when he came into the room with "Hello, my husband, hello, my man, hello, sweetheart." I kept still during those times, for I felt I was witnessing something I wasn't supposed to.

Aunt Lydia made Tebogo and me dance for them. My face grew hot because of their laughter, in spite of their cheers, but I would force myself to finish because then my aunt would take us in her arms and say, "You two will go far! Gaborone! Johannesburg! New York!"

OUTSIDE, I stood on the veranda, but I still could not see anything. I went up to the gate, leaned my body against it. Two boys came up the road talking loudly. When they saw me, they lowered their voices and turned and walked up to me. I recognized one of them— the one with the sides of his hair completely shaved off. He was fat, with round cheeks that made him look twelve and like he was on the brink of laughter. His friend was taller, wearing blue jeans and a T-shirt with the sleeves cut off.

"Eita," the boy I recognized said to me. I assumed the angry and bored look I reserved for boys. I continued looking in the direction of the wedding, as if they had not spoken to me.

"Aah, come on, baby," the tall boy said. "Come on, talk to us." He was just as tall as I. His face was pockmarked from pimple scars. His bright red Converse All Star shoes matched his hat, as if he had come straight from a kwaito music video.

"Baby?" I said.

"Okay, then, woman," he said, while his fat friend giggled. "What's your name, woman?"

"What's your name?" I asked.

"Sixteen," he said.

"What kind of name is that?"

"Tell her your real name," his friend said and giggled again, then looked at me. "Sixteen is his football name."

"Okay, fine," he said. "My name is Perseverance."

I considered using one of the names I kept in rotation for moments like these, simple common names that every other girl had—

Neo, Mpho, Sethunya. Sometimes I used Tebogo, but I thought it was sweet that he'd told me the name that embarrassed him. I told him my real name.

"So, where can one see you, Boikanyo?" he asked.

I hated when boys talked like this to us girls, using a voice that was not really their own, a language they still felt uncomfortable in. But I liked the way he rubbed his hands together, as if he were nervous to be talking to me. I liked his plum-dark lips.

"What do you mean?" I asked. I was embarrassed by all the people walking past, seeing me talk to the boys.

"If I want to see you, where could I see you?"

"I don't know." I shrugged. "I am always home."

He cocked his head to look past me at the house.

"I can come here and go knock on the door and ask for you?"

"No," I scoffed. Papa had already cautioned Tebogo and me against, as he called it, laughing with boys in corners. A heavily pregnant lady walked past, slow and lumbering, and I could feel my face growing hot at her lack of shame, showing that she had done it.

In the distance, I saw Tebogo walking back home. When she reached us, she opened the gate and closed it against the boys and stood beside me. She wrinkled her nose and said, "What's going on here?"

Sixteen's friend said, "Eita."

Tebogo looked at him and said, "Aren't you Mma-Tsiako's grandson? How is your grandmother?"

"Ao, sisi," the boy said and giggled. "Come on, we are just talking."

"You are needed in the house," Tebogo said to me. "Come." She grabbed my arm and pulled me behind her. I knew that she thought she was rescuing me from the boys, but I did not want to be rescued.

"Boikanyo," Sixteen called. "What do you say, BK?"

When we got into the house, we collapsed onto the sofa, giggling, careful not to wrinkle the cloths Mama used to cover the seats.

"I am going to tell my uncle," Tebogo said, "that I woke up and found you kissing a boy right here inside his house." I threw a cushion at her.

"'So, what do you say, BK?'" she said, imitating Sixteen.

"Voetsek," I said. "Tell me about the wedding."

"That bride, she is so beautiful, shem, but her hair."

"What's wrong with her hair?"

"It's just a pushback!" she said. "Can you believe it? Shame, so plain. I can't believe they think that hair is suitable."

I knew where the conversation was going, so I tried to avoid it. "What about the bridesmaids—what are they wearing?"

"Oh, they are wearing these nice bright-orange two-pieces, shem, the girls are all too dark for that color. Anyway," she said, getting up. "I am going to shower so I can go back."

"You just said the bride is plain and the bridesmaids' dresses . . ."

"It's still fun. I saw Peo and Mpho." My friends from school. I was sure that Sixteen and his friend had also been going to the wedding.

"Okay," I said. "I am going too."

"What about . . ." She nodded in the direction of the patient's room.

"But me, I also want to eat my youth," I said, and she bent over to laugh. We had started this thing where we talked about our age as if it were a tactile thing outside of us, a thing not to be enjoyed at leisure, a thing to be gobbled up.

"Okay," she said. "But I don't want to hear my name if you get into trouble."

While she finished dressing up, I went into the patient's room. She had turned over. I helped her sit up in bed, propping pillows between her back and the wall. I avoided her eyes. I held the bowl of milk and porridge up to her lips and supported the back of her head. I helped her lie back down.

After, I washed my face, and Tebogo and I went into Mama's bedroom, whispering as if she could sneak in and catch us red-handed. We darkened our eyebrows with eyebrow pencils. We drew a mole above our lips, the only identical feature on both our faces.

MMA-TUMO'S YARD, where the wedding was held, was like the other yards in our ward. Most had chain-link fences, sometimes with a hedge or tharesetala planted along the fence. Most had a main house in the center of the yard, flanked by smaller houses, sometimes an earthen hut, sometimes a one-room brick house or a two-and-a-half.

Mma-Tumo's had an earthen hut that she usually used as an outside kitchen. It had been improved before the wedding, a new layer of soil applied and decorative patterns drawn on the wall in different-colored clay. A new addition to the hut was the lapa, where the bride and groom would be given instructions for their new lives. The tent had been set up opposite the main house such that, from the gate, it obscured the hut. When you entered from the main gate, the tent was the matter of pride one saw first.

Tebogo and I went straight to the tent. The balloons on the entrance were half-deflated. Inside, a group of kids fought over the ones that had floated to the ground. The fancy chairs behind the top-table were unoccupied; the bridal party had gone to change into their second outfits. Bottles of wine littered the top-table and all the tables inside the tent. Ceramic plates retained leftover samp and cabbage and meat-stripped bones. The tent itself was half-empty. Most people had gone to watch a choir performing outside.

"Let me go outside," Tebogo said, "and see if I can see Auntie. If I can't, I will come get you."

I went to sit at a table at the very back of the tent. I looked around for Mama, for Papa, for Sixteen, for any of my friends. I hoped dessert would still be coming.

I wondered if the patient could hear the music from the wedding. The first two weeks the patient was home from the hospital, Mama took time off from work. During the day, she carried steaming bowls of bean soup and soft porridge back and forth between the kitchen and the patient's room. Women from the neighborhood trooped in and sat in the sitting room, talking in loud voices over tea Tebogo and I made: "Mma, wena, did you hear about Mma-Tsiako's daughter?"

"Owai, as for my uncle, Mma-Boikanyo, there is no person there either. We are just counting the days."

"I can't believe that I never heard that Rra-Etsile's little niece is gone."

"Oh, yes, yes, she is resting. Poor girl, she was in so much pain."

Inevitably Mama would have to bring out the pile of funeral programs she kept in a nightstand drawer and fish out the one that a visitor could not place. The women would look through all the other programs, sighing and clucking as their tea cooled on the coffee table. Then they would go into the patient's room, their voices low and reverent, coaxing her to tell them how she was feeling. I heard her—coughing, coughing. Her voice, hoarse and exhausted, murmured alongside and weaved with Mama's sometimes. Then her low laughter, different and new, was interrupted by coughs and my mother's gentle cajoling. When the women left the room, their voices returned to their normal loudness, and they called out to Tebogo and me to offer them a drop of water to prepare for the heat they would be walking out into.

Tebogo did not return to get me, so I walked around, keeping a wary eye out for Mama, Papa, or any of their friends. I saw Peo and Neo among the group watching the choir and walked up to them. They swatted at me playfully.

"Shee, kante, where have you been?" Peo asked.

"Just home," I said. "Protecting my complexion."

"Owai, what complexion?" They laughed. "You are still as black as coal."

"You are still as black as the tar on the road to Gaborone."

"You are still as black as those pots full of seswaa right now."

"You will still be black at senior school next year."

Their jokes stung, but were better than how they would mock me if they knew I had been wiping crusts from my aunt's eyes. I saw my father in the crowd of people dancing. He saw me midsong, smiled, and raised his hand to wave at me. Then I could tell he remembered I was supposed to be home, and he frowned, looking around.

"Sharp, I will see you," I said to Peo and Neo and walked away into the tent again. As I sat down, a surge of ululations started up. People who had been sitting under the shade of trees got up and walked forward, so I knew that the bridal party had changed and that they would be dancing back to the tent. I stood against the tent, right by the entrance, on the left flap where I would be able to see them when they came in. A photographer ran in, climbing on tables and chairs. The bride, her white veil gone, kept her face down. Her hair *was* in a pushback. She was like a magnet; everybody hurtled toward her and her bridal party but did not get too close, held off by her poise, her small and demure movements. She and her groom walked up to the top-table and sat down, flanked by their bridesmaids and groomsmen. The women had changed into blue German-print dresses with white embroidery around the sleeves. The men's shirts matched the women's dresses, but their embroidery was on the collars. Some of them, from the top-table, smiled and waved at faces they recognized. We all stared at the spectacle of their beauty and filled ourselves with the pleasure we got from it.

Just then Mama came into the tent. I wondered if Papa had told her about seeing me. I tried to move away, to flatten myself into the fabric of the tent, afraid to breathe. But she did not see me. She concentrated on her movements. She kept her arms pressed against her breasts in the way that all the older women did before dancing, then she moved her shoulders up and down, she moved her upper body side to side. She first bent her right knee, then straightened and bent her left. She moved the excess of her body, slowly, proudly, seemingly uncaring that her headscarf had slipped off her head to reveal her cornrows. She danced, her eyes closed, a small, private smile on her face that I felt uncomfortable witnessing. Somebody chanted, "Dudu! Dudu! Dudu!" and only after some moments did I realize that it was my mother's name that the voice was calling. Another shouted, "Does this child not have parents?" and a swelling of ululations answered him. I wasn't sure if the person meant the bride or my mother.

TEBOGO HAD FOUND a bowl of trifle for me. Sixteen and his giggling friend had discovered my spot in the tent and now sat across from me at a table. The scent of ginger beer and wine filled the tent.

"Your beauty," Sixteen said, "it fills me up."

I looked around for any adults I knew. It was getting dark, and most people had gone to witness the bride's final instructions for marriage. Both Sixteen and his friend got up when I did, but only he followed me out of the tent. Sixteen walked behind me until we were away from the wedding, then he ran up, grabbed my hand, and forced me to stop.

"What are you doing?" I asked him.

"At least give me your phone number," he said.

"Okay," I said. "You can only call during the day, when my parents are at work."

"Sure, sure," he said.

He held his arms open and I moved into them, into his hug that smelled of sweat and grease from all the meat he had eaten.

"Sure, baby," he said. "I will call you." He walked me to the gate. All the way, I was nervous that my parents would emerge from the darkness behind me.

SUNDAY MORNING, I woke up thinking of Sixteen. Then I wondered when my mother would discover that I had been at the wedding. I had gone in to see the patient as soon as I came back. She had shrugged the blankets off herself, and I had sat her up so she could slurp the porridge and drink the water I gave her. I had wet a washing rag in warm water and wiped her face, and laid her down so she could sleep. Mama had not even come to check in on me when she returned. Still, I felt compelled to make amends, and went into the kitchen to start on the soft porridge.

The fridge was crowded with bowls and plates with various cuts of meat that my parents had received at the wedding. A piece of liver in a bowl, some seswaa for my mother and mokoto for my father. Mama would be mad if I ate any of it without permission, but I wanted a taste.

As I was reaching into the bowl with seswaa, I heard a man's voice say very loudly, "May the Lord's Peace be with you!" I slammed the fridge shut and looked around.

"Peace be with you," the voice said again, coming from outside.

A man in a white robe stood in the yard. Beyond him, outside the gate, a group of people from my mother's church disembarked from a van. They came into the yard loud and boisterous, laughing among themselves.

"Mama!" I shouted.

The older women wore navy-blue skirts, long-sleeved white shirts, and blue capes over the shirts. The younger women and men wore white robes, with navy-blue sashes with the words FULL GOSPEL OF CHRIST thrown diagonally across their chests. All the women wore white starched hats perched atop their heads, because their push-backs and braids and cornrows would not allow the hats to be pulled completely down.

"Your people are here, Mama!" I shouted again.

The congregation stopped and rearranged themselves into a choir outside the house, the women in front, the men at the back. The men lowered their heads to produce the bass to support the women's voices. They clapped their hands and swayed in unison, and in a two-by-two procession walked into the house, their robes swishing back and forth.

Mama came out of the patient's room tying her headscarf and draping a shawl across her shoulders. She met them in the passage and stood in front of the room, matching her clapping hands to theirs and taking their song up. Papa, Tebogo, and I joined the procession at the end and into the patient's room, clapping and singing as well:

We are visitors in this world
We have a home up in heaven
This earth is not for us, friends
This world is not for us
We have a home up in heaven

The congregation arranged themselves around the mattress. Mama pulled the patient up so she sat against the pillows. She kept her face, thin and unrecognizable, down. My face grew hot in shame. The people all knelt down where they were and started praying. I knelt, my feet touching the cold of the door frame, sweat collecting in my armpits. I opened my eyes and looked at the patient. Her eyes were open, too, wide and lively against the tautness of her face. They were the same eyes of my aunt Lydia who had once pulled up her shirt to show me the large birthmark on her stomach—darker than her skin, shapeless like a stain. She looked at me, and I looked at her, and as the people around us prayed for her recovery, she smiled at me.

SIXTEEN called the house from a public phone the following Monday. We arranged to meet at the foot of the Botalaote hill, behind my old primary school. The hill separated the ward from the school and the cemetery. Even as primary school girls, my friends and I believed the hill sheltered us from the omniscience of our parents' eyes. On the school side, we could frolic as much and as roughly as we wanted and then, climbing back up and down to our homes, we assumed the obedient faces our parents needed.

Sixteen waited for me behind the school, looking through its fence at a group of boys playing football on the dusty pitch. I walked down slowly toward him, studying his body from behind—his legs, his arms, the contours of his chiskopped head, his neck melding into his back. I walked closer, looking at the way his butt protruded slightly in his tracksuit pants. I thought about his body beneath his clothes—his shoulders and chest, his thighs and knees, the only parts I could bear to think about. He turned around and smiled at me, and I stopped, a few feet away from him.

"Eita," he said.

"Eita," I said. I did not know where to look.

"Who is winning?" I asked, pointing to the shouting kids in the schoolyard.

"I don't know," he said, and I saw that he too was nervous.

"Come on," he said as he reached out his arm. We climbed up, veering off the path beaten into the hill. He stopped under a tree whose roots had split a rock open. He pointed to the right of the tree.

"What's this?" I asked.

"I found this place," he said. "I like it."

A rock jutted forward that one could climb upon and look beyond the school at the cemetery, beyond that to the tall Water Affairs building in the distance, to the small combis carrying people to the mall or perhaps far beyond that. Under the jutting rock was a kind of cave, cool and dark, dank with the leaves littering its floor. We crawled in and the faint shouts of the football-playing kids sounded a world away.

"So," he said. "I have been thinking about you a lot."

"Really?" I asked.

"Yes," he said. "What about you?"

"What about me?"

"I mean, have you been thinking about me?"

"Maybe."

He laughed.

"What have you been thinking about me?" I asked.

"You know, just that I, heish, I am feeling you."

The heat from my pleasure suffused my face and my neck. My heart beat loudly in my ears as he crawled over to sit in front of me.

"I mean, I love you," he said in English. I lowered my face.

"What about you?" he asked.

"Me too. I love you," I responded in Setswana, taking refuge in the lack of distinction between the words "like" and "love."

"Okay, come here." He sat me on his lap. He kissed my lips and I kissed him back, teasing his lips open with my tongue. I touched the back of his head. I slipped my hands down the back of his T-shirt. His back was sticky with sweat. That pleased me, as did his heart beating against my chest. We stopped kissing and just looked each other in the face, smiling like fools.

"So, I am your boyfriend?" he asked.

I nodded.

"No other boys, right?" he said. "I am privatizing."

TEBOGO said I was stupid for going out with Sixteen. A boy just a year older than me, a student, what good would he be to me, she asked, other than lending me pencils and pens?

"You don't even have a boyfriend," I said. We were in our room. She was lying on her bed, stretching her legs and then bending them so her knees touched her chin.

"I want a man with a car," she said. "He can drive me to school, drive me to the mall, give me money."

"An old man," I said. "Old leather." There was a heap of dirty clothes on the floor beside her bed. Her football boots, caked with mud, sat upended by the door.

"He can take me to hotels," she said. "So I can really, really eat my youth. Take me to a Miscellaneous game. Up the Reds! Up the Reds!" She whistled.

"I don't care," I said. "I don't want your games."

I knew that this—love and boys and relationships—was my own private experience, something I had over her, something for which she needed my knowledge.

"So, what have you two done, anyway?" she asked.

"I shouldn't tell you," I said. "Things grown-ups do."

"Please," she said. "You are a child."

"Oh, I am a child?" I said. "A child who was kissing her man yesterday."

I flopped my body back onto the bed and sighed luxuriously to show her that this was a feeling that she could not understand, something much more than could ever be put into words.

"I miss him," I said. "I miss my man." A pillow thudded into my face from Tebogo's direction.

OVER THE NEXT WEEKS, I snuck away from home. Again and again. I left after lunch and ran back just before my parents drove in from work. Sixteen and I, we returned to our little enclave, a way for us to be out of sight. Sometimes we climbed up and dangled our legs down the overhanging rock. Looking out at the cemetery, I would think, sometimes with envy, sometimes with pity, about how the lives of the dead would never again change. In the quiet of the cave, we entered a new world where Sixteen would soften his voice, call me "baby," swallowing mouthfuls of saliva, kissing my face and my neck, unbuttoning my shorts, pushing his always cold hands under my T-shirt to cup my breasts. He would take off his T-shirt and lay it on the ground for me to lie upon, and still the rocks would protrude through the shirt and poke into my back and my shoulder blades. I would adopt a baby voice, whiny and childish, and say, "No, no, I am not ready." I was afraid of what would come from his touching me like that, and I thought it was what I was supposed to do—to play coy, withhold myself from him.

On the afternoon that we made love for the first time, I returned home, leaves mashed into the back of my head, so ground into my cornrows that I was still removing flecks of them on the Sunday I undid my hair to plait it again. I was convinced that the oily smell of condoms had seeped into my skin. I thought my mother would know as soon as she came close to me, so I stayed in bed all evening with a phantom headache. But even when I had arrived home, I found Tebogo sitting up on her bed reading and she did not say anything. She looked up at me when I walked in the door and went right back to *The Collector of Treasures*. I knew now that one could feel different and new and still appear ordinary to the world.

There were some close calls, days when I miscalculated the time and arrived just after Mama or Papa got home. Then I would go to our neighbor and pretend that my mother had sent me to borrow salt or a cup of sugar, and bring it into the kitchen. I hardly ever went in to see the patient anymore.

One day, I opened the door and there my mother was, watching a soapie.

"Dumelang," I said.

"Boikanyo." She did not return my greeting. "Where have you been?"

"I wanted to borrow a book from Peo."

"Where is it?" she asked.

"Mma?"

"Where is the book you went to borrow?"

"She wasn't there," I said.

I saw her getting ready to yell at me, but at that moment the patient began a coughing spell. Mama tried to wait it out, but eventually she got up to attend to her sister.

In our room, Tebogo was sprawled on her bed; clearly, she had been listening. I thought she expected me to laugh about getting caught. I knew she herself had been sneaking out some days to go swimming at the Serowe Hotel pool. I knew she enjoyed the thrill of having this other life the adults knew nothing about. But I couldn't laugh about it, even though it seemed I had escaped my mother's anger. I sat on my bed. I bent down to untie the laces of my takkies and pushed them off.

"She asks for you sometimes," Tebogo said. "Lydia. When you are not here. Sometimes she asks to see you."

"I am very busy," I said.

"Hee, busy girl," she said. "Busy doing what?"

"Just leave me alone," I said. "Pretend I am not in your room."

"My room? This is your mother's house," she said. Then, when I did not respond, "You are so stupid."

"I don't want to see her, okay?" I said. "I don't."

"Okay, okay," Tebogo said.

THE LAST WEEK of December I ran home as usual before four thirty p.m. My father's van was parked outside the gate. A group of women sat out on the veranda, all wearing headscarves. Old men sat under the mulberry tree in the yard, their hats perched on their knees.

Their gray heads looked young and naked without their hats. I knew immediately. I went to find my mother.

In the sitting room, Tebogo was on the couch beside my father. My mother sat on the floor where the coffee table should have been, her legs outstretched, her shoulders heaving silently. Her head was bowed, her fingers splayed over her face, as if it held something private and unknowable. I went to her and laid my head in her lap and cried loud, hot tears. After a while I became aware of her fingers plucking leaves from my hair. Around us, I could hear women removing the sitting room curtains, could feel the evening light entering the room. I knew they would be applying ash to the windows, an announcement to the world that we were a household in mourning.

MANY YEARS LATER, I lived in Gaborone, only four hours away from Scrowe. I was childless and unmarried, shared my house and my life with a man, a photojournalist, a few years younger than me. I had traveled to Johannesburg, Berlin, New York, Kasane, Nairobi, Lagos, Bamako, Bahia, and many other places, sometimes for my work as a lawyer, sometimes for my own pleasure and curiosity. In Gaborone, my partner and I didn't go out much, wary of the younger people who had taken over all the best night-out spots, even the Sunday jazz bars. Instead, we threw small parties at our house. I cooked the simple food of my childhood—marakana that we ate soaked in milk or with goat stew, phane fried in just onions and tomatoes that we ate with bogobe jwa ting. I bought flowers and lit the fragrant candles that we kept in case of load-shedding: the house smelled of French vanilla and lavender and cinnamon spice. Our friends, lawyers and journalists, writers and professors, suffered the drive to Gaborone North. They brought wines and whiskeys bought during weekend trips to South Africa, for in Gaborone the cost of alcohol had become prohibitive. They exclaimed over the additions to our bookshelves and the fine art—photographs, paintings, sculptures—we were collecting. They filled the house with laughter. We drank and ate and sat around talking, trying to glean meaning from the art, the politics, the scandals making the news.

Often, the conversation would turn to that span of terrible years, before 2002, when everybody was dying, countless funerals every weekend, all families affected. We still could not, with all the travels and the education and the knowledge and the expertise accumulated among us, we still could not make sense of those years. So many dead.

I never talked about my aunt. Nor did I talk about Sixteen, who, I had found out, had died in Serowe when I was away at university. I told myself that their memories were mine to savor. Instead, I would often tell people about a boy I knew who died in our last year of primary school. A group of us students went to the funeral in our school uniforms and right after, when the other mourners went back over the hill, we crossed the dirt road to start our school day. Whatever group of friends I told, what always fascinated people was not the boy's dying but this image, this juxtaposition of school and cemetery, side by side, and a hill cutting them off from the ward. It was as if they thought that, away from our parents, we kids fraternized with the dead. There would often be one person who thought that I was embellishing, that I was making up these details for the benefit of a story, to create some sort of meaning. That skeptic seemed to assume that the hill—which I now knew to be just a hillock—the school, the cemetery were symbolic of something that I had overcome, something I had escaped. But the Botalaote cemetery was separated from Motalaote Lekhutile Primary School by only a narrow dirt road, and behind them the hillock cut them off from Botalaote Ward. Those were the facts.

Some days our teachers sent us into the cemetery with black rubbish bags to pick up litter. We went in, wearing our white shirts and cyan skirts, our white socks and polished black shoes. The smart among us took off their socks, rolled them into balls that bulged from their side pockets. Our feet sank into the red sand. Often we would have to stop and empty our shoes of the soil, but the grains would trouble us between our toes for the rest of the day. We picked up plastic bags and newspapers, Coke cans and condom wrappers, everything, to make the cemetery a place the departed could sleep in some beauty. Some of the graves were elaborate, with black marble headstones and engravings of the Madonna and child; a few were so old that there were just mounds of red dirt and a board with a name and a date of death. Most had a black cage-like enclosure with green netting hugging the tops of the mounds. Sometimes we would find plates and spoons on the graves, remains of food. Sometimes belts and ties, smoking pipes and other comforts, offerings to the deceased by those left behind, lest they forsake us.

A Good Girl

❦

One sun-dazed October morning, in the year I was nine and given to daydreaming, I watched my mother stab the soil in the potted plants on the veranda. She was stooped over her African violets and wax begonias, quiet except for the huffs of angry breath spurting from the tight line of her lips. It had been only two days since my older sister Boitshepho's return home from God knows where, and she and Mama were still staying out of each other's way. Me, I hovered behind Mama, drowsily rubbing the sand grains from the thin green water hose and eyeing her quick, fussy hands. My mother whirled around and snapped her fingers at me, and I pressed my thumb against the opening of the hose and sprayed and sprayed until we were interrupted by a shout from outside the gate.

Already, Mma-Pulane was pushing the gate open and complaining about the heat. She was a regular visitor to the house, once a month back then, Saturdays. She hoisted the Tupperware she held into the air, a brown canvas bag hanging from her other shoulder. Mama muttered under her breath, dropped the trowel, and told me to turn the tap off. When I returned, Mma-Pulane was watching Mama unfold the chairs that had been propped against the pepper tree in wait of visitors. I bent my knees to greet, in a show of my good manners.

"What a polite child, Mma-Temo," Mma-Pulane said to my mother and leaned down to kiss my cheek. But it was not just out of politeness that I greeted her. On the days Mama sent me to return her Tupperware, Mma-Pulane allowed me to sit at her kitchen table and eat whatever I wanted as I paged through photos of her daughter Pulane, who was twenty-two and studying medicine in Ireland. My mother did not acknowledge Mma-Pulane's compliment, but I bent my knees and held both my hands out, and Mma-Pulane placed the Tupperware on my palms and propped the bag over my shoulder. I knew without being told to make the tea. Every visit, the two women spent almost an hour drinking Five Roses and having a stilted, cursory conversation—asking after each other's children, complaining about the perpetually late rains, cataloguing the aches in their bodies. I could hear Mma-Pulane already as I turned to go to the house, her protests about the pain that haunted her shoulders. She was a pear-shaped woman with a small upper body that exploded into hips, then narrowed into thick legs, and it always astonished me that it was her shoulders, more than anything, that troubled her. Above her chest, her face was thin and sly, with a whisker sprouting out of a mole on her chin.

In the kitchen, Boitshepho sat at the table, still in pajamas, cutting an apple into slices. I did not speak to her. She wore her hair purple now, in shoulder-length braids. Every gesture concerning her hair was new—gathering the braids into a bun at the back of her head, tucking them behind her ears, shaking her head to loosen them into a purple waterfall. She was fifteen and had just come into her spell of teenage bad behavior: talking back, disappearing for days whenever she wanted, alcohol on her breath when she returned. I could not talk to her. She watched as I put the Tupperware on the table and the canvas bag on a chair. I set a tray out, placing on it two cups and two saucers, two teaspoons.

"Is Papa here?" she asked. Our father had left for a meeting at the Serowe Main Kgotla, but I did not tell her that. Whenever she came home late and knocked at the window of the bedroom we shared, her nails scratching the glass quiet as a splatter of grains, I rose to unlock the door, even when I'd promised Mama I wouldn't. Back in bed, I'd listen to her contented sighs as she untied her shoes and wiggled out of her jeans. I tried to imagine where she had been, what place disappointed Papa and angered Mama so. I stayed up for hours while she snored, until I heard the soft babble of the world hatching awake, and only then would I fall asleep. Now here she was, sitting at the table, nonchalant, her right leg outstretched across two other chairs, mottling peanut butter onto her apple slices with a table knife.

"Ooh, silence," she said, shaking her neck mockingly. "Did the devil run through the room?" Still, I did not respond. She did not know that when she was gone, Mama spent hours lying on the couch, complaining about heart palpitations and begging me to apply damp washcloths to her face.

"What's in there?" Boitshepho asked. I turned around to see her pointing at the container I had just set down. She leaned over, pushed the bag of salt out of the way, and pulled the Tupperware toward her. The aroma of ox liver fried in onions filled the room when she took off the lid. My mouth watered, but I knew Mama would throw the food into the bin untasted as soon as Mma-Pulane left.

"Lebelete le le," Boitshepho said suddenly, angrily. She turned to face me. "You know she is a whore, right, your friend?"

We were not permitted such language. "Stop," I said, "stop saying such things."

"Lebelete, lebelete, lebelete," she said. Her face was a fury and her breathing heavy. Her eyes dared me, and I looked away. Just as suddenly she seemed bored with our standoff. She offered me the plate of apples and I took a slice.

"Mama said it's because you are a teenager that you have lost your manners."

"I have no manners?" she asked. "Okay. Tell me why that woman is always here."

"She is Mama's friend," I said. "She told me that she and Mama went to school together."

"And you believed that." She laughed. I understood from her derision that Mma-Pulane had told me an untruth, a possibility I refused to consider, an adult veering from the path of absolute honesty.

"She is Mama's friend," I said again.

Boi stood up and reached into the canvas bag. She unfolded khaki chinos and a black blazer, draped the pair over the back of a chair. A white button-down shirt, a pin-striped button-down shirt, a white vest, black socks, a red golf shirt Papa always wore to work on Fridays. Draped them all over the other chairs. Her movements were petulant but fastidious, as though to insulate the clothes from a certain injury. When done, Boitshepho looked at me meaningfully. I grasped blindly for what her look meant to convey. Slowly, heavily, the understanding landed inside me, into my tightened chest. The kettle whistled its fury. A disorder of emotions unfurled from my belly. Seeing my tears, Boitshepho rolled her eyes. I pulled my T-shirt up to wipe my face.

"Keletso!" Mama called from outside.

"They want their tea," Boitshepho said. "Let me help. You forgot the sugar."

I went over to the cupboard and retrieved the silver sugar basin. I wiped its outside clean and burrowed a teaspoon inside. Boitshepho had poured the boiling water into a teapot and placed a saucer of tea bags on the tray. I lifted the tray under the witness of my sister and the disguised chairs.

"Don't say anything stupid," Boitshepho said, watching my face. "Give them their tea and come back here. Are you listening?"

I carried the tray out of the kitchen, past the sitting room, through the veranda. The brightness of the sun blinded me. I stooped over the tray while my eyes adjusted to the light. Mama and Mma-Pulane sat in silence. Mama had her arms folded over her chest, over the old T-shirt that she wore only to work in the yard. Under her arms, the soft folds of her stomach bulged. I bent my knees and handed Mama the tray. I lingered long enough to watch her hold the sugar basin up, turning it around to inspect its cleanliness.

Inside, Boitshepho stood by our bedroom window, watching the two women through the slit in the curtains. She put a silencing finger to her lips and motioned for me to join her. I wasn't sure what to watch for. Mama counted out her normal five teaspoons of sugar and handed the basin to Mma-Pulane. Mama poured milk into her cup and stirred. She took a sip of the tea, then spat it out. Boitshepho snorted out a giggle above my head. Mma-Pulane took a sip and her face contorted. Boitshepho laughed again, a low chuckle coming from her throat.

"I put salt in the water," Boitshepho whispered, her eyes alight with her mischief.

"Keletso!" Mama called.

"Did you see that?" Boitshepho said and imitated the contortions of Mma-Pulane's face.

"Keletso!" Mama called again. "Ke-le-tso!"

"Mma?" Boitshepho replied on my behalf, and that made me giggle.

It was a game we played sometimes, knowing Mama, unanswered, would quickly move on to the next name. As I laughed, I felt tears on my cheeks. I felt the ache in my chest, like the laughter was pressing down my throat, through the tightness in my ribs, pushing onto my bladder, making me want to pee.

I said, "Heish, now I have to make more tea."

"Yes," Boitshepho said. "And you are going to make it, aren't you?"

THAT EVENING, I sat in the kitchen, picking at the remains of the dough in the mixing bowl. My sister was at the stove, stirring green peppers, onions, and garlic into a pot full of beef. Dumplings bubbled in another pot. Now she took me into her confidence, emptying herself of the stories she had been hoarding. I was attentive in my listening; still, I could not grasp their meanings. Her words flashed quick and aquatic, silvery images banished from my head as soon as they formed, because of how fast Boitshepho was talking, how low the volume of her voice, how much she interrupted herself to laugh, pressing her hand to her chest, speaking things I had never before associated with her. She had pierced her ears even though it was forbidden for us, Batalaote, to pierce our ears. A *Motalaote's pierced ears will swell, morph into chandeliers of festering flesh.* But Boitshepho's ears were fine, and her earrings glinted between her braids as she spoke.

We drove to Palapye, Boitshepho said, and I tried to imagine her in a car that was not our parents', not our brother's. *Sylvia.* I pictured the singer. *Cresta. Girls fighting. Wig.* The heat in the room; I yearned to slip my T-shirt off. Sweat stung at my armpits. *Police.* I cut a corner off the cube of beef stock on the table and melted it onto my tongue and I emerged from my reverie to Boitshepho staring at me expectantly.

"I said, you know what I really want?" she asked.

"A house of your own," I said.

"Yes!" She was pleased, even though she had talked to me about this dream of hers before, of a house empty of our mother and our father. In my daydreams, we had chosen the paint colors, the television set, the chocolate bars we would stack by every windowsill. The windows were open and through them, I looked out to our neighbors', at the quiet little yellow house with the pale blue door, the outside light already on, the tharesetala growing in clannish clusters in the yard.

Boitshepho turned to me. "Don't say anything about this to your mother."

"I won't say anything," I said. She had started this thing of foisting our family onto me. Our mother was exclusively my mother; our father, my father.

"And your brother either," Boitshepho said. "You know how he is."

"Okay," I said, even though I wasn't sure what she meant.

There was no question of my telling Papa. Our father's head was full of dreams and ancestors, histories and names of the long forgotten, and every night he purged the stories into a black notebook. We kept him in this world of goodness and memory. We knelt to show him our school reports. We let him take us into the interior of the village, where the library was located, and he helped us choose the books he wanted us to read.

When I took in the water for their hands, my parents were sitting next to each other on the couch, each focused on their own work. Mama held a sheet of music, the new song for the schools' choral competition. She had changed into a green dress with big gold buttons. Her headscarf, pale yellow with embroidered green silhouettes of birds in flight, was draped over her knees and rose as she tapped her feet. She hummed to herself, stopping and starting, stopping and starting, moving her right forefinger to trace the highness and the lowness of the notes. Papa was bent over the coffee table, writing. Behind him, on the bookshelf, a mosquito coil unfurled smoke into the air, and it seemed to be pumping from the back of Papa's head.

"I have brought water," I said. Papa sat up and shut his notebook. He removed his glasses and smiled dreamily at me. I knelt before him, put the plastic bowl under his hands, and poured warm water over them.

Since the beginning of Boitshepho's wildness, we went out just the two of us, my father and I. Each time, I thought he would interrogate me about my sister's whereabouts. Instead we walked up Serowe Hill to Tshwaragano Hotel. He knotted together shifting stories about our people, the Batalaote. Sometimes he told me I should be proud that we were part of the Rozvi Empire, extending all the way from what is now Zimbabwe to Mahalapye. Other times he told me about the Ndebeles, how they had corralled and killed our people for disloyalty, how our people had scattered in their flight, fragmented into tiny skulking bands hiding wherever they could before seeking the protection of the Bangwato.

"That is how we came to be from here," he would say, gesturing around at the hills, at the ancient trees surviving the rocky ground, at the still heat and at Serowe itself. Papa would sometimes get overcome by the wonders of his revelations, that we had survived where our language had not, where we had failed to claim any land as ours. I was attentive and vigilant in my listening, but I never understood what any of those dead people had to do with me.

After supper, Mama asked us to practice the music with her. Because of these home sessions, we always knew the competition songs before our school friends. Boitshepho plonked herself next to Mama, and I grew nervous. I sang soprano like always, Boitshepho alto, Mama tenor, and Papa bass. Boi swayed and sang all her parts but intentionally sang a step behind us, making no attempt to harmonize her voice with ours. Papa lowered his music sheet to look at her, but Mama sang on undeterred. Every time she had to sing *La-La!*, Boitshepho opened her mouth wide and crossed her eyes. I saw that she meant to make me laugh, but I just wanted her to stop. Laughing would make Mama angry, and that could turn the evening into some other new thing. I wanted everything to stay the same, with Mama and Papa and Boi around me, and oh, if Temo were here too. I kept my eyes on my mother. I sang and stopped when she put her forefinger in the air and took the song up again when she pointed at me.

As we sang, I imagined that it was Sunday morning already, and I was sitting between Mama's legs; that my scalp did not sting as she subdued my hair into cornrows. I imagined that in our room, Boitshepho was ironing our church dresses and draping them on our beds, ironing our school uniforms and hanging them up to flutter at each end of the curtain rail at our bedroom window. On the veranda, Papa was whistling, shaving his beard with the better, natural light of outside. Here we were, already back from the hot tedium of church, already finished with our lunch. And there I was, waiting through Papa's self-effacing dreaminess and Mama's exacting long-windedness on the phone, waiting through the terse anger of my sister and now, see, it was my turn to talk to my brother, Temo. On the phone, I twirled the cord around my fingers, looking unseeingly at the flowery plates and cups imprisoned, until a special enough occasion, behind the glass doors of the room divider. I was laughing with my brother, bargaining for a bicycle if I came first at the end of term, even though I knew I spent too much time doodling sketches in my books, so I would never come first. Then Temo turned serious, summoned this secret between us, my duty to be a good girl and help Mama and Papa, now that they were going through these difficulties with Boi.

OH, I was given to such daydreams back then, much more than now. Sometimes hours of my lying on the veranda, somnolent from the bright summer heat. Sometimes a whole afternoon in my bed. Those were the days I started to notice Papa's nightly absences, his arrivals home just before dawn. He was hardly ever there during the weekends. I started to notice how, in his absence, Mama's whole body clenched tight, unfurling only when she retired to the couch and crunched trayfuls of ice cubes between her teeth. These were the days Boitshepho left, despite my mother and father pairing up to punish her. My parents argued behind their bedroom door, and I imagined that they were just volleying words at each other for fun and, indeed, when they emerged from their room, their arguments would be gone, their anger placed aside for their tenderness with each other. Mama called Papa *my friend*. Papa called Mama *heart, my heart, heart of a bull*, but it was the same thing he called everybody else, all the Batalaote he liked, for the heart is our totem.

ALL THIS was years ago. Three years, in fact, before Boitshepho gave in to the seduction of the Johannesburg we watched on the soapies and moved there all by herself. Seven years before Papa died from a cancer of the stomach. Nine years before I was admitted to UB and bade farewell to my mother to join my brother in Gaborone.

I thought often of that house of my sister's dreams in the peripatetic years of my life in the city. Years filled with roommates: Christian girls who went to open-air services during weekends and returned clutching bottles of holy water, buoyed by the prospect of miracles; girls who split their student allowances to pay rent and to send money back home; girls who guilted me into buying Amway, Golden, Herbalife, secondhand dresses arriving in bales from the UK and China. All over Gaborone, I lived with a series of these girls. Four years in the dorms at UB, where I studied humanities, which all the science and finance students called LeHuma, for the inevitable poverty that awaited those of us studying English and African literature and theology. After: Tlokweng, White City, Moguditshane, Block 5—sharing servants' quarters and two-and-a-halves, leaving every time the lease lapsed and the rent was hiked. The only evidence of our lives together was the portraits of these girls that I sketched into my notebooks. My roommates and I, we ran out of food and out of money to buy more. We watched pirated movies on our laptops: love stories and romantic comedies. We wanted love, and to be literate in love. We wished to fall in love with the men we watched in the movies. We wanted heartbreak, but only enough that our hearts required no worse cure than languishing in bed with a tub of ice cream. Some of the men we knew told us, *Ke go rata lorato la o ka swa nka go ja*, and we were afraid that they would love us to our deaths and that, even in our deaths, they would consume us. Some of the men we knew declared their love to us in English, the language a deception, a second skin they donned and shed as they wished. We fell in love with these guys, swept up in the slipperiness of their words, their declarations. We were in love. We thought we were in love. We felt sure it was love, this time. We made love after making them wait for months. We had sex with one, two, three guys in a year, parceling out pussy to convince them we were marriageable. We abstained from sex for six months at a time, for twice that, convinced it made us better, virtuous women. We fucked three, five, seven guys in one month, our bodies rapacious and unashamed. We fucked them on the same alcohol-fueled, laughter-drenched nights we had met them at a bar. We abstained, fearing disease. We wanted love, oh, we wanted love, but we knew, we had been warned, that for girls like us, love was dangerous, a bright-burning flame, it would lick us alive.

Whatever roommate I had, whatever house I moved to, Temo came over, current girlfriend in tow. He wanted to know what my rent was, he rattled the burglarproof bars at the windows and the doors to inspect their durability, he checked the neighborhood tuck-shops for illicit weed sales. Still, his house, whatever part of the city he was living in, was refuge; I could flee there to escape a sullen roommate, to wait out an unpaid bill, or just for a full bath frothing with bubbles.

But in 2014, after eight years in Gaborone, I was finally living on my own. It wasn't much, just a servant's quarters in Phase 4. My landladies lived in the main house up front. On the other side of my room, beyond the chain-link fence, was Kudumatse Road. During the day, the piercing hooting of combis and the trudging of cars was incessant; at night, trucks roared past. I felt barricaded in sometimes, the road on one end, the main house on the other.

At the end of that winter, I had received an invitation to a party at my brother's house in Phakalane, an actual card, its borders gold, mailed to my office at the Ministry of Youth and Culture.

ON THE DAY OF THE PARTY, I stood before the grandeur of my brother's house, fingering the edges of the card in my dress pocket. The white double-story rose before me into the cloudless vastness of the sky. The boundary wall, in matching white and topped with four strips of electric fence, meant that from where I stood, I could see only into the balcony overlooking the tarred road. It had been six months since the house was completed and Temo and his new wife had moved in. It was not that the house was extraordinarily big or more beautiful than any of the ones behind similar boundary walls. It was that I still found it hard to believe that my brother had risen to this—his own plot of land in this most expensive part of Gaborone, a house in this neighborhood where all the rich of the city were building homes. I have been told that as a toddler, back in Serowe, I used to await Temo's return from school by the gate, late afternoons, always anxious that I wouldn't recognize him in the army of blue-uniformed students who trooped past our house. I still found it hard to believe that same Temo had cultivated himself to this neighborhood. Gardeners came weekly to tend to the lawns in the front yards; the swimming pools in the backyards were always full despite citywide water rationing; bright-green JoJo tanks stood in wait of the mercurial rains. Every time I visited my brother, I wished Boi were still around, that the two of us could ridicule him about his big house in the suburbs and now, perhaps the greatest surprise of all, that he had married.

I pressed down on the intercom. Only Maru, the dog, responded, ambling over, lifting himself up to put his front paws on the gate, then looking side to side like a meerkat, until a gust of wind whirled through and toppled him off. The dust collected everywhere, on the roof of my mouth, under my tongue, in my eyes, on the dress I had bought especially for the party. I pressed the button again. I did not see the front door open, only Pauline's head poking around the wall of the double garage. She waved and walked toward the gate, stopping halfway. She was taller even than my brother and emanated the assured, bossy manner of a firstborn child, a certainty that the world would do her bidding, her only nervous habit a tendency to pull at her earlobes, which she did as she stood across from me in red shorts and a gray T-shirt.

"You came," she said. She sounded relieved, and I realized that she too was thinking of the last time we had seen each other, almost four months prior.

"I am a little early," I said defensively. The invitation had said eight p.m. for nine, and it wasn't even seven yet. "I thought, let me go and help."

"We have a planner and a caterer and everything," Pauline said in English. I had noticed, since learning that she had gone to private schools all her life, that she spoke in English to everyone: to me, to my mother, to attendants at filling stations. When we first met, at a brunch in a restaurant on the outskirts of the city, every sentence she had uttered was preceded by a territorial caress of Temo's arm, every sentence began with *we, we, we*, everything *we*, as if she had known him longer, as if she and Temo, together, were a dream conjured in ancient times, when the rocks were still soft. I had regarded her with some amused pity then, the way I regarded my Christian roommates, waiting for the membrane of their faith to be punctured.

"Let me open the gate for you," she said now and disappeared back into the house.

I removed my gift from the car and walked into the yard. Behind me, the gate slid closed. A pawpaw had splattered onto the pavement, its scattered seeds seeming to flee from the fruit. At the half-open door, I knocked and walked in, holding the gift against my knees. Standing at the door, I felt the brief terror of not knowing whether I was expected to slide off my shoes.

"See," Pauline said. Inside, the house revealed the secrets of its activity. A uniformed maid was finishing off the cleaning, darting here and there with a foaming bowl of water. Glasses and silverware and plates were arranged on silver trays at the dining table, which had been pushed to the wall. Through the back doors, I saw a man stringing lights up tree branches. On the patio, a table held a DJ's equipment. Round tall tables dotted the yard, and a woman wove through them, laying down golden tablecloths, and another followed her, staying the cloths with vases full of purple and white flowers.

"Babe!" Pauline stood at the foot of the stairway and yelled, her head tilted away from me. "Come here!

"He is going to be so happy to see you," she said to me. She was turned toward me, pulling at her earlobe and smiling hesitantly, and I saw then that she was trying to win me over.

"Baby!" she yelled again.

We had never been close. She was a year younger than me and self-possessed; she seemed to have absolute certainty about herself and her life. Being around her amplified my own bewilderment at the world. We had pretended to a brittle civility for a while, texting each other, cooking together over Easter in Serowe. But even that civility had splintered the last time I visited, when I came over for a long bubble bath and she told me off. *It's disrespectful*, she said, *you are a guest here.* A guest. I had stopped coming over.

"Ta-da!" She motioned toward me, and on the landing, my brother was peering down.

"Keletso," Temo said. He was the exact image of my father. The same lean frame, the same long arms, the gap in their front teeth. He even had Papa's dimples, which softened their otherwise hard, square faces. Watching him come down the stairs, I instantly felt at ease. He stood next to Pauline and they both smiled. She touched his chest, rubbed the back of his head, and gazed at me expectantly.

"Dumela, rra," I greeted him formally. People found our friendship strange. Temo was fourteen years older, and we had Boitshepho between us. But I had always looked up to him, and in the years of Boitshepho's transgressions, he had called often to speak to me, to remind me that as a growing girl I needed to take care of myself, to tell me that boys pursued only one thing and once they had it, they would discard an indecent girl.

"We haven't seen you in a while," he said.

"Work," I said. At twenty-six, I still kept my secrets from him, my drinking and my clubbing, the men I slept with. Always, I presented myself to him, as to my mother, as cocooned in virtue and chastity, patiently awaiting the preordained moment when the right man would choose me for his partner and my life could begin. I exulted in this elusiveness, imagining myself a shape-shifting trickster, legible only as I wanted. Temo had never kept his girlfriends from me, even back when he had many of them. So many women those years I first moved to the city, all fast talking and sophisticated, all light skinned with long straight hair, so different from me that I began to see that he did not conceive of women who looked like me as beautiful.

"Will you drink a Coke?" Pauline asked.

"I am fine," I said. Now that I saw she was remorseful, I was loath to let go of my righteous self-pity, which arrived promptly when summoned.

"And Boi? Crazy girl. How is she?" Temo asked.

"Where is she?" Pauline asked.

"She is fine," I said. "When I spoke to her she said she was visiting Miami."

"Miami?" Pauline raised her eyebrows. "Fancy."

I bristled, imagining traces of mockery in her voice.

"Is that my birthday present?" Temo asked about the frame propped against my legs.

"I don't know where the presents are kept," I said.

"I can take it up for you," Pauline said.

"What is it?" Temo asked. "I want to see what it is."

"Wait, no, not now," I said, but he had already bent down. I watched his hands untie the ribbon and tear through the wrapping paper. I cringed but turned the frame around. I had struggled over the pencil drawing of the two of them, which I had copied from a photo I had taken on their wedding day. In the photo, they were looking at each other in that way couples have of suturing a universe around themselves, even in a yard full of singing and dancing wedding guests. In the drawing, I saw now, looking at it alongside them, myriad mistakes. I had been too hesitant in my shading of their necks. In striving for photorealism, I had obsessed over their lips, their noses, their eyes, and still had failed to get them right, their lips somehow too sensual. I had shaded the background in lieu of the guests the camera had captured. Altogether, the drawing was flat and lifeless. As Temo and Pauline stared at their likeness in silence, I had the uncanny sensation that I had crossed some sort of line.

"I am still learning," I said. "I just thought, you don't really have any art on the walls, Temo."

"We love it," Pauline said slowly. "Right, babe?"

Temo just pulled me toward him again and ruffled my braids like I was still nine.

"We can hang it up right now," Pauline said.

"No, no," I said.

"I am sure we have some of those sticky hooks. Margaret!" she called for her maid and went into the kitchen. Temo shrugged in a boyish way, smiling, absolving himself of responsibility for any of the tense awkwardness in the room.

"Pauline," I said when she returned. "You don't have to do this."

"No, no," she said. "We want to put it up. Right, babe?" She had two white hooks, and she stuck them on the wall above the console table and balanced the frame across them.

"There," she said.

AT EIGHT THIRTY, Pauline pattered downstairs into the kitchen. Her dress was short and red and backless. Her feet were bare, their heels lifted off the floor as though she were a dancer in a music box. She wore a short black wig with a heavy fringe in a style we used to call the mushroom. Her teeth gleamed white and straight against her red lipstick. She looked very beautiful. I was sitting at the kitchen island, scrolling through my phone. She glanced at me and said, "People will be here soon, you should go upstairs and change."

I was obedient; I straightened my dress and walked upstairs. I locked myself in the guest bedroom and peered inside my handbag. Perhaps, by some miracle, a fairy godmother had folded a gown in there. I stayed upstairs through the intermittent buzzing of the intercom, and I heard the laughter and the rumbling deep voices of the guests as they came in. I agonized over what they thought of my sketch on the wall.

At the upstairs windows, I watched the backyard fill with men in their jeans and their array of pastel long-sleeved shirts, women in pencil skirts and shift dresses and heels, their shawls draped through their arms. I watched the intricacy of their choreography, the couples coming up to pump my brother's arm and hug his wife in greeting and then wandering off when another couple came up to pump my brother's arm and hug his wife in greeting. Some congregated by the food table, lingering over their sliced beef tongue, the mini pizzas, the seswaa. The DJ played old-school bubblegum pop—Brenda Fassie and the Big Dudes, Johnny Mokhali, Chicco—and the guests cheered as Temo and Pauline danced, their moves easy and light-hearted, lacking the competition of dancing at a club.

Some strange feeling, a feeling I couldn't determine, hung in the air by the time I arrived downstairs. In the living room I saw the women, all bobbing heads and gleaming brown necks, talking furiously.

"His divorce is not even official yet," one voice said.

"No, no, this girl is new. Brand new from the box."

"To bring her here."

"I would die. I would really die."

"Meanwhile, poor Miriam is filling my feed with inspirational quotes." And they tittered guiltily. I lingered, too nervous to join the women, too nervous to join the men outside. I hovered by the door, watching the men laughing and dancing with one another, their faces contorted into some remembered ecstasy, their bodies picking up the dance moves of their youths. Leaned against one of the tall tables was a curvy woman in a striking dress: floor length, the pink of the sky at sunset, voluminous sleeves buttoned at her wrists. She drank from her wineglass, oblivious or indifferent to her incongruity, nodding at the spectacle of the dancers. Her thin fingers were bird-like, picking through the coils of her short blond Afro.

As though alerted to my quizzical stare, she turned her head toward the door, where I was standing. Then she glided toward me and I was privy to the complete getup: the high neck, pussy bow, lace ruffles down her chest, and it was only when she was close enough that I could smell her vanilla-scented perfume that I realized I recognized her from photos in the newspapers. Oesi Pansiri. She was as famous a painter as one could get in Botswana. Smiling, she asked for the bathroom. Her voice was slow and syrupy and left me flustered.

"It's that door by the stairs." I pointed it out to her.

When she returned from the bathroom, she stopped to look at my drawing on the wall. I studied her to see what she thought of it, but the only change in her face was a slight frown. Out of some unknown impulse, I said, "It's mine."

"Mma?" she asked, turning around.

"The drawing. It's mine," I said. "I drew it."

She reconsidered the drawing. "I wasn't expecting to meet another artist here."

"I just draw and sketch sometimes."

"Look at this contrast between the stillness of these figures in the foreground and the movement of the lines in the background. It's quite compelling," Oesi said, nodding at me seriously.

I was a little embarrassed but emboldened. From the corner of my eye, I saw that my brother had walked in and was watching us. I remembered his phone calls of old.

"Do you have a business card?" I asked her, and she handed me her glass and fished a card out of her bag.

"This is my brother," I said to Oesi as Temo walked toward us, before he could say anything. "It's his birthday party."

"Oh, yes. The birthday boy. We met outside."

"What are you two talking about?" my brother asked.

Pauline materialized out of nowhere to stand beside Temo.

"Hello, hello," Pauline said in a silly singsong voice, her eyes darting from one face to another. We were all quiet.

"Silence," Pauline said. "The devil must have run through the room!"

Out of good manners, I laughed.

OESI LIVED IN PHASE 1, near a twenty-four-hour convenience store and a KFC that I frequented because it stayed open until midnight. She was waiting for me in her front yard, appearing spectral in another drapey voluminous outfit.

Now that I was here, I felt strange about having called her, but she had sounded enthusiastic about my coming over. I buried the melancholy that had made me dial her number and emerged from the car audacious and light.

"Do you know how many times I have been to that KFC?" I asked her.

"That place is the reason I have to start going to the gym," she said.

"Oh, come on," I said, and we both laughed awkwardly.

"Come in, come in," she said, in her unhurried way.

Her living room was colorful and burnished with the golden light of evening, which slanted in through her open curtains. She had a metal-gray three-seater couch and a pink love seat. Stacks of books sat on a low coffee table, and on top of the stacks were a pair of fragrant candles in squat glass containers. Across from the living room door were bookshelves, painted a dusky pink and laden with more books. But on the wall, above the shelves, was a large painting of two little girls, one hanging upside down, head to the ground, feet hooked around the seat of a swing, while the other sat upright, her leg on the ground, primed to kick off for flight.

"Did you make this?" I asked about the painting.

"I wish," she said. "I bought it a long time ago. It made me think of my sister."

We stood there for a while, looking at the painting.

"I have some water, Coke, juice, wine," Oesi said.

"I will have some wine."

"Oh," she said. "Don't you have work tomorrow?"

"It's a quarter to the weekend," I said, and she laughed. Then I laughed. I felt expansive and bold and expectant. She was at least ten years older than I was, but I felt we could be friends. I picked up a book on Coex'ae Qgam and settled on the pink love seat. I could live here, I thought.

She came from the kitchen with two glasses and a bottle of wine.

"I am always so excited to meet young artists," she said.

I could feel her eyes on me as I drank the wine. I wondered if she was amused or merely baffled by my presence. When I sensed her turning to me with a real question, I asked, "Can you show me your studio?"

She laughed, indulging me, and stood up. We walked to the servant's quarters in the back. It was slightly smaller than my room and was crammed with sketches and drawings and books, canvases stacked atop one another on the floor, canvases leaning against the wall. The single window was open, and through it we heard the sounds of the cars outside as though from a great distance. She unhooked a paint-splattered apron from the wall and wore it over her outfit. On a canvas on the easel, she had started a portrait, but so far, emerging from the white blankness she had managed only the brown whorl of a small ear and the ropy beginnings of a sinewy neck. When she saw me looking, she covered the painting. I walked around peering at the pieces she had on the wall, the sketches on paper, feeling simultaneously awed and disappointed. I was coming face-to-face with my own limitations.

"Were you drinking at your brother's party?" she asked me, when I held my glass out for a refill. "I can't remember."

I turned conspiratorial. "My brother doesn't know that I drink."

"Ah." She nodded.

"He doesn't even suspect," I said, laughing. "I have been drinking since my days at UB."

"We have all been there," she said.

"What do you mean?"

"You are being a good girl for your brother. We have all been there. Being good for our fathers and uncles and brothers, even our cousins and our boyfriends. They have no idea who we are."

I had the feeling that she was mocking me. "It's just easier," I said.

"It has to come to an end at some point, though, right? How old are you? You can't go through your life pretending to be someone else."

"I am not pretending anything," I said.

"Okay, okay," she said, as though quieting a bristling animal. She sipped her wine, keeping her eyes on me. The room felt hot suddenly, and I tugged at my T-shirt. I wanted to leave, but there was something about her life that I was not ready to give up, so I turned around and fixed my eyes on another half-finished canvas.

WHEN I arrived home from work one evening in October, I heard loud laughter coming from the main house up front. My landladies entertained a lot: dinner parties, house parties, braais I was never invited to. I maneuvered past and parked my Japanese import right in front of my servant's quarters.

"Dumelang," I greeted my empty room. I liked to think that what I saluted were the sketches of my family that I had stuck on my wall. But Papa had told me once that walking into an unoccupied space, one should always acknowledge the omnipresence of the ancestors. It scared me, back when the pair of us went on our walks up Serowe

Hill, thinking of the dead elders and their breaths watching everything I did. Now it was a salve. All the ancestors, known and unknown, benevolent and malevolent, long deceased and recently deceased, in here with me. I took my shoes off and plopped myself on the bed. I ignored the hunger gnawing at my stomach and scrolled through Facebook. From the main house came quick, furious bursts of laughter, like fireworks on New Year's Eve. I lay on my bed for a while and then grabbed my car keys.

At the KFC drive-through, I ordered a Streetwise Two and then parked in the bright lights of the filling station. I tore at the chicken, dunked the chips in tomato sauce. I ate it all, still piping hot, and chewed through the bones. When the box was empty, my fingers oil stained, I was disgusted with myself. I got out of the car, threw the debris in the dustbin, and walked to the convenience store.

A bell dinged above me as I opened the door. The fluorescent tube lights flickered, and the cashier behind the till raised her face to give me a perfunctory smile. I headed to the section with the toiletries to look for sanitary pads. Across from me, a woman in gray harem pants opened the refrigerator doors, stuck her head in and out, again and again, and trilled in laughter. It *was* hot. The kind of dry heat that we said was due to the gods withholding rain from us, to punish us for the rampant sins tied to city living. I turned around to watch the woman. It was Oesi, and she was putting on the performance for somebody else. A man, his back as familiar to me as the palms of my hands. Temo moved toward Oesi, her whole body now inside the open refrigerator. Still laughing, she draped her arm around his waist, and he lowered his head and kissed her lips.

The kiss felt inevitable. Still, my own body turned cold, a phantom hand pressing ice all the way down my spine. My chest tightened and I could not breathe. As if he could sense my presence,

Temo turned around. As he walked up to me, I could feel my face clenching into a smile, all of its own volition.

"Keletso," he said.

"Dumelang," I greeted him. Past his shoulder, I could see the cashier looking over at us. Oesi walked up to us with the same smile I had, all clenched teeth, all trapped eyes.

"Your brother has been sitting for me," she said.

"Nice," I heard myself say.

"We have just come from the studio," she said. "And now I am buying him ice cream to thank him. Do you want some?"

"I am fine," I said.

"Oh, come on."

"Seriously," I said. "I am on a diet."

"I am getting you ice cream. It's so hot. Everybody deserves some ice cream." She laughed.

My brother looked at me. "Go ahead and pay," he said to Oesi.

Temo and I stood amid the aisles while Oesi paid for the ice cream. She showed me the carton that was mine and left it by the till. She implored me to call her, she said she still wanted to see my work, and the door rang her out.

"Keletso," my brother said. "You know, don't you, that me and Pauline, we are trying for a baby. It's taking a little while, but we are trying for a family."

"Ee, rra," I said, even though I had not known.

"I know that you and Pauline have had your differences, but I know you are going to be a good aunt."

"Okay," I said, just like that.

"You are a grown woman now, Keletso. You hear me, don't you?"

"I hear you," I said.

"Good," he said, in English. Now he was himself again.

"Do you need money?" he asked, indicating the objects in my hand. He took out his wallet, slid P200 into my pocket. Then he left.

At the till, I handed the cashier my sanitary pads. She held them up to the reader. *Ding!*

"Twenty-four pula eighty-five," the cashier said. My hands trembled. I could feel my eyes filling with tears, so I kept my face down. I gazed into my handbag—there was my sketchbook and my phone charger, my mess of sweet and gum wrappers, there the pen that had leaked ink into the lining, the used airtime cards, receipts, so many receipts with faded figures for items I never ever remembered buying.

AT NIGHT, the city folded in upon itself, like a clever flower against nocturnal predators. How small and quiet, how thick the gathering darkness of night. On Old Lobatse Road, I zipped through the robots even though the light was red. In the dark, the unused parking lots in front of Trador Cash and Carry stood empty, as wasted as unploughed fields. I drove toward Kilimanjaro Shopping Complex and parked across from the butchery. I walked past the bone-white mannequins surveying the dark from the windows of the Chinese shops to Momo's. In the center of the complex, the wooden tables and colorful beach umbrellas used by the daytime vendors were chained to a jacaranda tree.

Inside, the usual selection of old white men sat at the bar for their lonely drinks and dinners for one. We had heard often that young girls flocked to Momo's in search of these men and their dollars and pounds and the visas to their home countries. I walked through to sit outside on the patio. With my first sip of Savanna, relief flickered in my head. Music tinned from the car boots in the parking lot, music spilled from inside the bar.

At the table behind me, a group of five men sat drinking and eating and, at intervals, breaking into raucous laughter. I turned around to look at them. One of them invited me to their table. They were quiet as I made myself comfortable. The man who had spoken extended his hand and said, "Ndibo."

"I am Estelle," I said.

WHEN I AWOKE, Ndibo was in the en suite shower. From his bed, I could hear the water and his whistling. Across from the bed was a giant painting of a woman playing the segaba. An air conditioner unit high up on the wall kept the room cool. My body felt sticky and sweaty. I stretched, savoring the pains in the insides of my thighs. I imagined I was in a film, a standing fan blowing air into my face and lifting my braids off my head. Here I was, sitting up in bed, white sheets covering my body, satiated, my skin shiny and glowing. I imagined that the man in the shower was my live-in lover, that I arrived home every evening, my expensive car purring into the garage, that I opened the door into the kitchen and said, "Honey, I am home," and he came down the stairs, his legs long and muscular in tight blue jeans, his arms brown and thick in a white sleeveless undershirt, that he pinned me to the kitchen counter, and that after, I wore his oversize white oxford shirt and sat cross-legged on the marble countertop and tossed grapes into my mouth while he made food.

The bathroom door opened, and I closed my eyes.

"Hey," Ndibo said.

He stood at the foot of the bed in an open white bathrobe. His smile was hesitant and bashful, his glasses misted over. His rounded fleshy shoulders touched me. His soft penis flapped below his tight, bulbous belly as he moved. Inexplicably, I felt sorry for him.

"Did I wake you?" he asked.

"I was just getting up," I said.

I felt shy, now that I was no longer drunk. He leaned into the bed, and I could see the sprinkle of brown moles poking out of his cheeks.

"Do you want to shower?" he asked. "I have spare toothbrushes."

I tried to think of what I had said to him the night before when we arrived from the bar, but all I could remember was loudly praising his house, his bookshelves, the paintings on his walls. Shame heated my face and I shut my eyes.

"You will feel better if you shower," he said.

"What time do you have to go to work?" I asked.

"Actually, I don't have any classes today."

"Classes?" I asked, incredulous.

"Yes," he said.

"How old are you?" I asked.

"I teach music education at UB." He looked at me like I should know this, like this information was etched on his forehead. "I told you this last night."

"Oh, yeah," I said, and he squinted at me.

"No classes," I said. "I really miss that about school. Free days."

"You could take a day off."

"I shouldn't."

"Do it," he said. "We can spend the whole day here, together. I am only leaving home in the evening."

When he went into the kitchen to make breakfast, I checked my phone. One message, from Temo. *Are u ok?* Delete. In a text, I told my friendliest colleague that I had a severe case of diarrhea. I showered and followed Ndibo to the kitchen.

We fucked against the counter, his hands kneading my breasts while I looked out the window at the guava tree dying in his yard. We fucked in his study. His fat fingers gripped the edge of the desk, his lips pressed warm kisses on my neck, and I felt a lurching in my chest, as if something in there clamored for exit. We fucked in his sitting room, the curtains flapping all over us, hot air gushing in through the open windows. In the study again, his grunts failing to cover the smack of his skin against mine. In the shower. On the floor. On the stairs. He begged for rest and we went back to bed, attempted to piece together the previous evening.

"So, no boyfriend?" he asked, eventually.

"No."

"I am not sure I believe you," he said. "A girl like you, so young, so beautiful. I am sure there are many people who love you."

Out of nowhere I was overwhelmed by emotion, a sudden unhinging of grief. I pressed my hand to my chest, kneading at the ache, trying to contain the sound of my crying. But he turned his face down to me and swept the braids from my eyes. I kept my eyes closed, felt the tears on my cheeks.

"What's wrong?" he asked. "What did I say?"

I couldn't speak; I buried my face in his armpit, into the smells of his sweat and his flesh.

"Oh, Estelle," he murmured. "Estelle. Estelle. Estelle."

EVERY EVENING I made my way to an empty home, my only company the drawings I had sketched on bright white paper. Some nights, when I was not afraid, I switched the lights off and could see the luster of the paper in the dark. Most nights I couldn't switch the lights off. I hoped intruders, burglars, rapists would see the lonely square of light from the window and think that in that lit room were people who stayed up all night, talking, making love, offering each other warmth.

Returning from Ndibo's, I saw the sketches anew. Beyond the failures of technique, I saw their falseness. Our being a family felt like another duplicity. I thought about my father and the stories with which he had offered me a glimpse into our past. They were meager and deficient, his tales, I thought that night, if they could not provide us with ways to be in the present, with tenderness and love and honesty.

WHEN BOITSHEPHO answered my video call, she seemed angry, distracted. I hadn't talked to her in months, and when I saw her face, with a new ring in her brow, I felt the niggling resentment I always felt talking to her.

"Le teng?" I asked formally, conferring on her an elderhood she did not deserve.

"I am fine," she answered in English. She leaned into her screen and adjusted the eyebrow ring.

"How is everyone?" she asked.

"They are fine."

"And you?"

"I am fine. Everyone is fine."

"Okay," she said, sighing loudly, biting her lips in a way that made me feel she was impatient to get off the call.

"People want to know when you are coming home," I said to her. Years after Papa's funeral, she had left Johannesburg to move to New York, seduced by the yellow taxicabs in all the movies. She changed cities often, searching for something known only to herself, and not finding it, she packed her things and left. Again and again. I had just come into this irrational belief that were she to return to us, everything would be restored: all of us together again, Papa still alive.

"Soon," she said. Her standard answer whenever I asked about her return.

"Soon, like next month soon, or next year soon? Or never soon?"

"Soon, like when I decide to come back soon," she said.

I stared at her resentfully. "Boi, do you remember Mma-Pulane?" I asked.

"That witch," she said, smiling. "How could I forget her? She brought us food every month, probably trying to poison us so she could move into our house."

"Don't say that."

"I am joking," she said.

"Why was that even okay? How could Mama allow that woman into her yard?"

"Mama was just doing what she had been taught. Do you know what they tell you when you get married? That you shouldn't question your husband if he spends a night away. That a man is an axe to be lent around. What else could Mama do? She was just raised that way. And Papa with just his one other woman, and the woman is respectful, that fucking witch. She treats Mama like she is a senior wife. What could Mama do? It was just a different time."

"Shame, Mama."

"You know if it was me, I would have stabbed him in his sleep."

"Don't say things like that," I said.

"Ao mma, I am obviously joking," she said.

"I am just saying. Papa has passed away. You can't say things like that."

"Okay, Mother Teresa," she said. I resented this too and fell quiet.

"Actually, there was a day when Mma-Pulane came to the house when it was just me and Mama," she said. "She knocked and Mama did not open the door. It was so strange. Mma-Pulane knocked and knocked and knocked and then gave up and left her little bowl of scones on the veranda."

I watched my sister's shoulders as she laughed and tried to parse through my feelings about Mama's small rebellion. It was funny, but I felt a chip of anger, small and sharp, in my belly.

"Temo is cheating on Pauline," I said. "I think."

"Already?" Boitshepho said.

"I saw him at an Engen the other day, with a girl," I said. "They were just acting really strange."

"Who is she?"

"I don't know her," I said and heard how easily my lie sat beside the truth.

"Poor Pauline," Boitshepho said. "O, Batalaote, Batalaote." It comforted me, hearing my sister's oath, the call of help, of surrender to our ancestors.

"Why did I see them?" I asked her. "I wish I had never seen them."

"What are you going to do?"

"Why did it have to be me seeing them?" I asked her again.

"It was just a matter of time. Men who cheat are stupid and careless."

Sitting in my room after hanging up my phone, I felt the cold, sharp anger. I dredged it up from the recesses of my gut, felt its foreignness on my body, and I did not know what to do with it.

BY MARCH, the rains still had not come. The city was parched and desolate, grimly bearing the merciless sun. I needed reprieve.

The A1 stretched before me, and in the distance, the unrelenting late afternoon heat shimmered above the road. On either side, gaunt cattle grazed on the dry brown grass. I arrived in Serowe after dark. At my parents', no lights were on. I parked under a mulberry tree, rousing indignant clucking from the chickens sleeping packed together in the wire-mesh coop. The door was unlocked, the TV was muted, the actors gupping their mouths silently. Mama slept on the couch, my father's coat covering her legs. I was afraid for her. I knelt beside her and shook her shoulder. She startled awake.

"Mama," I scolded her. "Aren't you afraid of thieves?"

"Boitshepho?" she said.

"Where do you see her?" I asked, then, hearing the unkindness in my voice, I said, "It's me."

"Keletso?"

"Yes, mma." It was always me.

She sat up, rubbing her face. Something about that gesture made her seem much younger, and I adjusted Papa's coat on her legs.

"I was dreaming of your sister," she said. "She was wearing that yellow dress she used to like, remember?"

I remembered the dress, yellow with bell sleeves. The last time I had seen her in it was during one of her disappearances. I had been sent to buy meat from the butchery at Sesakgaleng, and walking past a parked red Camry, I heard Boitshepho's voice calling my name. I turned around and she was leaning with her arm out the open window. She stuck her thumb in the air. *Ja*, she had said to me, and I had stuck my thumb back, too shy to walk over to the car.

"What are you doing here?" Mama asked. I got up from the floor to switch the lights on. So much of the house remained unchanged—the same room-divider unit, the same bookshelf full of encyclopedias, the same unused floral plates. The world could shed its skin to reveal fragile new flesh and this house would still look the same.

"I came to see my mother," I said.

"And you children, there in Gaborone, are you well?"

"I am fine," I said. "As you see me."

"And your brother?"

"Mama, are you asking me for lies?" I asked. "You know I haven't seen him."

My mother fell silent. It had been four months since I had cornered Pauline after yoga at the botanical gardens. I had been fueled by the sharp alien anger inside me. Pauline had looked me in the face while I told her, opening her water bottle with her teeth. Then she turned away from me without speaking. When I left, I saw her in her car, head to steering wheel. She had not accompanied Temo to Serowe that December. My brother had spent the festive season going for angry runs up Botalaote Hill, through a heat wave and unseasonal dust winds. I heard that he had stayed at a hotel for a while, but that he was now back at home. We hadn't spoken in months.

THE MORNING bore the ancient soundtrack of my childhood: the rattle of my mother's grass broom as she swept the yard, the clink and clatter of cutlery and teacups, the low murmur of her singing. I burrowed into the warmth of my bed. The glare of the morning sun was diffused through the curtains and landed softly on my face. This enchantment was broken by the sound of my mother talking and laughing with someone. That got me out of bed. I opened the bedroom door and peered out, and right away my mother saw me.

"Aren't you coming to greet?" she said, and I walked out into the passage.

Mama was sitting with Mma-Pulane. On the coffee table lay a tray with dirty cups and saucers with leftovers of bread.

"This is a woman now, Mma-Temo," Mma-Pulane said, looking up at me. "Soon you will be calling us for a wedding."

"Dumela, the mma," Mma-Pulane said when I stood unmoving in the passage.

"Ao, where are your manners?" my mother asked. "Did you leave your manners in Gaborone?"

In the rare times Mama and Boi got along, after Mma-Pulane's visits, Boi would ask, *What did she want, that witch?* and Mama wouldn't scold her for her disrespect; instead she would mutter, *Who knows?* When I walked into the sitting room, a girl was standing in front of the dining room unit, peering into the photos my mother had displayed inside the glass doors. When she saw me, she stopped and stared, unblinking.

"Who is this?" I asked.

"This is my lastborn," Mma-Pulane said. "Katlego, sit down, what's got into you?"

I walked over to sit next to my mother, and Katlego walked over to sit in the chair opposite.

Her gaze was unabashed but not insolent. I took in her dress, her white sneakers with knee-length socks.

"Katlego," Mma-Pulane said. "Did you wake up in the same house as Keletso?"

"Dumelang," Katlego said to me in response.

"How old are you?" I asked her.

"Eight," she said. Eight wasn't old enough to be my sister.

"She is in standard two now," Mma-Pulane said.

"Do you want some tea?" my mother asked. "Mma-Pulane brought diphaphatha."

I was exhausted. I closed my eyes and put my head down on the arm of the couch.

"Keletso," my mother said. "Where does it hurt?" She pressed her hand to my forehead.

"Maybe her body is not feeling so nice," Mma-Pulane said. I heard her getting up and felt her hand on my face too. Their silent eyes pinned me to the couch, their acquiescent bodies stooped heavily over mine.

"O, Batalaote, Batalaote," my mother muttered under her breath, like prayer.

"Has she eaten anything?" Mma-Pulane asked. "Maybe she ate something bad." A hand on my forehead, another hand on my cheek. I couldn't tell her hand from my mother's.

Small Wonders

In the year she was mourning her husband, Phetso Sediba faced, every time she left her house, a series of small wonders at the stubborn, unchanging ways of the world. Some days it was the group of boys who met at the culvert across from her house that surprised her, that they would still gather there, mornings before school and evenings before heading home, to smoke and talk loudly and jostle at one another, falling silent only when she walked past. The jacaranda trees in her neighbors' yards still grew their wild purple blooms, their trunks home to the blue-headed lizards whose bobbing Phetso felt mocked by sometimes and other times pitied by. Other days it was the primary school girls who stunned her, in their little gray skirts and heavy matching stockings, their shiny faces, their backpacks beating an unending rhythm on their backs, still trotting past her gate without seeing her.

Even here, under an acacia tree in the center of the Kgale View office complex, when Phetso had braved people's swiveling stares and their tapering conversations to join the queue for the lunch vendor. Even here, a wonder.

There was a group of men who met for lunch every day; some

stood, some sat on a pack of jumbo bricks with pieces of cardboard protecting the seats of their trousers. Their arms would often be stretched to avoid staining their shirts with beetroot salad juices and coleslaw and straying oil from their fried chicken. Holding their foam containers at a distance, they were immersed in their own strange choreography. Whenever Phetso walked past, the men interrupted their loud football talk and fell into a reverent silence, as though her clothes bestowed a sainthood upon her. She did not come out that often, not anymore.

It was September and the dust winds had finally swept in, dislodging the tail end of a long winter. A gust of wind buoyed a flurry of dust upward and skittered a Coke can against the paved parking lot. The leaves from the acacia tree fell intermittently and so the vendor's silver chafing dishes could not be fully open. In the queue, a man in front of her was shouting into his cell phone, complaining to his contractor about having to buy additional cement bags. He did not interrupt his conversation to order; instead, he pointed a stubby finger at the chafing dishes holding white rice, then beef stew, then bean leaf morogo. On his tight lilac shirt, a sweat stain was sprawling toward the small of his immense back. The folded softness of his head meeting his neck reminded Phetso of Leungo. She wanted to reach out to touch the sweat-slick folds, feel them between her fingers. A wonder, that Leungo's neck would show up on the body of a belligerent stranger. Phetso watched the man walk away, holding his lunch pack away from himself, his phone still stuck to his ear.

The vendor was an old woman Phetso had bought lunch from once and thereafter felt forever tethered to, guilt-stricken whenever the errant idea of buying from another vendor visited her. All she knew about the vendor was that she was from Mochudi and a ZCC member, this latter from the glittering silver star on the green badge pinned to her chest. Additionally, Phetso knew that the vendor's food was not so good: her fried chicken too oily, her samp and beans stiffening into lumps when cold.

"Rice and chicken?" the vendor asked when she moved up the queue.

Phetso nodded. The woman dished out the rice, the spinach, and the beetroot, then without pausing from her activity, she said in a low voice, "It must be time now. It's been a year. You, in those clothes. I remember it was just after my oldest had her second son."

"Mma?" Phetso was taken aback. Most people didn't speak directly to her about the clothes. Most people only gazed at her with pity and shock and fear, wondering, she knew, how one so young could have a dead husband. Before the vendor, Phetso stood still, but inside her something was hurtling upward, from the depths of her belly to the top of her head.

"In truth," the old woman continued confidentially, her gloved hand rummaging through the fried chicken pieces. "In truth, I thought you wouldn't take a whole year. You are so young. But I don't know how they do things there in the north."

"No soup," Phetso said. She felt a little dizzy, a little too warm, pinprick tingles all over her face and on the tips of her fingers. She put her twenty-pula note on the table and turned away without saying her thanks.

EVERY MORNING THAT YEAR, Phetso had examined her outfit in the mirror in the cramped sitting room of her BHC low-cost. She had done it before too, draping her pencil skirts and cowl-necked tops, her miniskirts and shift dresses, her skinny jeans over the back of the couch to try one piece after another, shimmying in front of the mirror to the music spilling out of the TV, while her husband, with his flustered stuttering, complained that they would be late. How often she had been surprised, then, by the revelation that this was what life was, those unobtrusive moments: coffee brewing in the kitchen, her dancing before the mirror while her husband hovered nervously, anxiously, urging her to get ready for a job she was ambivalent about. Leungo had always tried to be helpful, bringing more tops, a different pair of shoes, and Phetso would still settle on skinny jeans and a white shirt. Sometimes he couldn't help himself, Leungo, seeing her dancing with a pencil skirt on, no top, no bra, and then they would be late anyway.

Now her entire wardrobe for the year had been reduced to just three items, bought for her by Leungo's brothers, in accordance with tradition: the loose, below-the-knee midnight-blue dress with a gathered waistline, the matching midnight-blue cape that fell to midback, and a cut of fabric of the same hue, which she wound every morning over her hair. She had even had to forget her collection of strappy heels and knee-high fuck-me boots, replacing them with a modest pair of Bata canvas takkies. Tying the scarf around her hair and the ends of the cape around her neck, Phetso had the uncanny sensation, sometimes, that she was putting on a disguise, like an embryonic superhero whose powers would one day announce themselves, if only she bided her time long enough.

PHETSO WORKED FOR an engineering firm, in an open-plan office perpetually overbright from the long fluorescent lights on the ceiling. At the rear of the room, she sat with her back to the wall, feet caged in by the metal legs of her desk. Whenever she raised her eyes from her computer, it was to the bent backs of the junior engineers she shared the office with. Before her bereavement, the men had openly flirted with her despite her wedding ring, arguing, mischievously, that it had been proven by their forefathers that an affair would only revitalize and strengthen a marriage. After, they grew uncomfortable and silent around her. Months later, their loudness and bantering with one another had returned, but she remained unseen. In the back, she entered data into a computer, numbers whose significance she barely understood. She had taken the position of a temporary data entry clerk, thinking that it would ease her through a couple of months of unemployment while she looked for a job better suited to her humanities degree. Perhaps working for a publisher or a public relations firm. Now it had been over two years and she had ceased searching, instead acquiescing to a life of entering the prices of cement, asphalt, and concrete for the far-flung roads and bridges the engineers designed.

When the phone at her desk rang, she knew immediately it was her mother.

"Phetso, your family in Serule have been calling me." Her mother's voice was loud and agitated, the way she always sounded on the phone. "You don't answer their calls?"

"I don't have my phone with me all the time," Phetso snapped, and her colleagues turned to look at her. "Mama, I can't talk right now," she said and hung up the phone before her mother had a chance to respond.

AT THE END OF THE WORKDAY, waiting for her cab in the parking lot, Phetso was seized with the desire to walk the edge of the curb, like she had done as a girl, her arms a straight-out cross to keep her from falling. When she reached the end, she turned and walked back in the opposite direction. Two cleaning ladies in green uniforms walked toward her, laughing between themselves. Seeing her, they stopped talking. She watched them walk past, all the way to the small gate that led to the combi stop. She wondered if they harbored any of the old beliefs, that her bereavement rendered her unclean, a carrier of an archaic disease, that the world needed protection from her.

In the distance, pink light suffused the rim of the sky at some far-off horizon of the city. It would be a year soon. How strange, a whole year of his absence. Days in which she had dazed through the city she and Leungo had made their home. Soon she would have no reason to wear her mourning clothes. Not that she had *needed* to wear them. Not really. Not anymore. Many women no longer did it, believing it cruel and old-fashioned. But in those first bewildering days, her mother had insisted. *There must have been a good reason for our people to do this*, her mother had said. *Better to do things the right way.* Besides, in the wake of her loss, Phetso had needed something. She couldn't have slipped back into the world, her pain camouflaged in her miniskirts and bright lipsticks, just another carefree young woman in the precarious city. No, her grief had been unfathomable, she had needed it confessed and laid bare. Like those religious orders who fasted, knelt for hours, wore sackcloth, self-flagellated. Mortifying their flesh in pursuit of penance. She had needed *something*. It had its uses, her mourning garb. But soon she would no longer have its announcement of her grief, its protection. The thought of it, of her unveiling, rattled her. How would she enter the world anew?

A new impulsive desire made her stand up, her heart beating and her hands sweating. She followed the two cleaning women past ChemInc and the beige double-story offices shared by a law firm and a struggling newspaper, through the small side exit out of the complex. Out in the world, a cacophony of noise and smells. Combi drivers still stuck their torsos out the windows to scream their routes. She turned on Old Industrial Road toward Old Naledi. She ignored the stares of the people who swiveled to look at her as she walked past. She ignored the phone ringing inside her handbag. By the time she crossed the railway line into Old Naledi, her scalp and the backs of her knees itched from sweat. She never ordinarily would have wandered through the township by herself, but she knew that her clothes gave her some protection. So she walked on, through the hodgepodge of painted and unpainted houses, the shebeens and tuckshops, all the way past the makeshift market where the fishermen hung their rows upon rows of butchered fish. She searched people's faces, seeking . . . she wasn't sure what she was seeking. Perhaps grief that matched hers. This too was a wonder, in a city where the public hospital was so full that patients lay crammed together on the floor, in a city running out of grounds to bury its dead.

BACK HOME, she stood in front of the mirror in the sitting room. She took her clothes off—first the cape, then the dress and the headscarf—dropping them onto the floor. Her body slackened, losing its coiled stance, no longer poised for the world's watchful eyes. She changed into a velour tracksuit, like she would have worn when Leungo was still there.

"Husband," she said out loud. She was in the kitchen, opening her nearly empty fridge, looking through the cupboards she had not replenished with food. "Husband, I stopped by the market and bought fish for dinner. It's fresh from the Gaborone Dam. I won't burn it, I promise. And if I do, don't return me home to my parents."

She chuckled to herself. It had been one of their jokes. Her ineptitude in the kitchen. His mock-threat that he would send her back, a defective bride, not worth the number of cattle he'd paid for her.

"What about this steak in the fridge?" she asked. "You want that? You want a full roast chicken? I just don't know if I have the energy for that. You are going to have to make do with this yogurt, dear husband."

She carried a saucer full of crackers and a cup of rooibos tea to the couch.

Husband. She had said the title freely before they were married. She had had his number saved under the name *Hubby* on her phone a month into dating. But after their wedding, she was giddy with the taste of it on her tongue, disbelieving that the boy with whom she had lain for hours in her dorm room bed, laughing over stand-up comedy specials, now bore this weighted title—husband. And what his title rendered her! Wife. How could she, who would buy a sheer top on final sale over a cut of beef for dinner, how could she be a wife? Yet she had known, since she was a little girl, of the many selves folded inside her, lying dormant, emerging as needed. There was the self who showed up when her father came to pick her up from her mother's house over school holidays, who sat prim and silent in the back of the car. *She* finished her food with no fights. *She* was quiet when she played by herself, mouthing the words when she gave herself a stern talking-to in front of the mirror. She had always been relieved to return to the looser self of her mother's house, the self who sprawled on the mat to watch *Superman* and *Recess*. Growing older, still another self, the partying girl that she was with her university friends, calling each other *dearest, my dearest dear* in imitation of one of their Anglophile university professors. *Well, my dear. See, my dearest.*

Despite her circumstances, her body was another wonder. In the middle of the night, her desires still woke her from the depths of a dream. Before, she would have reached for him. She would have woken him from his slumber, putting his hand between her thighs, counting on his always immediate excitement. Now she woke up reaching for herself, for the slickness of her body, and was desperate through her need, but once satiated she felt guilty. She kept herself awake with her guilt and her shame, burning so hot that she had to kick the blankets off her body.

ON SUNDAY, when Phetso opened the door, Stella was bent over struggling with the clasp of the T-bar strap on her heels.

"Help, help, help," Stella said. She was the only one of Phetso's friends who still came over, after church, with fatcakes and fresh potato chips.

Phetso laughed at her. "Every week you say you are throwing them away." She herself was cozy in her velour tracksuit and bedroom slippers.

"They are such beautiful darlings," Stella said, clasping the shoes to her chest. "And they make me look so good. But the pain." She left the shoes in the kitchen. In the living room, she shimmied out of her pencil skirt.

"Look." She showed Phetso the welt rising from her belly, above her pink lace boy shorts, where the skirt had cut into her skin. She unstrapped her bra and used it to fan air onto her chest. They walked into the bedroom, and Phetso opened the closet. Her side of the closet. His side she avoided. She brought out a pair of leggings, a long gray T-shirt, a pair of gray joggers, and Stella reached for the joggers and the T-shirt. Dressed, Stella ran her hands through Phetso's clothes, still hanging in the closet. Phetso watched Stella's hands and felt her chest begin to constrict. She had thought that she would look forward to the end of the mourning period, to wearing her own clothes again—her favorite red coat that Leungo had surprised her with, the wide-legged jumpsuit she had found on their Easter trip to Maputo. But now every time her mother called, she found it difficult to breathe.

In the sitting room, Phetso slid her wedding ring off and dropped it in an empty glass vase. The two sat on the couch, tearing the fatcakes into chunks, laying three chips side by side, drenching them in vinegar and dotting them with red chili flakes, then enveloping them in the bread. The food transported them back to the years when they were dorm roommates. Stella had been there when Phetso met Leungo at the refectory their first year of university. The two had secretly called Leungo "the Man That I Love," imitating a character on their favorite soapie. Stella had gently poked at her about being a Kalanga bride who would be expected to bolt away during the wedding so the groom could run after her. Phetso had imagined herself running, giddiness filling her chest, the wind whipping through her locs running and laughing and running.

Phetso did not tell Stella that there were days now when her mind fooled her, when her hands mindlessly poured a second cup of coffee, and she rolled onto his side of the bed, expecting the solid warmth of his body. They switched the TV on to some gospel music show they never actually watched.

"Your mother called me," Stella said.

"What did she want?"

"Come on," Stella said. "She is worried. You don't answer your phone. You don't talk to anyone."

Phetso concentrated on her fatcakes and chips, on her ice-cold glass of Oros.

"She told me that every time Leungo's family comes to collect his clothes, you lock yourself in the house."

"They didn't tell me they were coming," Phetso said.

"Dearest," Stella said, "you know that when you don't answer their calls, they just call your mom."

Phetso felt again a shortness of breath, the return of a tightness in her chest.

"You know they just want to make sure of . . . everything," Stella said. "Make sure everything is completed. You know, closure for everyone. And that everything is done the right way."

"Do you ever feel like even the elders don't really know what they are doing?" Phetso asked. "They are just making things up as they go along."

"What do you mean?"

"Everybody is pretending there is a pure and right way to do things, that we have to have this ceremony right now. Right at this moment. Or else. But if we were doing things the right way, the old way, you couldn't even visit me. I couldn't even go to work."

"Well, the world has changed."

"Exactly. That's what I am saying."

For a minute, Stella regarded her in silence. Then, "Tell me what you are saying."

"I am just saying," Phetso said, "what if I need more time?"

"You don't want to postpone this. Dearest, oh my God, P, I wish I could tell you what you want to hear. But none of this makes sense, right? Nothing in the world makes sense. The fact that Leungo is not here makes no fucking sense. Akere? But this, ceremonies like this undressing, this cleansing, this is the only way we know to make sense of . . . this confusion, this complete mystery. I mean, we can say that it's God's will. But we don't know why God willed Leungo's—why it's Leungo who is no longer here. But with a ceremony like this, we can accept that he is gone, and know that we have mourned him, and move on. I really think you have to do it. For his parents. And his siblings. And his relatives. Otherwise, this mourning period will go on and on. And everybody will be stuck in this purgatory of bereavement."

Through her tears, Phetso felt unable to articulate something essential to Stella, that she was twenty-four and alive and where, before, she had known what she was heading toward—a bigger house full of the chatter of children, a plot of land somewhere outside Gaborone— now she had nothing to look forward to.

"You can't postpone this," Stella said, handing her a tissue.

But what if she could, Phetso thought; what if she had secret powers to postpone it forever, into the next life, into infinity, to guarantee that she would forever be tethered to Leungo?

"Chomi, just do what they want," Stella said again. "Just do it for your parents and Leungo's parents. Just do it to satisfy them. I mean, you already did everything the traditional way."

It was true, though even their wedding had faced some obstacles. Her mother had been resistant, worrying about her age, warning her that marriage was far from what she saw on TV, warning her that at twenty-one her life had yet to begin. During the magadi negotiations, her father and the great-uncles she saw only at funerals demanded more and more cattle, axes, knives, a house; Phetso had to threaten to abandon the whole negotiation. *This is not 1924,* she had shouted at her father. *If you don't rein your relatives in, the two of us will just go sign a document at the district commissioner's office.* In the end, she had been glad that she had gone the traditional route, the two celebrations in Serowe and Serule. Such a strange sensation she had had, of being watched and exalted by everyone. She had felt as though she were watching herself, sitting in the lapa, surrounded by the married women of Botalaote Ward, all in their blue leteise and their blue-and-white megagolwane and headscarves. She had known to keep her head bowed as the women came to give her her instructions for marriage. She had known to sob softly, out of decorum, to show her modesty, but not too much, so the pictures wouldn't be spoiled. In Serule, when her mother-in-law knelt in front of her with her blanket, everything had slowed and quietened, even the chatter of the unmarried girls leaning from outside the lapa to catch a glimpse of her, even the ululations of the women seated behind her. Phetso remembered the two flaps, above her head, behind her, and the weight of the blanket around her shoulders. She had felt, despite herself, that she was part of *something*, something ancient and unbroken, steady.

Perhaps it was that feeling that had led her, after the funeral, to shave her head, even though it wasn't much done anymore. Her mother had spent three weeks with her in Gaborone, to adjust her to life without the deceased. It should have been longer, the time of her readjustment, three months at least, but who could spare the time? Her mother needed to go back to work. There were other rites that they had not performed that Phetso had read about. She was supposed to have entered the house backward, for example, her first entry after the funeral, her bare feet stepping on an uncured goatskin mat. She was supposed to have chewed some kind of root named sekaname and spat it at the crossroads, at the cattlepost, at the farming land, at all the homes she visited. But they had not made her do that. Surely there was a way she could prolong these last moments of being tethered to Leungo, prevent them from being swept away by time.

"Once I take these clothes off," Phetso said to Stella, "then I have no relationship with him or his family. We might as well have never been married."

"That's not true," Stella said. "How can you say that?"

"Everybody keeps telling me that I will get married again. That I will move on with my life."

"Dearest, you don't have to get married again. Maybe you will, maybe you will be lucky. But you don't have to think about any of that now. You just have to do this."

WITHOUT GABORONE, it's possible that she and Leungo never would have met, Phetso thought sometimes. Had they not been in the city at the same time, in university at the same time, was it possible that they could have spent their entire lives ignorant of each other? Then they never would have had their places in the city—their club, their butcher, the cobbler who put new heel stoppers on her shoes. Their bar, one they used to frequent so much that they and their friends called it their sitting room. *Are we going to the sitting room tonight?*

On Friday after work, she abandoned her cab again and crossed the road into Kgale View. She walked past the flats, identical in their off-white and gray paint, then through Phase 4, where the yellow town houses were hidden behind boundary walls on which were stuck broken bottle shards with the jagged edges pointing toward the sky. She walked to a small shopping complex with a butchery, a hair salon with the name Turn Heads Here, an internet café, and their bar, their sitting room.

There were only two customers inside, in the cool dark of the afternoon, two men, already inebriated, dancing together to a song blaring from the jukebox. Behind the bar, a new girl in a burgundy weave was bent over a cell phone. The girl looked startled when Phetso came in and waited before walking over to her. Phetso ordered a beer. When she was halfway through the bottle, one of the dancing men walked over and sat across from her.

"Are you supposed to be here?" the man asked. When Phetso ignored him and kept drinking, he asked, "Who was it?"

She looked at him. He was sweaty and had a chipped front tooth. A tiny golden hoop glinted from each of his ears.

"It was my husband," Phetso said. It was the first time she'd talked about him with a stranger, although she knew that they all knew, all the people who saw her, because of her clothing.

"What happened?"

Then a fully formed lie slipped out unbidden, like in the days when guys at bars just like this one would ask for her name, and she would present herself anew. Felicity, she would say. Or Tebogo. Ludo. Fifi.

"He was old," she said to the drunk man. "Much older than I am. I married him for his money."

"You must be rich."

"His children are fighting me for the money."

"No!"

"They are. They want to take all the houses. The house in Phaka-lane. The house in Mokolodi. Even the one in Cape Town. They want the savings accounts. But I am his wife. And they are old, all older than me, they have their own money."

"There is nobody greedier than a rich person."

"I keep asking them, what about me? Can somebody think about me?" She felt a glimmer of pleasure deep in her belly.

"That's why I am here," she continued. "I am drinking my stress away. The case is in court next week."

"Ah, but don't worry. Don't stress. You are going to win. I can tell."

"Really?"

"You are going to win," he said. "Believe me."

She took a sip of her beer. "Are you a prophet or sangoma or something?"

"No. I just know. I have a feeling, in my body. You are going to win. And when you win, you should come back here and buy me drinks."

He left to go dance again with his partner. When Phetso ordered another drink, the girl sullenly raised her head from the phone. She put the beer in front of her without a smile, without a word. In a minute Phetso's dancing friend was back, his hand on her shoulder. Phetso was afraid that she had gone too far.

"But even if you don't win, my sister," he said. "Even if you don't win. It's fine. You are young. Look at you. And life is long. Ask me, I know. You are listening to me, right? Listen to me, I know."

"I am listening," Phetso said.

BY THE FIRST WEEK OF OCTOBER, the quiet, relentless summer rains had returned, and in their wake wild yellow flowers bloomed all over the city. Phetso spent nights in erratic sleep, coming awake in the dark to insistent rain. She searched her memory of The Day for premonitions. She had thought they had the kind of love that was written about, the kind of love that warranted signs. She should have gotten an uncanny feeling even before he left for Serule that weekend. She should have begged him to stay. She should have convinced him that he could see his parents another time. She should have called. She should have asked him to stop at Kaytees, provided him a moment of serendipity, so he could have reached that spot minutes later, the cow already having crossed the road. She should have known the moment his car hit the cow and flipped through the air. Instead, at around the time he died, she was falling asleep on their couch watching *It's Pimpin' Pimpin'* for the seventh time.

AFTER HER TALK WITH STELLA, Phetso had thought about what she would do when she invited her sister-in-law, the one who lived closest to her, in Mochudi, to come over. She would keep her head and voice low, as befitting a mourning wife. She would invite Mma-Tirelo in for tea and they would commiserate over their sorrow, the loss of their beloved. She would have all of Leungo's clothes ready. So she was shocked, on Sunday afternoon, when she responded to a knock at her door, expecting Stella, and found Mma-Tirelo instead.

Mma-Tirelo was angry and dry-eyed and she did not even give Phetso a chance to greet her.

"How many times must I call you?" she asked. Behind her the sky was turning a deep orange and Phetso could hear her neighbors calling for their bulldog. *Princess! Princess!*

"Must I spend time calling you when there is so much work to do?"

"Mma-Tirelo," Phetso stammered. "I didn't know . . ."

She looked back in the direction of the bedroom, where her phone was. From where she stood at the door, she could see her unmade bed, the duvet gathered in peculiar mountains and valleys. Mma-Tirelo looked up and down at Phetso's clothes, the leggings and crop top that left parts of her body exposed.

"I am here to collect my brother's clothes," Mma-Tirelo said.

Phetso led her to the bedroom. She watched as Mma-Tirelo ran her fingers through all the shirts Leungo had bought for his job at the accounting firm that he had worked for since his graduation. Mma-Tirelo pushed a bedside table in front of the closet and climbed up to remove the two suitcases from the top. Phetso, unable to breathe, turned around and walked into the bathroom. She locked herself in and sat on the toilet seat. She listened to the staccato of Mma-Tirelo's shoes, moving with the certainty of her duty and responsibility, between the closet and the suitcases flung open on the bed. She imagined her collecting all of Leungo's clothes: the jeans, the chinos, the T-shirts, the socks rolled into the bedside drawers. She imagined her stuffing the clothes in the suitcases without pausing to savor the vestiges of his scent. Phetso's throat was raw. She wept. Every time Mma-Tirelo called out to her, she flushed the toilet. She felt the seat vibrate under her and its noise fill her ears. A knock on the door. She stopped sniffling.

"Phetso," Mma-Tirelo said. Phetso did not answer.

"I know you hear me talking to you," Mma-Tirelo said. Still Phetso kept quiet. She felt silly, a child, and regretted locking herself in.

"Okay. I am leaving," Mma-Tirelo said.

Phetso opened the door.

"I have never seen behavior like this," Mma-Tirelo said. She was breathing loudly, wiping at a sweat mustache with her hand.

"Sorry," Phetso said, chastened.

"You are not the only person who misses him," Mma-Tirelo said. "We miss him too."

No one could miss him as much as I do, Phetso thought.

"I am leaving tomorrow," Mma-Tirelo said. "Five a.m. I thought we could leave together. You spend the night in Mochudi and we leave first thing in the morning."

"I have to go to work."

"You didn't ask for days off?"

"I have work I need to finish," she said, but even she heard the starkness of her lie.

"I can take the bus on Friday," she said.

She watched her sister-in-law wheel suitcases full of Leungo's clothes into her car, then she walked into the bedroom to look at the gaping, half-full closet.

THE LAST WEDNESDAY before the ceremony, her phone wouldn't stop ringing. Her mother's calls were relentless. Stella's calls. Mma-Tirelo's calls. Phetso couldn't focus. She needed to escape the office, so she took a combi from Kgale to the Gaborone bus station. Where she alighted from the combi, there was a low redbrick wall that people sat on, waiting for their T-bone steaks and their boerewors to be done on the braai. She walked past the rows of taxis facing north, their open doors like metallic wings heaving in the heat. Everywhere she looked, masses of people occupied their own worlds, indifferent to her sorrows.

From the bus station, she walked over the bridge to the Main Mall. She arrived at dusk, just as the mall was assuming the lonely and empty face it wore in the evenings, after the vendors packed up and the office workers hurried to catch their combis. Behind Debswana House, Phetso waited for the traffic lights to change. An old man was sitting on the steps of the Labour office, his clothes darker against the yellow paint of the building. Immediately she pitied him, the way she always sorrowed at the sight of elderly people in Gaborone. Why were they here, subjecting themselves to the mercurialities of life in this city? Where were their children? He was, she saw as she approached, a tall man with a straggly gray beard and a black hat, wearing a gray jacket over an olive-green shirt. On the lapel of his jacket was pinned the little square of black fabric that marked him. As she walked past, the man doffed his hat at her.

ON FRIDAY MORNING, she watched a man in a bright yellow T-shirt and shorts walk down the length of the Serule-bound bus, a stack of Hungry Lion boxes in his arms. Behind him, a tall, gaunt man leaned into every seat, showing his selection of faux-leather wallets, business card holders, and passport pouches, then loudly berated an old woman for declining to buy his products. Phetso opened her book as the bus moved out of the station. She wouldn't be able to read, but she wanted to revel in her memories of Leungo waking her up with the news in his forthright and simple way: *I think it's time I sent my uncles to your family.* She had merely smiled and nodded, hidden her giddiness, forgetting altogether the romantic TV proposal—bent knee, ring concealed in some kind of dessert or book—that she had always vaguely expected. Instead, she nodded at his words and said, very rationally, that she would call her aunt and her mother with the news and they would in turn call her uncles, who would wait for word from his uncles. She had wanted to laugh, responding to him, for even though his words were good and true, she had felt, somehow, that the idea that the two of them could invent a new life, unencumbered by their families, was only a kind of game.

AS IT PULLED INTO the Palapye station, the bus became a magnet that vendors hurtled toward and squirmed against, holding up plates of fried chicken and potato chips cut in thin disks, trays of Simba chips and warm fizzy drinks. Phetso reached across and closed the window against their desperate faces. She got off the bus to stretch her legs. None of the vendors approached her, but she walked up and bought peanuts and a bottle of water from a boy still wearing his school uniform, his gray tie loosened around his neck. The bus drove on for another hour, and then they had to get off and sink the soles of their shoes into a shallow well of medicine that would stop them from transporting foot and mouth disease. The officers were flustered, seeing her clothes. Quickly, a separate plastic bowl with the medicine was provided for her, and she lowered first one shoe, then the other into the bowl. Along the road, seemingly from nowhere, women sat beside pyramids of watermelons and buckets of dried salted phane.

THE YARD was somber when she arrived in Serule. Most of the women were in the sitting room of the main house, watching the news on the television. The sofas had been pushed all the way back to the walls. Instantly, Phetso remembered the week before the funeral, when she had spent her days in a darkened room, prostrate on a mattress surrounded by old women. Every time Phetso had shifted her body or sat up, they all asked if she needed anything—more tea, more porridge, another phaphatha—and then sank back into their stillness when she refused their offerings. Now she knocked on the open door and walked in.

"Phetso, is that you?" her mother asked, her voice bright with relief.

Phetso saw Leungo's mother look away.

Mma-Tirelo turned the television off. An old woman struggled up and came to relieve Phetso of her bags.

Another asked, "Does the patient come alone?" and they all clucked disapprovingly at her confirmation. She felt, rather than saw, them leading her to one of the mats. A blanket was brought for her to cover her legs, and another for her shoulders. Once she was veiled to their liking, the old women took up their positions again and gossiped in low voices. Phetso lay among them, allowing their murmurs to wash over her body while she waited for her instructions.

THE PLACE where she was to be undressed was a single room behind the main house in the yard, hemmed in between the tharesetala fence and the pit latrine that nobody ever used. Leungo had paid someone to build the room before he and Phetso got married, and three years later, it was still unpainted and gray, still had no proper ceiling and at night its corrugated iron roof popped and snapped as the temperatures changed. Since they lived in the city, the room needed neither beautiful nor comfortable furniture. It was just to satisfy tradition. They had only used it once a year when they went home for Christmas. The room was bare except for a chest of drawers and a single bed pushed right up to the wall. This was where Phetso spent the night.

By dawn, Phetso was already up, fully clothed, sitting and waiting on the bed, which she had made. Outside it was dark and quiet, and the light of the moon washed in through the window. Soon a quiet, urgent knock came at the door.

The woman who entered was familiar to Phetso, one of a contingent of older relatives whom she had had to meet before her wedding. Phetso was not sure what was expected of her, so she just sat on the bed and watched the woman haul in a metal tub and place it in the middle of the room. The woman closed the door behind her and came back momentarily, lugging a bucket full of hot water. She moved slowly, breathing loudly and raggedly, due to her exertion and her corpulence.

The woman had to be a widow to be performing this ceremony, but she still wore a simple gold wedding ring. Phetso watched her from the bed where she sat. The old woman untied a small plastic bag from the ends of her headscarf and pinched the herbs inside the bag and dropped them into the water. It smelled like lawn and the gata-la-tshwene tea that her mother used to make. The old woman straightened up with a groan.

"The water is ready," she said to Phetso.

Phetso stood up but was unsure what to do.

The old lady gestured at her and Phetso took off her clothes—first the cape and then the dress and the headscarf, everything except her underwear—and dropped them onto the bed. She put a foot into the water. It was so hot that she was nervous it would scald her skin. Yet she put her other foot into the tub and then eased down into it, her back meeting the cold surface and the hot water rising to lap at her buttocks. She closed her eyes and felt the older woman scooping up the water with her hands and pouring it over her back, then down her arms, down her legs. Her calloused fingers pressed into Phetso's neck. It was so early that there was no other sound except for the old woman's breathing and the trickle and splash of the water.

The old woman groaned again, straightening up. Her face was dark and glistened with her sweat. The towel she unfolded and held up still bore the imprints of pegs on its edges. Phetso rose from the water and walked into the towel. She dried herself, wondering if the herbs would make her skin itch, wondering when she would be allowed to have a normal bath. Behind the towel, she slid her underwear down and off and stepped from it.

As Phetso dried herself, the old woman unfolded clothes from a plastic bag.

"Your uncles in Serowe have bought you these clothes," the old woman said with formal solemnity, "to show the end of your affliction."

Then the woman handed Phetso the clothes, one by one, saying as she did:

"Receive this, panties.

"Receive this, a bra.

"Receive this, a skirt.

"Receive this, a shirt.

"Receive this, socks.

"Receive this, shoes."

Phetso put each item on: sky-blue cotton panties; a brown cotton bra, slightly big on her; a German-print skirt that fell below her knees; a white long-sleeved T-shirt; sky-blue socks; and a white version of her midnight-blue canvas takkies. She put them on, one after the other, like a child learning to dress for the first time. She felt slightly ridiculous in the too-long skirt, which swallowed her frame. But the woman only looked at her with what seemed to be satisfaction. When Phetso was done, the woman poured the dirty water back into the bucket and lugged it outside.

Phetso stayed where she was, in the center of the room her dead husband had built for them. She was unsure what to do. It was still dark, but she could hear the sounds of activity around the yard. There, a man chopping wood. There, an intuitive goat bleating its apprehension. There, the murmur of women preparing water and food. Soon, she knew, her husband's relatives would show up and distribute his clothes among themselves, talismanic little pieces of him they could latch on to forever. An uncle would rise, soon, to thank them for coming to bring to completion this sad chapter that they had all suffered. He would remind them that the family had gathered a little water to quench their thirst and sate their hunger. Go *weditswe, go weditswe*, he would intone, the words a final salve, and the family would disperse, some back to their jobs in the city, some back to the cattlepost; still others would linger to take care of the leftover bread and meats, to take care that everything was in its right place.

Out there, the world was back in its order, steady and unsurprising; out there, the great body of her people had drawn from its well of earned wisdom and had been restored to wholeness. Sequestered in the cocoon of the room of her cleansing, Phetso was envious. She rubbed her sweaty, childish hands on the German-print skirt. She had hoped for more from the ceremony. Rising from the water, she had thought she would reach a different state of maturity, one without her faithless dread or her bewilderment or her unanswerable questions. She wanted to feel calm and whole, all her lonely and disparate selves coalesced into one. She wanted a moment, perhaps it was still coming, when she could feel herself step into a redeemed world.

Dark Matter

◈

In Makalamabedi, their names were entwined: Tumo and Nametso in the classroom, heads puzzling over maths problems; Nametso and Tumo at break time, basking in the sun and eating their bowls of bopheya; *Tumo! Nametso!* shouted into the darkening evening by their mothers when neither had arrived home. Their mothers were teachers at the same primary school in the region of Makalamabedi north of the Boteti River. Both were transplants brought to the village by work, living in the teachers' quarters within the school compound. The quarters shared a forlorn look—peeling yellow paint, rusting corrugated iron roofs—but Tumo's mother had been in Makala-mabedi longer, thus her accommodations were bigger: two bedrooms, an unfitted kitchen, and a bathroom with no indoor plumbing. As early as two weeks into their meeting, Nametso's mother would turn up apologetic at Tumo's mother's house, evenings, carrying a light cardigan and a Tupperware lunch for her daughter. Before long, people entangled the girls, calling the one by the other's name. But they were nothing alike. Tumo had wide-set eyes in an oval face, dimples in her chubby cheeks. Brimming with incessant chatter, she was aware, already, of how her smile startled adults' faces into laughter even when what she said was naughty. She trained her dimples and eyes on everyone, like a pair of torchlights, then wickedly imitated the teachers and adults for Nametso in the privacy of their play. Nametso envied Tumo this ability to issue spontaneous words from somewhere inside her, with no prior thought. In contrast, Nametso had to gather first the one strand, then the other strand of her thoughts before getting the courage to open her mouth. She wished, sometimes, that her thoughts could be received in the world without the necessity of her speech. Nametso was devoted to Tumo. She wanted nothing more than to be within Tumo's orbit of many excitements. For example: Tumo and Nametso sneaking around to go swimming in the river they had been prohibited from. A willful deception, which haunted Nametso though it had been her idea, Nametso's, that they squeeze a bit of body lotion into a plastic bag before going down to the water; they always returned from their playing smelling of cocoa butter and camphor. Tumo and Nametso squatting down to shit, then spreading their excrement between two pieces of rock and holding the rocks aloft, calling down bouquets of buzzing flies. Tumo and Nametso climbing up mopenoene and mmupudu trees to sing to boys in classes higher than theirs—*Ekse mosimane / N-kadime / Tshipi-e-ntsho / Ke palame.* Nametso's mother loved her daughter's new exuberances, her arrivals home full of endless and breathless stories, so many that Mma Pilatwe, an inveterate daydreamer, was rescued from the obligation to respond and could rely on her store of exclamations—*Ao! Ijo! Heelang! Waitse!*—as her daughter went on and on and on.

ONLY MUCH LATER does Nametso realize that the "tshipi e ntsho" in their treetop song had less to do with riding a bicycle than it did with riding a bbc. Nametso is sitting in the back of the car, from Sir Seretse Khama International Airport, peering out the window at a lone cyclist on the shoulder of the road, when the memory washes over her unbidden. Laughter emerges from deep in her belly; she covers her mouth with her hands. Sitting next to her in the back is her niece, Sethunya, white heart-framed sunglasses propped on her cornrows, who steals a smiling furtive look at Nametso. Sethunya's mother, Onthatile, squints at them both through the rearview mirror and asks, "What?"

But Nametso cannot respond. She is bent over, convulsing.

"What?" her younger sister asks again from the driver's seat. She is sludging through Thursday evening traffic. "What is it? Don't deny me news, you two in the back."

Nametso waves the question away. It is August, and though diffused by evening, the light of the sun is incandescent inside the car. Onthatile is squinting as she asks, "Baby, what's your aunt laughing at?"

"I don't know," Sethunya says, "she just started laughing, just, just, just." Sethunya giggles a little, glancing askance at her aunt, whose face seems different from the one that video-called every month to her mother's phone.

"Your aunt is a writer," Onthatile says, as though that explains everything. "Did you know that? She writes books."

Listening to her sister, Nametso can't contain herself. Laughter continues to bubble out of her, the sound escaping from her body without aid, turning into an ache in her chest. At the airport she had been overcome by the miracle of her homecoming. Behind her, ten years of a life, an ex-boyfriend, the roommates they had shared a two-bed apartment with, colleagues at her underpaying adjunct job, the writer friends with whom she had shared monthly Thai dinners where they gushed over Ginzburg and Ba and Shields and Morrison and assiduously refrained from discussing their own works in progress; all that was behind her. Ahead, just beyond the customs officer, who, glancing at her passport, greeted her by name, was home. She had been so overwhelmed by her arrival that she had neglected to use the bathroom. Now she feels the achy throb of her urine-filled bladder and she crosses her legs. Her eyes prickle with tears and she tilts her head backward to stare at the roof of the car, even as she continues laughing. She has wandered into some kind of delirium, she fears. It's not just the bicycle. Or the erstwhile inappropriateness of their childhood song. It's everything. What she remembered as swaths of grassy open fields in the city are revealed as new neighborhoods, blocky double-stories rising rigid behind tall boundary walls and electric fences, high-rise office buildings sun-gleaming so far from the city center, new strip malls sprawling one after another, gobbling up space, the swarms of cars in the parking lots around the shopping malls. Everywhere, ugly yellow excavators, cranes against blue sky, painstaking men raising mammoth buildings from the earth. At the traffic light, a group of riders in matching helmets and powerful motorbikes take off past the car in an extravagant roar and zoom into the darkening horizon. Even they make Nametso recall Tumo, the semester she had decided she was an adventurer, saving up for a trip to bungee jump at Victoria Falls. Turning into her Block 6 neighborhood, Onthatile has to ram onto the brakes and come to an abrupt stop. Ahead, revealed in the headlights, a herd of cattle marching across the road with the leisure of matrons accustomed to reverence. Nametso stops laughing, with relief. Not everything has changed.

At her door, Onthatile runs into the house to disarm the security system. When she returns her heels are off and her skirt is unzipped.

She is less contained, her smile hesitant and expectant as her eyes search her sister's face. Nametso studies her sister back, her large, open face, her closely cropped hair, which she guesses is not due to any affinity to the new trend but for the convenience. Her simple gold earrings have the same dangling heart-shaped ornament they used to covet in the sales adverts that came with the free *Daily News*. *18-karat gold. 24-karat gold.* Nametso feels light dazed, welled up and tender, like she could be tipped into tears by anything at all.

"This is where we have been suffering life," Onthatile says shyly when she wheels Nametso's matching luggage inside. She gestures toward the open-plan kitchen, dark-wood fittings, and gold-plated hardware, toward the living room, the TV playing some Disney show, an enormous couch in a buttery brown, cushions stacked against one another. Everything spotless. Everything where Onthatile wants it to be. Even Sethunya's rucksack on the couch and her school blazer draped over it seem placed there just so. Nametso is moved, seeing the effort her sister has taken, the evidence of care.

"If this is suffering," Nametso says to her sister, "I will take some."

"It's just a little shack," Onthatile says. "Somewhere for me and Sethunya to lay our heads."

Nametso has, of course, not forgotten this strain of self-deprecation that seems seeded into the marrow of every Motswana, but it has been a while since she has seen it deployed in real life.

"At least," Nametso says gently. "You have tried. Mme would be proud."

In a bedroom off the living room, there is a pink guitar with white strings on an ottoman in the corner, posters of wide-eyed blond girls Nametso does not recognize plastered on the wall.

"You will use Sethunya's room," Onthatile says. Sethunya collapses her face and purses her lips into a pout. Onthatile doesn't notice; she pulls her daughter toward her and chucks her under the chin. She says, "And Sethunya will sleep with me, remember, baby?"

"I am ten," Sethunya responds in English, thrusting her hands into the air and pursing her lips in a way that, Nametso understands, has earned her laughter. Indeed, Onthatile laughs and rubs Sethunya's head. A gesture that surprises Nametso. This is not the kind of mother Nametso expected her sister to be, all softness and laughter, tolerant of petulance.

"I can't believe she is ten," Nametso says. "I mean, how is it possible that she is ten already?"

"It's terrifying, isn't it?" Onthatile says. "How the years rush past? Sometimes I feel like they are after me, that the years are chasing me, you know, like if I am not careful, if I am not smart, I will wake up one day, old, having accomplished nothing at all, made no mark on the world. But at least I created this little parcel for myself," she says, patting her daughter's head again. "Before long, this one will be going to secondary school, then university, then maybe I can rest."

Switching to English, Onthatile says, "But you are not too old to have sleepovers with Mummy, are you, baby?"

"Ugh, Mummy," Sethunya says, "do I have to?"

Onthatile looks at Nametso and says, in Setswana, "Will we survive these white children?"

Six years into their life in Makalamabedi their mother had impulsively left teaching and moved them to Selibe Phikwe, where she had hoped to make a living as a tailor. There, the sisters had first encountered the kinds of children they called white. They were always Batswana, sometimes even Batalaote like themselves, but their lives had been incomprehensible to the sisters. They were children who went to private schools and spoke English all the time, children with a lifetime of eating cornflakes and bacon and eggs for breakfast, whose parents seemed besieged by the onslaught of their offspring's back talk, children who claimed pollen allergies and wielded asthma pumps at playtime, who had no chores and could squander a whole day watching TV, lifting their legs so their maids could scoot beneath and sweep under them. Nametso can't tell from her sister's smile whether she is proud or embarrassed.

"Don't be naughty," Nametso says to her niece, and Onthatile glances at her sharply.

"When I was your age, your mom and I shared everything," Nametso tells Sethunya.

Sethunya has a soft, chubby face, the darkness of a plum, and a protuberant forehead that gives her a defiant expression when she looks up at Nametso. She stares, blinking her large eyes slowly, holding her mother's hand in both of hers.

"We had to share a bed and a bath. Sometimes we ate from the same plate. We shared everything. Dresses. Everything," Nametso says.

"Dresses?" Onthatile laughs. "That might have been Tumo."

That's right. When she and Tumo were ten, Onthatile would have been just four years old. And when Onthatile herself was ten, Nametso would have been in Selibe Phikwe Senior Secondary School, chasing her sister away whenever she wanted to straggle after her. In those new days of boys and surreptitious cigarettes at the park, Onthatile had been nothing but a pest, full of sensible warnings and threats to tell their mother. Here she was now, with a day-to-day reality that Nametso cannot fathom—a mortgage, life insurance, unit trusts, savings accounts, monthly payments on the new car, monthly contributions to the motshelo with the ladies in her department at work, contributions for bridal showers, baby showers, kitchen top-ups, housewarmings, school fees, a regimen of extracurriculars for her daughter: dance, guitar, Kumon, Mandarin and French classes, presents for birthday parties, play dates at the movies and the water park. Not that Nametso is too surprised at Onthatile's grim competence. Her sister had determined at fourteen that she would be rich. She had drawn up a budget for their mother. She used to chase away the women who came by selling Golden and Amway and Tupperware. And yet after enumerating all her bills, Onthatile had still bought Nametso's one-way ticket home. The ticket price a loan, money that Nametso has promised to pay back.

Thoughts of the money crowd Nametso's head like dark little menaces, but she pushes them off, electing instead to sit heavily on the bed. Onthatile pauses from her chatter about their cousins in Serowe, the last of Sethunya's clothes in her arms.

"You have been traveling for two days," Onthatile says.

"I have," Nametso says.

"You must be jet-lagged."

"I am," Nametso says. "On top of everything else. I just have so much fatigue."

This admission Nametso offers as a tentative opening to a conversation she hopes they will have, a taxonomy of all the mysterious ailments of her mind, all her debilitating anxieties and depressions, but at the admission Onthatile's face shutters closed and she presses her lips together. They have yet to discuss the phone call, which had started routinely enough but had ended with Nametso in great, gulping tears, confessing to her sister her conviction that she would die so far from home. From the impatience with which she had enumerated her bills, Onthatile's voice had morphed into full-on alarm. But all subsequent phone calls had been practical: account numbers, dates of arrival, the merits of taking the longer route via Doha rather than directly to Johannesburg or Addis Ababa. Now, sitting in full physical health across from her sister, Nametso is ashamed, certain her sister thinks she invented her illness, like a truant schoolgirl. She wishes she could explain how she was asphyxiated beneath her worries, too removed from the clarity she needed to face any day.

"You are sharp, though, right?" Onthatile says, turning at the door, face perched atop her daughter's clothes. "You are all right? You are okay?"

"I am home, at least," Nametso says.

Onthatile closes the door behind her.

Eighteen hundred dollars. Almost P20,000. She had emptied her American bank account but still arrived in Gaborone with a fraction of the amount. If she got a good job, she could pay the money back within months, no problem, but how long would it take to find a job? Mostly, Nametso is confounded at what has become of her life. What has she made of thirty-nine years? Perhaps the time had arrived to face her life, not with the rash impulses of her youth but with acquiescence. Already her every decision is weighted with risk and consequence. Everything assigned meaning. Once, running out of her apartment for the bus, she had fallen and scraped her knee and hands, and later she had spent hours wondering what lessons there were to be gleaned from the fall. Perhaps she needed to Slow Down. Perhaps to Pay Attention. Another time, walking in the Californian city she had ended up in, she had been lost, her phone battery dead and night descending. She had heard a voice say her name, clear as day, the way it was meant to be said. She had turned back and in turning had remembered her childhood, how it had been said that a name echoed in that way, with nobody around, meant that you had become unrecognizable to your ancestors; the call an invocation requiring only one response—a revelation of the self.

UPON WAKING her first morning back, Nametso is bewildered by the quiet. She misses the voice of her boyfriend practicing his Spanish via Duolingo, as he often did at that hour. *¿Me lo escribe, por favor? No hay dulzura aquí*; his voice trailing after the garbled voice of the woman on the phone. Ex-boyfriend. They had come to a very civil and adult agreement.

Out her sister's window, a gentle rain teeters through sunshine. The piss of the sun, they used to call that kind of rain, with a childish awe at their own bravado, insulting so grand an entity. The smell of the earth seeps into the house and Nametso is overwhelmed by an old craving. She opens the windows and the door, and the smell is everywhere. In the US, she had often woken up tormented by a hunger for just this fragrance. She had been bewildered by just how many miles she could walk with nothing but pavement and tall buildings and trees encircled by pavement so that, sometimes, she doubted the existence of earth beneath the buildings. In her sister's backyard, the pinpoint prints of the raindrops on the ground are like goose bumps on flesh. She digs up a clod of earth, below the surface where it is cool and dry, and it crumbles in her hands. She digs up another and holds it up to her nose, and inhales deeply. Her tongue darts out, craving the grainy creaminess of the earth, but Nametso can't bring herself to taste it.

OVER THE WEEKS, she gorges herself on Chicken Licken hot wings. On Eet-Sum-Mor and Romany Creams and Tennis biscuits. She drinks cupfuls of Five Roses, taking her top off so sweat can trickle down her chest and back unencumbered. She walks to a roadside vendor to buy roast mealies. She pairs plain sorghum porridge with milk for dinner and Sethunya asks to order in pizza. She boils short-grain white rice and eats it with just mayonnaise and tomato sauce, and Onthatile laughs at her, saying surely she cannot miss that food of their poverty. Still, they stand in Onthatile's kitchen sharing a plate of the rice, girls again. In a nostalgic daze Nametso buys a bag of mosutlhwane, and the smell of it in the pot resurrects those school days of splashing in the river with Tumo; she throws the mosutlhwane out without eating any of it. She buys sour milk and eats a cupful with just a little bit of sugar sprinkled on it. She cooks soft sorghum porridge with dashes of lemon juice, but the tartness is not the same as real ting, tart from weeks of fermentation, foaming at the mouth of its container. Nametso eats with the vigor of one wishing to propel herself to the past.

THEY WERE A PICTURE, Tumo and Nametso, in matching drop-waist dresses, gifts sewn by Mma Pilatwe, wailing beside a truck loaded with precarious furniture. Two years, almost to the day, since they had met, Tumo's mother had been transferred to a school in Orapa.

Bomma, you have cried your tears, Tumo's mother said. The sun will set with us waiting for you two to stop crying.

You can visit, Mma Pilatwe told her daughter, in her airy voice of a daydreamer.

Onthatile, six years old, reached for her crying sister and said, Namza, Mme says you can visit. Namza swatted Onthatile's hand away.

Orapa is not that far, Mma Pilatwe said. We get on a bus and one-two, one-two, we are there. And you can write to each other. Don't you want to receive a letter from your friend? Don't you want to go up in assembly and get your own little envelope and a beautiful little stamp that you can keep forever and ever?

A vision materialized in Nametso's mind, of her name being called in morning assembly and her, in her green tunic, walking up to receive an envelope addressed to her, observed by the whole school. *Vaya, vaya, little envelope, and land in the hands of Nametso Pilatwe*, it would say on the outside of the envelope, in the fashion of the day. But even that vision proved small comfort in the face of the truck driver press-press-pressing the hooter and Tumo's mother saying, Night is nigh, and Tumo climbing aboard the truck. Nametso turned away, determined to not-wave, to not-see Tumo's face. Instead she ran home to burrow inside her mother's bed and cry herself to sleep. When she emerged five hours later, the sky loomed low, its amber light seeping through the sieve of clotted clouds, alien enough that Nametso believed she had dreamt the whole episode. She wandered over to Tumo's and stared, lip trembling, at the curtainless windows, the gaping house.

Nametso sent letters:

Dear Tumo,

Yesterday our class went to the Nhabe Museum in Maun. We travelled there by combi until we arrived. At the museum we learnt about the Batawana and their chiefs, like Kgosi Letsholathebe and Kgosi Tawana. We also learnt about the Bayeyi and the Hambukushu, who used to rely on the Thamalakane and Boteti rivers for everything.

Dear Tumo,

I am excited to tell you that I have joined the Young English Speakers Club. We are not allowed to speak any

other language during the day except English. Mr.
Mpulubusi brings us the Daily News and books like the
Famous Five, the Faraway Tree, and the Hardy Boys. I think
you would like George. She is my favorite.

Dear Tumo,
For this year's Commonwealth celebrations, I was chosen
to represent Singapore. Singapore gained independence on
August 9, 1965, just a year before Botswana. While
Botswana is a landlocked country in Southern Africa,
Singapore is an island city-state in Southeast Asia.

And always, at the end of the letters, *I miss you. Respond please.*
Your best friend, Nametso.

EVERY MORNING, Nametso walks into the kitchen to find that Onthatile has left a newspaper out, as well as coffee and tea and sugar,
sometimes powdered milk or biscuits, various other treats. She ex-
plores the neighborhood, walking farther and farther each day, past
the new private hospital and the new private college, past the small
shopping complex with a Pizza Hut, past the large posters advertising shows at nightclubs whose names she doesn't recognize. She
walks with the slow astonished air of a convalescent. She remembers,
seeing groups of young men at a car wash, to tuck her cell phone
into the waistband of her leggings, to conceal it beneath her T-shirt.
Back in the house, she occupies her hours with a daily routine of
cooking and cleaning and watering the plants in the yard. She reads
out of a habit of reverence, of seeking penance and solace; a faithful
page from Flaubert, a comforting page from Achebe, an energizing

one from Head. The day still wide and expansive, she has no more excuses to keep her from work. Work being a 127-page novel manuscript, five years in the making. Riffling through her marked-up hard copy, she is moved at the esoteric marginalia she left herself: *mythos—totem—heart—literal, translate names of trees?????*

She suffers from intense fits of nostalgia for the city she lived in, missing the heat and scent of fabric softener emanating from the blocks she walked past, missing how her body would intuit the bus's approach to her stop on late nights and jolt her awake. Even the mercurial weather she had never stopped complaining about. In memoriam, the habits she had adopted in that city are diminished and softened: the choreography she had mastered to avoid human shit on the street, dirty needles; stepping around homeless people on her way to barre, turning away at the sight of police. Instead, she tells her sister about the city and its many moments of beauty: high-rise buildings shrouded in early morning fog, tiny corner stores where you could get your fortunes told, how one could partake of cuisine from across the world and queue outside marijuana dispensaries in the light of day. She talks about her wind-whipped beach days and hikes up rolling hills. Only with her sister is she this loquacious, so she talks and talks and accepts Onthatile's brief flashes of smiles as tokens of admiration. Onthatile hears all about museums and bookstores and art galleries and the endless high-end stores where one could buy a handbag for the price of a plot of land in Serowe.

"You know what's coming next?" Nametso asks. "Smartphones that respond to your thoughts. Computer-aided telepathy."

She has slipped into a remembered role, of predecessor, sophisticate, a pioneer lighting up a path for her baby sister. Her sister, who had been sensible, easily shocked as a child. At Nametso's moments of generosity, of admitting her into the mysteries of teenage life, Onthatile would listen devotedly, mouth slightly open. Her guileless face would sometimes betray her, with a frown of disapproval or disappointment, at some of Nametso's stories. The stories had been full of embellishments and Nametso had savored, back then, those disapproving looks as evidence of the distance between herself and Onthatile, distance characterized by her daring and her sister's lack of it. Now, Onthatile toggles between nodding smiles toward Nametso and leaning down to listen to Sethunya, who lies prone on the floor, who raises her head once in a while to speak to her mother in a whisper concealed behind her hands. Nametso has noticed Sethunya doing this at other times, chattering away into her mother's wonderstruck face but immediately lowering her voice when Nametso steps into the room. This hurts Nametso. But she reprimands herself for her own silliness, taking seriously the whims of a child. Watching Onthatile's face light up to what Sethunya is whispering in her ear, Nametso falters. She waits for her sister to return to her.

When she does, Onthatile mentions her plans for the money loaned to Nametso. She wants to develop the yard, she says, raise the value of the house. She was thinking of a patio in the back, tiled, with some kind of roof structure, maybe an in-built braai stand for get-togethers during summer nights.

"You will get your money back," Nametso says. "I will pay you."

Onthatile is leaning down into whatever Sethunya is whispering into her ear.

"I am going to pay you back," Nametso repeats. "I am not going to be a burden."

"Burden?" Onthatile asks. "Did I say anything about being burdened?"

Nametso *has* been shocked that even with the loan to her, Onthatile's life seems to have continued uninterrupted—no tinned pilchards and half loaves for supper, no unpaid school fees, no end to Sethunya's afternoon extracurricular activities. We should all be auditors, Nametso thinks resentfully.

"As soon as I get a job," Nametso says.

She says, "I don't mind helping out more, around the house. Did you see I cleaned at the back?"

"You don't have to do anything," Onthatile says. "You don't have to compensate for being here."

"Tomorrow you will be saying that I am just sitting around watching your TV and eating your food. Let me help here and there until I have found something."

"To be honest, I *was* supposed to hire a driver, for Sethunya," Onthatile says. "Her new swimming classes are not on her school campus. And now . . ."

"I will take her," Nametso says, and Sethunya shoots a hurt, betrayed look at her mother.

EIGHTEEN YEARS OLD, newly arrived in Gaborone, Nametso was in an interminable queue of hundreds of other first-year students waiting to open bank accounts for their monthly government allowances. She stood toward the end, within the heat and hubbub of the UB Student Union Hall, feet throbbing, long past complaint, just resigned to the small forward movement of bodies, when across, ahead of her in the queue, Nametso spotted Tumo. In a moment the queue, the chatter, the smell of Russian rolls and fresh chips receded. It had been six years since Tumo had clambered into the truck in Makalamabedi, but Nametso felt, again, like the ashy, dusty-limbed girl of ten, holding a bouquet of flies aloft. That dusty-limbed girl watched a new Tumo and her friends, indifferent to the people around them, talking loudly in English, their accents the nasally twang of private school students and TV presenters. She was much taller, this Tumo, with a long neck and elegantly protruding clavicle. The cascading waves of her weave grazed her bare shoulders. Her face was smooth as a pebble as she listened to her friends, but her impertinence lay fallow and obvious to Nametso. It was a testament of how much she had known Tumo that Nametso understood instantly that she made fun of her friends behind their backs, that she studied their words and imitated them the way she used to their teachers. The nonchalant expression was new; the head cocked to one side, eyes never leaving the speaker's face, it had been arrived upon in the intervening years. It convinced Nametso that Tumo knew the effects of her telegenic face, that she was conscious of people watching her, that she was holding herself aloft as a shimmering object to be admired. Nametso's face heated when she remembered the formality and sincerity of those letters she used to send—*I miss you. When can I come visit you in Orapa?* She would not reveal herself, Nametso decided; she would remember her old friend from afar. But as the queue trudged ahead and curved, she and Tumo were suddenly face-to-face, a tunnel-sized space between them. Tumo's eyes flicked past her face, then flicked back.

Tumo said, Oh my God. She said, Nametso? Tumo seemed unsure what to do and raised her hand in a wave. Tumo's friends, affronted at the withdrawal of attention, turned to look at the interloper. Nametso responded with a wave of her own. Then she crossed the chasm of years and space and walked over. As in their childhood, Nametso waited silently for Tumo to speak.

How is your mom? Tumo asked. How is your sister?

She is fine. They are fine.

Good, Tumo said, smiling. Good to see you.

Nametso crossed back to her side of the queue.

Once in a while, they saw each other—in the refectory; late at night at the Humanities computer lab; outside 411, the on-campus bar, when Nametso's friends from the UB Writers' Workshop hung out with students from the Travelling Theatre, which Tumo was a member of. Tumo would imitate her African Literature professor—*Well, now, laaaydiez and gentlemen, notice the sort of imagery Momplé uses here*—and, with her eyes closed and lips downturned, her whole face somehow assumed the professor's countenance, and the group wouldn't stop laughing. At those times, witness to Tumo's old mischief, Nametso glowed with a secret territorial pride, born out of her exclusive possession of their history, their treetop songs, their bouquets of flies. Yet Tumo had also acquired a new way of holding herself, a serious way, a knowing way she wore with casual authority. It made Nametso feel impossibly young, ignorant about the world. Nametso had only a vague sense of sophistication, which, in her mind, tallied with womanhood. It was a mysterious kind of intelligence, elusive and unseen, like dark matter, impossible to earn through one's own efforts. Those who had it seemed to possess a complete knowledge of the workings of the self and the world. Such as Tumo. There was just so much Tumo knew already. The necessity of a personal scent, ways to smilingly rebuff a man so she wasn't exposed to his anger, the wisdom to fully be a part of her several friend groups yet set off on her own, as she did most afternoons, disappearing to interviews and auditions at TV production houses.

One Thursday, late at night, when Tumo gathered her things after their hours outside 411, Nametso stood up too. They set off, the loud drunken voices of their friends receding behind them. It was one of those deceptive Gaborone nights, balmy for hours, then quickly turning vicious and cold. Goose bumps rose on Nametso's arms and she crossed them over her chest, shivering. Tumo unfurled a burnt-orange scarf from her handbag and wrapped it around her own shoulders. They walked in silence. It was the first time they had been alone together since Makalamabedi. Nametso ransacked her mind for a story, memorable and fascinating, but came up short.

What dorm are you in again? Tumo asked.

Block 449, Nametso said.

Is that one of the old ones?

Yeah, Nametso said.

In their silence, Nametso searched again for a story, perhaps about her dorm, or her roommate, a girl from Maun who prayed morning and night in the singsong accent of their childhood.

I am in Las Vegas, Tumo said, referring to a coveted new block of dorms.

My boyfriend is a lawyer, Nametso said.

Really? Tumo asked, pausing and turning toward Nametso.

Law student, Nametso hastened to correct herself. He is a law student, first year.

What's his name?

Goodwill, Nametso said, her face hot. Goodwill Garebamono. He is from Motopi.

Tumo raised an eyebrow. A lawyer, she said. Just remember your mom won't like a fancy hotel wedding. She wants to be cooking magwinya at the fire.

They laughed. Tumo slowed down, so Nametso did too.

I am going this way, Tumo said, smiling at her. Her smile was like a great wave of light washing over Nametso, throwing her into sharp relief, and she stood still, awaiting instruction from Tumo.

Bye, Namza, see you next week, Tumo said.

Good night, Nametso said cheerfully.

She walked on by herself, strangely invigorated, smiling at Tumo's evocation of her childhood nickname and the joke about her mother. The dark of night was inky, despite the tiny squares of light from the windows in the dorms. She walked past the eating area outside the new refec, where, on one of the tables, a couple was kissing. *My boyfriend is a lawyer.* Nametso shivered, rubbed her hands on her arms; their conversation replayed in her head. By the time she arrived in her room, she was humiliated. She was convinced that Tumo would never again smile softly at her, call her Namza.

Still, increasingly, when Tumo returned from her auditions, she went to Nametso's room and they fell asleep next to each other, on the tiny hard single bed, just like they had when they were ten. Sundays too she knocked on Nametso's door to recover from her weekends and they lay side by side, catching up and drafting text messages to their boyfriends, getting out of bed only for meals at the refectory. They were just eighteen, then nineteen, then twenty, and everything should have been ahead, but already Tumo felt defeated by the smallness of their country. She dreamt of other continents, more romantic cities encircled by the dark shimmer of rivers, nights filled with the bobbing jewels of lights, cobblestone alleys to bike through. She was a theater studies major. Her mother had protested, threatened, cajoled; her mother had warned her she was wasting the years of her youth. Her mother's generation had had jobs waiting for them upon completion of their studies. They had had their ennobling duty and obligation. They had been animated by the facts burnished by repetition into myths: twelve kilometers of paved road at Independence, only twenty-two university graduates at Independence. Who could think about dreams when there was love and devotion to nation, when there was a still-new country to build?

We were born in the wrong country, Tumo was fond of saying. She took for granted what she, what her generation, had been taught of their country's exceptionalism; she could parrot its accomplishments by rote: the happy accident of a subterra packed full of diamonds, the restraint of the Independence-era leaders who had built schools and hospitals and roads and rendered their country a miracle for its escape of the resources curse, the oasis of peace in a continent besieged with wars. All that, all that, she could repeat all that and believe it, yet she believed too that their country was tight-fisted, the life it promised too small.

I want to be onstage, Tumo would say, sick with her yearning, sighing and tossing around on her bed. Nametso was moved on those days, watching Tumo, for she had not fully recognized till then that there were things Tumo was lacking, things that she wanted, things she had difficulty acquiring. Too, Nametso was amused at Tumo's performance of her frustration, her absurd theatricality, which lent her yearning falseness, an air of inevitable defeat.

If it happened that Nametso's boyfriend, Goodwill, the future lawyer, was in the room with them, Tumo would banish him from the bed to the study desk.

Do you know how smart she is? Tumo would ask Goodwill furiously.

He was a thin, shy boy who often resorted to covering his face with his long-fingered hands when confronted with this kind of inquisition from Tumo. In her eyes, despite his prospects, his cardinal sin was what she called his SRB—*strong rural background*—which manifested itself in his coarse accent and his continuing distaste for any food unlike what he had grown up eating.

Had Nametso been born anywhere else, Tumo would say, she could have been an astrophysicist or neurosurgeon or something.

Those times, the contagion of Tumo's dreaming was inescapable, and Nametso too suffered from impatience and contempt for the smallness of her life. She too was seized by the idea that they could not amount to anything inside the cloister of their provincial desert, that it was the gaze of the world turned upon them that would bear testimony to the beauty and fullness of their lives.

IS IT POSSIBLE that she once found this city inscrutable? Now, even with the tall buildings in the new CBD, she sees Gaborone for what it is, a scrappy upstart of a city, punching above its weight; a national habit. Gabs City, Magheba, Motse Moshate, they used to call it. Is it possible that she was once that young? She had taken combis everywhere, buying cheap jewelry and clothes that never lasted beyond a year. When she went back home, her mother would hold the dresses and tops up to the light and point out the faulty seams, the cheap material.

The city admits Nametso back without resistance and she arrives at Sethunya's school far too early. The campus is still and eerie, so she retreats into the car in the empty parking lot. When the other cars arrive, the parents, in their business suits and leggings, wait in the walkway and on benches across from the parking. Nametso gets out of the car and paces back and forth. Finally, an unseen bell tolls and a swell of voices spill out of the classrooms. There they are; the children, in their little maroon-and-white uniforms, they run and trip all over the place, they hold hands and walk with arms around one another.

"See you tomorrow!" they shout. "Bye!" they shout in their tiny voices. "Sharp-sharp!" "Bye, Loapi! Bye, Motheo! Bye, Shamiso! Bye, Thomas!" "Hello, Mummy," they shout. "Daddy!" "Mama!"

Amid this chorus, Nametso sees Sethunya skipping hand in hand with two other girls. Waiting for Sethunya to search her out,

Nametso notes the clamminess of her palms and acknowledges for the first time her queasiness at the prospect of spending time alone with her niece. A lot could go wrong, she thinks. Nametso waits for the girl to find her. When, eventually, Nametso calls her name, Sethunya hurtles forward and throws her arms around Nametso's waist.

"Oh, hello," Nametso says, something welling up in her chest. "Hi. Hi, baby. Hi," she says, tentatively, holding the girl, rubbing her back.

In the car, she asks, "Who were those two girls?"

"Umm, my friends?" Sethunya responds, in an imperious tone Nametso will come to call her sassy American TV voice.

Nametso glances at her in the rearview mirror and sees that she is wearing her sunglasses.

"I was just asking," Nametso says.

"I told them about you. I told them that my aunt was coming from America."

"What did they say?"

In Sethunya's pause, her seeming deliberation over her friends' appraisal, Nametso finds that she is holding her breath. But Sethunya only shrugs and says, "Nothing much.

"By the way," Sethunya continues, scooting up from the back to put her head between the front seats, her sunglasses lowered, looking at Nametso over the top of the frames. "How long are you going to be using my room?"

Sethunya's eyes are squinted and her lips pursed in that familiar pout. It is not just mischief that Nametso sees in her niece's face, but a knowing slyness.

"Seriously?" Nametso asks.

"My things are in there," Sethunya says. "My clothes and my guitar and my books."

"You can still go in the room for them."

"I just want some privacy," Sethunya says. "I am ten, you know."

"Oh, I know! Ten!" Nametso says. But she reconsiders her sarcasm. "I am probably going to be there until I find a job. A good job."

"And when are you going to find a job? Wait, so you are not going back to America? Are you going to live here forever? Oh my God, are you going to live with us forever? Am I ever going to get my room back?"

Nametso is taken aback by the malice of the questions. She is dismayed too, by the stab of dislike she feels toward her niece, her pursed lips, her big forehead. She feels herself on the verge of a spiteful remark.

"You talk a lot, don't you?" she says instead.

"I *am* a chatterbox," Sethunya confirms, and when Nametso glances back at her she sees that yes, her lips are pursed in that particular way that means she is very pleased with herself and secure in the armor of her adorableness.

The swim school is within the vicinity of the technical college, her sister has told her. Nametso used to take combis past the college, in the penitent months following her breakup with Goodwill and during her slow painful severance from Tumo, to visit a new church friend who lived in Kgale View. Keeping her eyes on the road, Nametso finds the college and, past the campus, takes the left turn at the T-junction, then another left at a tuckshop. The new luxury apartment block is straight ahead and to its right is Water Babies. The building is small and unassuming, half-concealed behind a wild untrimmed hedge.

The front desk is a low table, behind which sits a man in a sleeveless olive-green safari jacket, who greets every child by name and scribbles into a spiral-bound notebook. Sethunya holds on to Nametso's hand.

"Oho," the man says, studying Sethunya's face. "A-ah. This is not a face I have seen before. Hee, mma. Mma? Mosadimogolo? Who are you? Tell me who you are." Sethunya clutches Nametso's hand and doesn't say anything.

"She is new," Nametso says. "Sethunya Pilatwe. This is her first class."

"Aaah, Sethunya. Mosadimogolo Sethunya," the man says, licking his forefinger and turning the pages of the notebook. "You want to swim?" He asks, "You want to be like a fish in the water? Hmm? Are you not scared of the water? Hmm? Speak, old woman. You don't speak? Are you not scared of the water?"

"Umm, no?" Sethunya says in her American TV voice.

"She was slow to learn, at her school," Nametso explains. "These are just extra lessons."

"Ahaaa, Sethunya Pilatwe," the man says, writing something down. "Here you are. Welcome, Sethunya. Go in there, go and ask for Petros."

Past the front desk, the indoor pool. The scent of warm water and chlorine. A woman in an orange sari talking softly to her sobbing child, who does not want to wear his red swimming briefs. A father pacing back and forth, talking loudly on his phone. Petros, one of the instructors, shows them to the girls' changing room. Changed, Sethunya hands Nametso the rucksack full of her discarded uniform. Nametso sits on a bench and keeps her eyes on her niece. Sethunya struggles, she leans heavily on the blue foam raft, she kicks her frantic feet, she is tipped over and her head disappears below the water. When she emerges, she is furious and spurting extravagant amounts of water. Oh, Nametso thinks. She wishes she could send a message of encouragement. She gathers the force of her thoughts and directs them to her niece. Lighter on the raft, she thinks. Hold the raft away from your body. Try again, she thinks. Yes, that's it. That's it.

All around are children holding on to the rim of the pool, kicking their feet, raising a white spray, an incessant roar. At the shallow end, two toddlers cry loudly as the instructors dip them gingerly into the water, and another floats around serenely, buoyed by the inflatable rings around her belly. Then Nametso is unable to breathe. She rises to walk outside. The air, hot and dry, free of chlorine and noise, is consolation. Nametso waits in the car until her niece comes outside in her swimsuit, dripping water, saying, "Did you forget that you have my towel?"

ONE NIGHT, their last year at UB, Nametso arrived unannounced at Tumo's room, finding only Tumo's annoyed roommate. Nametso said she would wait. So long, she waited. Finally she surrendered to sleep. Awakening, she saw that the room was illuminated only by the study light at Tumo's desk. Tumo stood there, in the middle of the room, examining herself in the mirror on the inside of the door and muttering to herself. Before I was a person, she was saying, I was just a girl. Nametso sat up. Out the windows the streetlights glowed yellow. Beyond that, everywhere, was dark. The whole world was still, except for Tumo muttering to herself. It's never any use, Tumo said in a deeper voice. Nobody ever wanted me to tell my own story. What was she doing? Nametso wondered. But she did not utter a word; she continued watching until Tumo startled and turned around.

Did I wake you? Tumo whispered.

What time is it?

Two a.m. maybe? Tumo responded. Rehearsals took too long.

She turned back to the mirror. Go back to sleep, she said, and Nametso lay back down. But then she remembered why she was in Tumo's room in the first place and started crying. Tumo sat next to her on the bed.

I missed my period, Nametso said. The words, uttered out loud, were stark and confronted Nametso with her inexperience, her failures, her unworldliness.

How long? Tumo asked, sitting next to Nametso on the bed.

I don't know. Maybe like seven weeks.

It could just be stress, Tumo said. Exams.

I took a test, Nametso said.

Not to mention her sensitivity to smell and her constant craving for dirt, her new impulse to carry a plastic bag full of lumps and clods of earth to classes, throw them into her mouth, let them come apart under her tongue.

What do you want to do? Tumo asked.

I can't have a baby, Nametso said.

In the morning, Tumo called a friend, who called another friend, who gave her the number of someone who knew a girl who had just had to buy abortion pills from a woman who worked at a private clinic. That evening, they met with the nurse, an unsmiling put-upon middle-aged woman, who had parked her car behind Tumo's dorm. First, Nametso had to take the mifepristone, which, she had read, would block her body's progesterone and halt the fetus's growth. Tumo watched her place the pill on her tongue and then swallow it down with a can of Coke. Nametso returned to her room and waited some hours before downing the misoprostol and taking to her bed to await the cramping and bleeding that would empty her uterus. In the dead of night, she was woken by the roiling pain of her cramps, but she had not bled.

Tumo said, There is a private doctor in Mogoditshane, but it's going to be expensive.

It was only then that Nametso texted Goodwill. The three of them waited for the end of the month, then cobbled together their student allowances. Thereafter, Goodwill was superfluous; expendable. It was Tumo who accompanied Nametso to the clinic. Upon their return to the campus, Nametso was no longer pregnant.

"DID I EVER TELL YOU about this amazing class I took on shibari?" Nametso asks Onthatile one afternoon, six weeks into her return. Nametso is unmoored and restless; injured from another afternoon in which her manuscript wouldn't yield to her. She has waited all afternoon for her sister and her niece, and now that they are home, Nametso itches with that long-ago feeling, of scandalizing Onthatile with her stories.

"You do know what shibari is? No? It's Japanese rope bondage, an ancient art."

Onthatile flashes a panicked smile at her daughter, who is engrossed in another show on the television. Nametso tells her sister how she went to the class all by herself, on a rainy night, wearing a leather trench and chunky heels, tightly laced. How she bent her head away from the rainy wind, but it still softly pelleted her neck. These were things that she did only because she had known Tumo, and desired to meet life as Tumo had, with boldness and curiosity. So she sat among the others in the class. Conspicuous, the only Black person in the room. Her hands shook so hard she could not make head or tail of the knots. Nametso turns now to her sister, knowing Onthatile will gently reproach her for what she calls her adventures. But her sister is again leaning down into the sanctuary of whatever nonsense Sethunya is whispering behind her hands. Nametso falls quiet and sits back on the couch, overcome with the sensation of being alone amid the debris of a disappointing party.

With Sethunya held captive by the TV, Onthatile turns to Nametso.

"Namza, I am not trying to be somehow," Onthatile says. "But I have to ask how your plans are going."

"My plans?" Nametso asks bitterly. She knows her sister. Her grim pragmatism. Her affinity for vision boards and five-year goals. *When you fail to plan, you plan to fail. Winners never quit, quitters never win.*

"Maybe you have heard something," Onthatile says. "I don't know what kind of work you are looking for."

On Sethunya's show, a cartoon character has been struck with a log and lurches around, head crowned by a constellation of stars.

Her sister is still being magnanimous. "Or printers? For your book? I know somebody from my job who has printed a book. *Marriage and Money for the Modern Woman.* That's the name of the book. I could ask her who her printers are.

"Here is what we'll do," Onthatile says. "I will talk to that lady about her printers and how much it costs. The two of us will come up with a marketing strategy. It shouldn't be that difficult, I took a marketing module in varsity. We'll just print your book and sell it ourselves. Cut out the middlemen. You could make a lot of money."

"Maybe," Nametso says. She is tempted by the ease of her sister's words, yet "print" seems such a malevolent word.

Onthatile retreats. She says, "I am just trying to figure out what you are planning to do."

"I am keeping my ear out there, for a job," Nametso says.

Since her return, Nametso is staggered by the self-indulgence of her years away. She had arrived to writing residencies with the piety of a pilgrim. She had sequestered herself into wood cabins, wintry rural retreats, months at a time, pursuing something elemental yet elusive, the language to make meaning of her life, mastery over the world.

"I never should have left," Nametso says.

She had meant to be away for three years, surely enough time to write and sell, in a major deal, a novel and a book of short stories. She had done the residencies, the fellowships, until she ended up in a city where she couldn't leave the apartment without carrying a light cardigan.

"You always were a little bit of a dreamer," Onthatile says wearily. "You and Mme both. How do you do it? How can you leave everything to chance?"

"So you think I made a mistake?" Nametso asks. "You do, don't you? You think I was stupid. You do. Tell me."

Her sister is now a woman who doesn't cower before hard decisions, and Nametso is unsure if what she requires from her is punishment or salvation.

FRIDAY MORNINGS, Onthatile takes a cab to work, and Friday afternoons, Nametso picks up Sethunya and takes her to swimming. Now Nametso knows to bring a book, to wait in the car. Once, immersed in a story set in Manitoba, Nametso is startled by a familiar peal of laughter, and her heart races. She braces herself for Tumo's teasing wide-set eyes at the car window. But it's just another loud laughing woman in Gaborone. After swim practice, Nametso drives around the city, ghosts of her past emergent everywhere. In the back of the car, and everywhere else, her niece chatters on and on.

"Do you know who I love most in the world?" Sethunya asks. They are stuck in traffic by the Molapo Crossing robots. Sethunya has scooted up so her face is between the front seats again and she fills the car with the sharp scent of chlorine. Her hair is mussed and wet despite the swimming cap, and she dabs at it with the edge of the towel draped around her shoulders. Her sunglasses are clipped onto the damp T-shirt she has replaced her swimsuit with.

"Who?" Nametso asks. Despite herself, a tiny flame of hope.

"Number one, God. Number two, Mummy. Then my best friend Kitso and my best friend Skylar."

"Poor Skylar," Nametso says.

"No," Sethunya says, giggling, "they are both number three."

"Okay. And number four?"

"Daddy. But honestly, I don't like going to his house over school holidays. He wants me to read the whole day, he doesn't want me to watch TV. And he just always wants to cut my hair."

"I notice I am not on the list," Nametso says.

Sethunya giggles into her hands and falls backward onto the seat. Nametso laughs too, happy to share in the bright, voluptuous pleasures. It is like emerging into restorative air. But even when Nametso stops, proffering her contented little sighs, Sethunya keeps on, hiding her face in her hands to muffle her laughter.

"Okay, it's not that funny," Nametso says, but her niece laughs and laughs, and Nametso's amusement sharpens into a kernel of doubt. Is Sethunya laughing *at* her? Nametso is swept, without much resistance, into an old habit of private and vicious judgment. Bitch, she thinks, she is such a little bitch.

IN THE INTERVIEWS she is called for, Nametso hears herself speaking too quietly, words sticking to her throat. She tries to impress the interviewers, brandishing the faraway cities she has been to. But without fail, they are all incredulous that she turned her back on life in America. In the last week of October, she interviews for the position of subeditor at a private newspaper. The editor has sleepy eyes, pops his chewing gum loudly, and swivels his chair back and forth, looking at her with some suspicion. Her heart beats too loud. Her hands are anxious trembling birds in her lap; she is ten again.

"Why did you come back?" he asks, smiling as though to catch her in a trap. "Huh, you haven't been keeping up with the news about us there in California?"

"I have, of course," she says, though she hopes he doesn't ask her to elaborate.

"There is nothing but hunger here," he says. "There is no money. You left all that money there and came back here? Why are you here?"

She starts to explain about her novel, rejected now by numerous publishers, and the agent who had dropped her, how the prospect of querying more agents had seemed insurmountable. But even to her, all that now sounds arcane and distant, legends from a past life. She hasn't even touched her writing in weeks. What she really wants to talk about is botho. She wants to talk about the homeless, whom she had walked past, even in the freezing rain, to step into her apartment. She had acted as though their lives, their humanity, were extricable from hers. She had failed to recognize them as human when she averted her eyes from their suffering. In that failure, she herself had become less than human, undeserving of any care. That was what she had felt: abandonment, indifference, a sense of life mattering too little. She wants to tell him how the conviction had become deafening in her head, that she would die, and that in her death, her body would lie undiscovered, uncared for in so foreign a place.

"I missed home," she says instead. "I missed everything. My family. The sun. The rain. Everything. My jaw got tired of speaking all that English."

When the editor laughs, she knows she has flattered him and his innate belief in the exceptionalism of their country, that despite everything, this is the luckiest country in the world.

She is here, she tells herself when she leaves the interview. She is home. She went out into the world, vast and mysterious though it was. She had left everything behind. But this is her home, she thinks. These are her people. This is her very own life. The thought fills her with grief. She takes a familiar route through the Main Mall, wades through the mall's usual noise and flurry, its heat and the seething aroma of street food, of overripe morula fruits plopped to the ground. A crowd has gathered in front of one of the bank buildings. She joins the crowd as others disperse from it, and she hears the roar of motorcycles and the revving of engines at rest. Concealed inside the half-moon of the crowd are six women, in pink bandannas and black leather pants and steel-capped cowboy boots. The women are all elderly. Perhaps the age her mother would have been, were she still alive. Three of them wave clipboards around, the other three mount the motorcycles or pose against them for photos. Nametso stands among the crowd for a while, gawking with surprise and delight at the women who are, it is revealed, due to embark on a ride from Gaborone to Francistown to raise funds.

Extricated from the crowd, walking away, Nametso hears an insistent voice calling her name. She turns, her heart in her mouth, and sees that it's one of the women, approaching with the heaviness of a premonition.

"Heelang, heelang, heelang," the woman says. "This is you?"

She hugs her for a long time and when she lets Nametso go, she has tears in her eyes.

"Is this you?" Tumo's mother asks again.

"This is me," Nametso says.

"I see you," she says. "You are a woman. I didn't know if I would ever see you again. Nametso? Look at you, you have that little absentminded face your mother used to have. You know, I still have a dress that she made me? All those years ago, before she quit teaching. Your mother, she used to talk and talk about this seamstress business. She would say, 'I am going to quit teaching and work for myself, do something I enjoy.' And I used to tell her, 'The only people who can do that are those whose fathers own cattle.' I said, 'You are supposed to work a steady job, build a foundation for your children and the children should build on that foundation and maybe, maybe, their children can be the ones to do all that playing.' Look at your friend, heh? She stopped all that drama nonsense and now she is an accountant. Did you know that?"

Nametso knows what Facebook has revealed: Tumo in small theater productions at Mantlwaneng, at Maitisong, at the Little Theatre; Tumo's new devotion to Christianity, a biblical verse on her wall every morning, videos from a Malawian preacher she called Man of God; Tumo's return to school. Nametso herself has posted only what she wanted people to see; her dispatches from abroad: photos from Big Sur; photos of herself in Times Square; photos of kale salads, ramen bowls, matcha lattes; photos of her throwing a ball of the first snow she had ever experienced.

"But your mother," Tumo's mother continued. "I was not surprised to hear she had quit. I am telling you, you have that little preoccupied face she used to have. Hee, Nametso, so, you are here? I thought you were living in those cold countries."

"I was. But I have been back for some months."

"Ehe? And yours?" Tumo's mother asks. "She is hiding you.

She wants to keep you her little secret. She never told me that you were here."

Nametso emits a short, dry laugh. "I am not sure she knows that I am back."

Tumo's mother is careful. "You haven't called her?"

"Not yet," Nametso says quickly. "But I will. I will. I am going to call her."

"You girls used to be like this," Tumo's mother said, her fingers twisted into entwined snakes.

"And then?" Nametso asks, gesturing toward the woman's black leather pants, her boots, her pink bandanna. "Are you a rocker now?"

"When you get your pension, that's when you start living," Tumo's mother says, turning in a circle to show off her outfit.

NAMETSO RECALLS, with startling vividness, an evening many years ago, when Tumo had dragged her to a recital by an all-male Russian ballet company, in Gaborone for two performances only. They were just second-year students then. Nametso recalls the low hubbub of voices and occasional bursts of laughter outside the theater. She recalls her shock at the number of white people who had shown up for the show; she had never before seen so many white people in Gaborone. All around, elegant people in sparkly earrings, evening dress, heels. Tumo had asked Nametso to dress up, and she had worn the least casual outfit she owned: a mustard ankle-length A-line skirt with black piping at the bottom and a cream tube top; an outfit that, they both liked to joke, was a siren song for gaunt Rastafarian men. Whenever she wore this outfit, these men would call to her, *Queen! Nubian Queen! Empress!* She would never find the right man with that kind of look, Tumo told her often, intentionally forgetting about

Goodwill. Nobody wants to fuck an empress, Tumo would say. After the show, in the walkway outside the theater, Nametso tugged at Tumo's arm. She asked, Did you really like that? But Tumo didn't answer. She grabbed a glass of white wine off a tray held by a white-gloved waiter. Tumo sipped and wended her way through the crowd, smiling at everyone, eventually stopping to talk to two white men in dark suits.

That was magnificent, wasn't it? Tumo said, smiling, her face animated in a new and bright way Nametso had never seen. It embarrassed her, the effort Tumo was making, desperate and false, and Nametso laughed nervously. Tumo kept talking, and Nametso kept laughing, mirthlessly. Eventually the men asked, Is your friend okay? In the cab back to campus, Tumo asked Nametso: What's wrong with you? Just a conversation, a normal conversation, and you act like a child?

Nametso looked out the window of the cab, the city zipping past them.

Why did I even bring you? Tumo asked.

Nametso saw then, in the flare of her nostrils and the trembling of her lips, that Tumo was angry.

Why did you? Nametso asked. If I am so rural and I embarrass you so much, why did you bring me? You could bring your friends and listen to them *twing-twing-twing* all night.

The world is much bigger than Gabs, Tumo said. Don't you understand that?

Tumo's perfume hung heavy and intoxicating in the car. Nametso beheld Tumo as though for the first time: her pixie-style wig, the red chandelier earrings which, Nametso knew, came from a Chinese shop but appeared expensive on her, her black minidress and black heels. Tumo looked no different from the other people outside the auditorium; she sounded just like them too, with her TV-presenter accent. Tumo's beauty had settled, no longer the chubby-cheeked, soft, and dimpled beauty of their childhood. The understanding came to Nametso, all at once, intact, that Tumo's beauty was culti-vated now for a particular trajectory she was planning for her life. Everything she wore was calculated to seem either effortless or put-together enough that it conjured the decadence of sinking hours into dressing. In the back of the cab, with the streetlights bobbing blurrily ahead of them, Nametso became conscious of the long stretch of her own life, unknown to her and ahead of her. Beside her, Tumo was quiet, furious and spent, removing her earrings, leaning forward to direct the cabdriver to her dorm.

OCTOBER STILL: all the beauty of the sky is thwarted by the harsh afternoon sun. The brilliance of the day mocks Nametso, who is le-thargic and over it, paying little attention as she drives through the city. Since the interview, since her encounter with Tumo's mother, Nametso feels tender, thin skinned; everything grates at her. Through the car window, Nametso is startled at the sight of dull sardined houses, for she has somehow driven from Kgale to Old Naledi.

"I don't know if my mom would want me here," Sethunya says from the back seat.

"You know your mom is my younger sister, right?" Nametso says. "You can't use her as a threat."

"By the way"—Sethunya scoots up to put her face between the front seats—"if you are older than Mummy, then how come you don't have your own house? Oh, yeah, you don't have a job, I guess, so you don't have any money. When you get a job, will you get a house? Who will live with you? You don't have a husband. Also, you don't have a child. When you get a job, will you have a child?"

"That's a very rude question to ask," Nametso says.

"Why?" Sethunya asks.

"Because," Nametso starts.

"Because," Nametso says.

"Well, because," she says, then glances at her niece. Again, in Sethunya's eyes, she sees amusement at her faltering, and in her pursed lips, the knowing slyness. Nametso raises her hand from the steering wheel and pushes it through the air. The back of her hand sinks into Sethunya's soft cheek with a satisfying thud, which is followed by a startled silence inside the car. Sethunya gasps and heaves in air and wails. Her hands shaking and breath choppy, Nametso drives on.

A WEEK LATER, Nametso hurries home in the late afternoon with news of a piece job, which she hopes will mollify her sister. The week has been long and difficult. Nametso had never seen her sister so cold, so angry, her words icy daggers: *We never hit her. You can't know what it's like to be a mother.* Onthatile had never before been so impervious to apologies. Nametso hurries home as thunder rumbles in the distance. Heat still presses oppressively on the day. Suddenly, a summer storm. It falls heavily, intensely, drenches Nametso as she runs blindly homeward. But by the time she reaches her sister's gate, the rain has stopped, the sun out already, the sky blue again. At the gate, she wrings rainwater out of her dress, laughing as though the weather is a grand gag thought up by a mischievous god. She had missed this, all this, the smell of wet earth all around her. In her sister's backyard, she uses a stick to dig deep down, where the clods of dark loam are

128

barely damp, still crumble under the pressure of her fingers. Nametso places a piece of the earth on her tongue; allows it to dissolve to its discrete particles. She closes her eyes to savor it as though it were a sacrament.

SO MANY years and months and hours had elapsed without Tumo and Nametso speaking, save for one short, self-conscious message Tumo had sent to Nametso's inbox—*Hi, I hope you are well! Who is sponsoring your studies? Could you please help me find scholarships?* Nametso sent her links to scholarships for African students; all available were for those wishing to study agriculture, leadership and development studies, STEM. Otherwise they were mute to each other, exiled from one another's lives, although Nametso harbored the belief that their lives were inextricably bound. She thought so when Tumo posted a photo of her magadi ceremony: she and her new husband in matching blue leteise, captioned *We are nothing without His Grace.* This was just weeks before Nametso called her sister. In the photo, Tumo's face was tilted up to her husband's, her smile small and mysterious. Nametso stared at the picture for a long time, studying it, convinced she alone could divine something concealed behind Tumo's smile.

AND NAMETSO believes so, months later, in a Woolworths at one of Gaborone's new malls, when she looks up from selecting a caramel cake for her niece to the sight of Tumo standing before the housewares, talking to that same man in that magadi photo, smiling up at him, her hand lifting from the trolley to flick a speck from his jacket. Tumo's features are filled out, her face soft, absorbed completely in her conversation with the man. Once Nametso thought Tumo knew everything there was to know about being a woman in the world; that she could grasp, could master, all the enigmatic and luminous matter that could make a life. Across the shop, Tumo looks the way Nametso feels: grown, surrendered to whatever happy accident life would bring next. Because Nametso knows some things too. It's only because Nametso knows that she sees this plainly in Tumo's face.

Bodies

I still go into the city sometimes. When it cannot be avoided, I, as we used to say, very-nice myself. I powder my face, paint my lips red, and subdue my body into skintight jeans. I brace myself for the city center and its deceptions.

This time, it was the pain in my body that was unavoidable, and so I found myself amid the music and the voices of vendors.

"Ausi! Ausi!" An insistent male voice made me bristle. "Mama! Ausi! Ha'e sorry."

A much older man in navy-blue overalls stood beside me, smiling. The old contempt born out of a *lifetime* of parrying admirers rose in my chest, and I hardened my face.

"I was saying, Mama," the man said. "You have been staring at this place . . ."

"Oh." I laughed. "There used to be a pharmacy here."

"Botsogo," he confirmed. "Owai. They closed down, what, maybe it's been one month, two months."

Corner Supermarket, Capitol Cinema, that bar behind the President Hotel, now Botsogo Pharmacy. Two women—their full faces gleaming with youth and laughter—walked out of the Chinese clothing store that had replaced the pharmacy. Another pair, bankers probably, click-clacked past us in pantsuits, sipping from green plastic bottles. The best breakfast in the city—fatcakes and tripe—used to come from Mma-Malebogo's table, outside Trinity Church, next to the morula tree where men used to gather to talk football.

The old man had propped a cigarette in his mouth. He struck a match and cupped his left hand over the flame and the cigarette. I watched his hand, its taut skin covering the protruding veins, its soiled nails.

"You needed something urgently?" the old man asked. A headache throbbed above my left eye.

There are new remedies and supplements coming into the market every day, all promising the same things—to cleanse blood, to relieve headaches and pains, to lower blood pressure, to boost energy. Phuza-O-Phele, Energy Boost, Black Health & Detox Tea; even the old monepenepe, whose bark and roots my mother used to steep in hot, darkening water, has now been crushed into a powder and packaged. Yet I cannot find the remedy that I am looking for—not in the pharmacies, not on the tables of the street vendors, not in the bags of the black-market women who trade illegally in foreign currency and abortion pills. It was supposed to have the curative powers to purge the body of all its minute pains, this remedy. It would be like wiping the slate clean, eighteen years old again.

The old man was still staring at me. In the small of my back the persistent tenderness awoke, thrummed, and I reached around to massage it as if to quiet an inconsolable child. The old man walked away to expel the smoke from his mouth and shrugged at me. Without looking at him or the China Trade clothing shop, I turned and headed toward the combi stop.

———

NOBODY knows the origins of this remedy, but posters advertising its many benefits taunt me from the backs of combis and the sides of tuckshops. Sometimes I find leaflets about the remedy rolled into hollow pipes and poked into the diamond-shaped holes of my mesh-wire fence; sometimes I find two or three flyers littering my front yard. If I had the new supplement, I could get rid of all these small pains. Sometimes I imagine they must be floating in from a merciful time, back when my friends and I, when we talked about it—at our jobs, at parties, having drinks that we never paid for at hotel bars—we talked of grabbing the city, as if by its neck, and having it right here, right in the palms of our hands.

IN MY NEIGHBORHOOD of Gaborone West, there was a boy, Thuso, Thato, whatever his name was, who would not stop bothering me. He was unfortunate, really. Braces on his teeth that he'd had since he started secondary school. Skinnier than the homeless dogs that scavenged in our neighborhood. His skin —the color of undercooked fatcakes—would have been his saving grace, were it not for the black scars littering his face, probably from pimples he had split open.

He was sitting on the stoep of his mother's house when I returned from the city, and leaped up when he saw me.

"Ausi! Ausi!" he shouted at me. A familiar, quick anger stirred in me.

"Sorry hoo!" he called. "Ausi! Sorry!"

I whirled around, watched him jog toward me. His oversize T-shirt, its orange loud, billowed around him. The boy reminded me of count-less other boys throughout my life, grasping above their station.

"Ausi?" I asked. "Didn't I tell you that my name is not Ausi?"

"Askies," he said.

"Do I look like an ausi?" I asked. His eyes traveled from my face to take in my pink halter-neck top, my tight-fitting dark blue jeans, my heels.

"I am nobody's auntie," I said. Nobody's mother. Nobody's wife. There are no names to lend to me, no names to decorate mine with. But the boy has been taught that a woman's name, on its own, is not enough. So every time he needed to talk, this issue of my name hung between us.

"I am sorry," he said again. "I just wanted to help."

He reached out and coaxed two of the plastic bags from my fingers.

"Careful," I snapped. The bottles in the black plastic bag clinked. He straightened up and looked at me in surprise. I enjoy a bottle of Autumn Harvest wine now and then, nothing wrong with that. As we walked over to my house, giving a wide berth to the pungent puddles on the ground, dodging four little girls playing football in the street, he blabbered on and *on* about a neighborhood watch group he and his friends were starting. They had a WhatsApp group for it and everything, he said. As a little boy he used to come around pushing a wire toy car, asking for money for ice pops. Did he ever remember those days of his lisping and wiping mucus from his nose with the sleeves of his sweaters? Though perhaps I was mistaking him for other boys pushing other wire cars. There had been so many visitors back then, when my house was always open to little neighborhood children, to the girls I befriended in bar bathrooms just because I liked their hairstyles or their dresses, to the men who were dying to make all of us love them.

He stood aside and watched me as I pushed the gate open with my hip. At the door, I put my plastic bags on the stoep and reached out for the ones he had.

"Thank you," I said. He just stood there holding the bags in his hands.

"So," he said. "You should give me your number."

He hoisted one of the plastic bags up and hung it from his shoulder, and produced a cell phone from his pocket.

"For the group." He rubbed his right nostril, squirming under my gaze.

"Okay. Sharp." He cleared his throat. "Take mine, ge. So you have someone to call if something goes wrong. This neighborhood is not safe anymore."

I DO NOT need the boy to let me know that my neighborhood is no longer safe. I have been living in Gaborone West for twenty-four years. Despite my mother's warnings in my teens, despite her speaking of the city as though it were a live, snarling thing lying in wait for girls like me, I boarded the bus from Serowe as soon as I wrote my Cambridge exams. My first year in the city I lived in Old Naledi in a tiny one-room house with four other girls. We went to the pit latrines at the back, we knelt to boil water and cook on a Primus stove, we slept three on the bed, two on a mattress we slipped out of sight during the day. Our favorite dresses and tops fluttered all around the room from nails someone had hammered into the wall. Our room, the Mansion, we called it, seemed to always be writhing and heaving under the weight of all our bodies, our Sheen Strate and Blue Magic, our wigs, our lipsticks, our perfume, our sweat, our laughter, our worries, our conviction that we could tame the city. We looked for jobs during the day, and at night we dressed up in our best clothes and went to parties and waited for the men who would fall for our charms. Girls moved in, eager for excitement, clothes, everything new. Girls moved out when they found good-paying jobs or husbands or cheaper houses.

Finally, at twenty-two, a last refuge from years of moving between Old Naledi and Bontleng and Tsholofelo, I moved in here, when Gaborone West was *the* city. When the city council bestowed the streets with strange names nobody bothered to learn. I was here when they installed the first streetlights, when kids and adults alike spent evenings under the poles soaking up the orange light bathing the asphalt. I was here when this was the place aspirational government officers nurtured their middle-class dreams. I was here. Who would have known that Gaborone West would become the first stop for the late-coming villagers impatient for the city's new jobs and pleasures? My neighbors built lodgings for all those looking for cheap accommodations: one yard, one long house with seven, eight separate units going for P100 each. At night, candlelight blinked from each room, as if from a train floating imperceptibly through mist. Shebeens sprouted up all over the place, becoming the spots for drinkers of cheap home-brewed alcohol, for knife fights every weekend, for heart-wrenching screams in the middle of the night. The neighbors who could afford it ripped out their mesh-wire fences and raised boundary walls to shield themselves from the devastation settling into our neighborhood. That is how I came to have a yellow brick wall on my left and an unplastered wall on my right and my old fence hanging limply at the front. The final insult was when the kwaito kids reduced my beautifully named Gaborone West to G-Wawa.

G-WAWA Neighbourhood Watch:

Max: WARNING!!!! Watch out for TWO MEN pretending to be from Water Utilities, needing to come INTO your HOUZ for maintenance. Then stealing TVs, Radios, PHONES!! Ask for ID's b4 letting anyone into ur houz!

The following day, the boy brought me four overripe mangoes that bruised at my touch.

"We have a tree in our yard," he said.

I accepted the mangoes. I considered them his apology for calling me Ausi. I cupped my hands the way my mother had taught my sister and me, and he pressed the fruits into my palms one after the other.

"Please," he said. "Tell me if I can get you anything else."

"Why?" I asked.

He laughed, using his hands to cover his mouth, and I thought of the old men and women back in Serowe who used to press my hands to their lips, to their cheeks, to their despicable wrinkles.

"Why?" I asked again.

He saw that I was not laughing and stopped.

"We are neighbors, akere," he said. "We have to take care of each other. That is why we are starting this neighborhood watch."

G-WAWA Neighbourhood Watch:

THUSO: Ladies, plz be careful, don't use the passage going towards the Route 4 stop late at nyt. Somebody had their phone and handbag stolen there! Plz plz plz, just go around the longer way! Or call me or Max or Dipsy go go khapha. Or stay home. Better safe than sory.

When I was a little girl, my mother would rouse my older sister, Boipuso, and me from bed early Saturday mornings, saying, "Who will bury you? Who will close your eyes upon your death?" These were never questions, just admonitions meant to coax us into trekking behind her to funeral after funeral and into taking food and fetching water for men and women whose children had neglected them into a lonely old age. My sister and I would look at each other and struggle to keep straight faces, the idea of our dying laughable. I was disgusted by the moles and folds populating the old women's faces. I was disgusted by their tongues, how they lapped in their empty mouths at the memories of their long-fallen-out teeth. At their sight, I would elbow Boipuso and murmur under my breath about witches.

The years went by, and I turned thirteen, then fourteen, then fifteen, and my body was revealed to me. It became all I thought of: its gifts and surprises, the pleasures it doled out to me and others. I discovered that I was a girl who had beauty—perfectly curled eyelashes over brown eyes, a dimple puncturing the smooth blackness of my face, muscles in my legs, and my hands with their tiny half-moon nails, their fingers so chubby the skin stretched out taut and shiny, my palms so soft my mother grumbled they announced my laziness.

Discovering my beauty made me bold: on Friday nights I started locking the room my sister and I shared, and on Saturday mornings when my mother knocked I dragged the blankets over my head. Boipuso was weaker; she could not bear to listen to our mother's angry knocks. She trudged behind our mother to her latest project, tying the same headscarves on her head, throwing the same shawls onto her shoulders, wearing the same sensible shoes. I stayed home with my father, asking him questions about the year he spent working in a gold mine in Johannesburg. I listened to his stories about the men from different countries all sardined together in hostels, their languages bumping up against one another to create a new language. I dreamt about leaving Serowe, leaving my mother, leaving her commands. I wondered what a girl like me could make of herself in the city, of the new life awaiting unexplored just four hours away by bus.

When I went to Serowe again, it was after ten years, for my father's funeral. I left the city in the full protection of my learned ammunition—my makeup and store-bought clothes, my conviction that I knew so much more about the world than my family did. So many years away and now there was a brickhouse in almost every yard, all painted the same pale yellow. That did not stop Serowe from looking small and desolate, with scraggly grass in need of rain. In my old home I felt I was some kind of giant girl hankering after her childhood toys. I met a man my sister introduced as her husband, and I immediately compared him to the men I had known. I met their child, my niece, who followed me around but would not say anything to me. My mother—from her room of mourning—sent my uncles to tell me that my father died heartbroken from my staying so long in the city. I stayed in Serowe for as long as expected and respectable, and then I took the bus back. Riding into Gaborone and seeing the Onion Tower poking its head above the city, I felt I could breathe again.

> G-WAWA Neighbourhood Watch:

> THUSO: Bagolo, Thieves broke into Mma-Mpho's tuckshop and took money and drinks. Pls if you have any information, cm 4ward.

Days had passed when the boy again knocked at my door. When I saw him, I propped my body against the door frame. The sun was out and he squinted against its brightness. He reached for his back pocket and pulled a flyer out. I grabbed it from his hands and he chuckled nervously. It was nothing about the remedy. Instead, it was about this neighborhood watch, a manifesto of some sort, about community and neighborly love and taking care of one another.

"We have a meeting tomorrow at the community hall," he said. "We are trying to get as many people to come."

He had a peculiar way of tucking his lips back into his mouth and using his forefinger to scratch at his perfectly manicured hairline. My eyes were fixated on his hands, which were large and unblemished, his fingernails clean. I stepped aside and invited him in. His eyes wandered around. My home, through his eyes, was small and pitiful: the threadbare couch, whose shabby spots were covered by yellowing cushions; my television set, still in the old tube style and broadcasting only BTV and the religious channels; the rug on the floor faded from its original bright orange; the lingering smell of pilchards; the glass half-full of wine sitting on the floor. He sat down on the white plastic chair across from the television.

"Maybe I can read this for you?" He waved the pamphlet for my benefit.

I shrugged and lay back on the couch, listening to my body, as my mother used to say. The boy had a strong voice, but he stumbled over the words. I wondered who had written the manifesto for the group. Now and again, I reached down for my glass, sipped my wine, and luxuriated in the pleasant drowsiness lapping over my body. His voice went on and when I closed my eyes, he sounded just like my first boyfriend, Phatsimo. The same deep voice, deeper than his slight body promised. The same hesitation over words he was not familiar with. The same eagerness to finish reading the paragraph, the same impatience and incessant asking of "Are you listening?"

Phatsimo had kept up futile fights against my advances. He would swat my hands away when I tried to move his face to mine. All he ever wanted to do was help me with my homework, because he had his future all planned out: plan A—finish school, get a job with the army, build a house for his mother; plan B—finish school, get a job with the diamond mines, build a house for his mother. I could see his serious face, how he would pull at the flesh on his throat when concentrating.

When I opened my eyes the boy was still hunched over in the chair, reading from his document. I watched him as he lengthened his middle finger to push his glasses back onto his face. I drained the wine in my glass, turned around, and fell asleep with the voice of Thuso, or Thato, or whatever his name was in my ear.

G-WAWA Neighbourhood Watch:

THUSO: Dumelang bagolo. Plz we are still asking 4 people who will be in G-Wawa 4 Easter 2 volunteer to keep watch. We hv 2 so far. Me & Max. Plz we need more people. Remember, G-Wawa is our home. Only we can take care of it.

I had started on my second glass of wine, watching BTV with hope for any news of the remedy, when BPC plunged the neighborhood into darkness. Almost immediately after, I heard tentative knocks on my door.

"Who is it?" I called.

"It's me." A tremulous, disembodied voice, like the voices on the radio. "Thuso."

I stayed quiet, my mind zipping through faces in my head. Thuso. Thuso. Thuso.

"Mma-Tshiamo's son? I gave you mangoes?"

"Oh," I realized. "Thuso."

I unlocked the door.

"Where is the fire?" I asked.

He laughed.

"I just wanted," he said, "to make sure that nothing happens over the load-shedding. You know Ausi K, three houses from here? They were robbed last time the electricity went."

"I am a witch," I said. "I am not scared of the dark."

"I am the scariest thing in this neighborhood," I said.

But I was pleased that he had come.

A lone besieged candle in the corner struggled to keep the room alight. A triangle of light on the wall, as if a deity had her arms pushed wide open. He sat on the plastic chair. I offered him my wine; he said he would have just one glass. I watched him take the first sip, a grimace zipping like lightning across his face.

He sat in my sitting room, telling me about all the new names the BPC had acquired since this load-shedding business began: it was no longer the Botswana Power Corporation, but the Botswana Pau! Corporation, Buy Paraffin and Candles, Be Patient Comrades, Botswana Proudly Chinese.

At his jokes, I laughed and laughed. It had been so long since my laughter had mingled with another person's. I felt it building inside my chest, and I expelled it, loud, free, wiping the tears from my eyes, slapping at my chest the way my mother used to. The silence after was warm and expansive.

"I am growing older tomorrow," I told him.

"Serious?" he asked.

"Yes."

"So," he said. "What's the plan?"

"Owai," I said. "I don't get excited anymore. I have eaten birthdays. I have a lot of birthdays piled on top of this head."

"Still," he said. "We should celebrate." I could not breathe as I waited an eternity for him to move from the plastic chair and join me on the couch, to reach for my hand, to caress my face. In the dark, I waited and I waited.

His rejection, which I saw in his refusal to reach for me, stung.

I wanted to tell him that there had been a moment there, once, when this city had been mine, when I had been young and beautiful and knowing, when I had been wanted.

I wanted to tell him that I have known bodies. I have known men. Tlotlo. Derek. Tabona. Mothusi. Shawn. Thabo. Zachariah. Wadzha. Emmanuel. Moshe. Reginald. Tlotlego. Hugh. Phala. Lekgotla. Moreri. Tiro. Goodwill. Isaiah. Boipelo. Tshepho. Katlego. Moses. Frederick. Billy. Nchi. Thabo. Baboloki. Kabelo. Bushy. Raymond. Temo. Leruo. Kagiso. Ndiye. Simba. Paul. Lesego. Men. *Bodies.* My body still holds dear its memories: of the weight of another's body, of the feel of a shoulder, of being slick with sweat, of ragged gasps of breath in my ear, of a hand stilling the back of my head for a kiss. When *he* came around here, I could see the little-boy body he camouflaged in those oversize T-shirts, his teeny-tiny waist where his belts held up his baggy jeans, his hands undeserving of touching any part of me, his little jokes meant to soften me.

The lights flooded the room. My face was hot. It always embarrasses me when the lights come back on, no matter what I am doing.

"Go home," I said.

I did not open my eyes, but I felt his hesitation. I did not see it, but I sensed him raising his head, propping his glasses back up on his nose, frowning maybe. I sensed him standing up and heard him as he opened the door then clicked it gently into place.

I sat in the room for a long time, drinking glass after glass of wine on an empty stomach.

Some nights, I can't help it. My regret swirls where once there was joy. I start to wonder if my mother had been right, that the city would devour me and spit me out. That you should never trust the things men say when they are courting you. Nor the words they say during lovemaking. That men think themselves gods when they desire you; that men promise to not only buy you trains but to build railway lines too.

That I should not forget about home. That I should know my people. Perhaps if I had listened I would still be with Phatsimo. He used to walk me home from school, all the way to Botalaote even though he lived in Dinokwane. He was so convinced that we would get married that even back then he called me mother-of-my-children. He joined the army and I came to the city. I never went back home after my father's funeral. We never saw each other again. I wonder if I should have left when I lost my job.

"KO-KO."

I put my pillow over my head.

"Koo-ko."

I shut my eyes even tighter, but the knocking continued, getting even more desperate. Then my phone began to ring.

"Ko-kooo!"

Oh, Thuso. Around the room, all the damage from the night before: specks of vomit clinging to my duvet, my clothes, my shoes, my radio, my plastic daffodils, vomit on the full-length mirror on the door.

I was in no condition to be seen. In the mirror, a despicable face, hair clumped and matted, eyes reddening with each throb of the head. I listened to the knocking, my heart thudding in my chest. The knocking and the ringing phone alternated. Eventually he stopped calling and just rapped at the door, the knocks alternating between frenzied and quiet. I lay back on the bed and closed my eyes but could not go back to sleep. Very soon I realized that tears were sliding down my face. I was no longer sure if Thuso was still out there, or if the sound in my ears was just the echo of his earlier knocking. After a while, I realized that it was no longer Thuso I was thinking of. It was my mother, it was my father, it was my sister and her child. It was all my friends who had turned their backs on our lives, on the city. All those girls who returned to Serowe, to Mmadinare, to Makalamabedi, to Molepolole. They had gone back to working at the family tuckshops, back to night school, back to toiling at the lands when the rains came, back to working at their marriages. They had been driven back home by unexpected pregnancies, by duty, by disappointment, by disease. I wondered if, waking up to the wide expanse of their days, they ever thought of me, still here, biding my time for an age when my city would again gaze, as a witness, upon me.

Homing

❖

The three women in the kitchen of the large Phakalane home did not look much alike, but they were sisters. Their unlikeness extended to their demeanors—the bearing in their shoulders, the timbre of their laughter, their gazes at one another. They had gathered on a Sunday, a day replete with sun and light and the bright heat of a Gaborone summer. The youngest sister, Sedilame, was hunched over her phone and straddled the lemon-yellow bar stool at the kitchen counter. Her legs were a deep brown and seemed impossibly long and sullen as she dragged her feet on the floor. She was ignoring the blackened pot next to her on the counter, its handles melted down to nubs. Her back was turned toward her sisters, who were laughing and chattering on and adding to the national inventory of complaints about the heat. These two—the oldest and the middle—were closer in age and affection and, even on this afternoon, appraised each other with fondness and the blunt meanness of women sure of their place in each other's lives.

The middle sister kneaded at the soreness in her older sister's bare yellow back. She was the shortest of the three, the middle sister, her body trim from predawn kickboxing classes she took at a studio in

BBS Mall. She had clawed her way to a top position in the communications department of a bank and now crammed her days with the mollifying tedium of work. She had been the last to arrive, radiating her nervous energy. After greeting their mother and her nine-year-old nephew, she had shepherded her sisters into the kitchen, where she lacked the patience, or grace, to stand still. She paced around, sniffing at the rancid odor of smoke still lingering in the air, opening cupboard doors, picking up the blackened pot—the evidence of their mother's condition—and putting it down, knocking her knuckles on the three watermelons on the counter. She was the one who looked most like their mother. On her desk at work was a picture of their mother outside Teacher Training College, twenty-four, in a denim miniskirt and black leatherette boots, her face forthright (or defiant), staring down at the camera. Her colleagues divulged the recurrence of that same expression on her own face. Her name was Boitumelo.

"Do you even look at yourself anymore?" Boitumelo asked, smoothing the gather of jowls under her older sister's chin. The oldest laughed, continuing to dab her face, her neck, her décolletage with a dishcloth filled with ice cubes. This was her home, the kitchen counter where her sons had their lunches during the week, where they confided in their maid about their days and the small unforgivable betrayals of friends. Her name was Lebogang, a name her sisters still called her, even though she had been a mother for eighteen years. She had quit her teaching job after the birth of her second child, to sell dresses, weaves, and shoes from her car boot and, increasingly, through Facebook. She wore one of those dresses now, a maxi dress, its spaghetti straps unhooked and hanging limp and relieved on her bosom. She was so light skinned that, in her wavy Brazilian weaves, she was often mistaken for Coloured and, once, for the daughter of a wealthy cattle rancher from someplace deep in

Kgalagadi. Lebogang sat at the other end of the kitchen counter, closest to the living room door, from where she could hear her son Leruo in conversation with her mother. He sounded exasperated.

"Mme, have you forgotten already?" he said. "I just told you Papa is not here."

Their mother was surprised. "Ehe? I asked you already? Ijoo, sorry, my baby."

"Leruo, manners," Lebogang called in English. She and her sisters would never talk to an elder the way her sons, lacking patience and discipline, often talked to their mother. What the three sisters did have in common were the manners they had learned growing up in the same house in Serowe, with a woman quick to pluck a mulberry branch to strike their bare legs. They knew to refer to their elders formally, in the plural, and still kept it up, even after so many years in the south, in Gaborone, where younger people called to their elders in the naked, combative singular. They knew to never inquire after an elder's health, lest they constrain the elder between a lie and embarrassment. They knew that difficult words became more palatable face-to-face, which was why they had gathered in Lebogang's kitchen. Out in the world, they knew to defend one another as only sisters could. But on the occasions when they fought, when they were bewildered by one another's miserliness or moroseness or impatience, they would each wonder, maliciously, if the miserliness or the impatience or the moroseness on display was a trait inherited from a father.

They were sisters, but each had a different father.

Each had, at some point in her adolescence, gone through her own private anguish of asking their mother for a name. (Oh, who but these sisters could understand that terrifying curiosity, the specific guilt of asking their mother to ransack her heart and memory for, to put it plainly, the names of the men she had slept with; to insinuate that she, a respectable woman, once smoldered with desire?)

"Bomma, chop-chop! The day is almost done," Boitumelo said, clapping her hands like a PE teacher. "I am here. We are all here now, even your friend over there, always on her phone. Heela, mosadi, your phone is not going anywhere!"

"Boitumelo, no," Lebogang protested weakly. Boitumelo had inherited their mother's face and her capacity to work from sunrise to sundown, but the abrasive manner she must have picked up elsewhere. Lebogang feared this abrasiveness deployed against Sedilame. Lebogang always felt the need to protect her youngest sister, although she was never sure what exactly she needed protection from. Even as a child, Sedilame had harbored her private sorrows, which Lebogang could neither divine nor ameliorate. Sedilame was born to a mother wearied by the world. She had had better opportunities than her sisters; back when the government sponsored everyone's university studies she had left for England to study mining engineering and returned after a year, pro-Black, Pan-Africanist but degreeless. Lebogang often found herself angry at Sedilame, for the guilt and pity she elicited; for her shyness, which Lebogang interpreted as victimhood; for her sensitivity, which she found naive. She was impatient with Sedilame's habit of dissolving into tears at any moment, like white women on TV. *Is it blood or water you are shedding?* their mother used to ask her, sometimes angrily, sometimes tenderly. Yet, at funerals, Sedilame still wailed along with the children at the accumulation of red earth over the casket, over the body of an uncle or a grandmother.

The sisters were forty-eight and forty-three and thirty-five.

Each had, in adulthood, suffered the anguish of searching for her father, with results so different the sisters hardly ever talked about them. Boitumelo, for example, had found her father retired and living in his home village of Nlakhwane, a man who still fondly asked after her mother. He had introduced her to his other children and to his wife; Boitumelo was on that family's WhatsApp group now and showed up in wedding photos, on Facebook, with people her sisters knew nothing about. Sedilame had waited for years, with the vague romantic conviction that her father would make his way to her. At twenty-nine, she had pored over the phone directory, called each Maun landline listed under her father's surname. At the only meeting they ever had, at a food stall in the Gaborone taxi rank, her father had clasped her hands in his and prayed quietly, fervently, and Sedilame had the distinct sensation that he was ashamed. Lebogang had been too late; all she could do was weep into the overgrowth covering a grave.

Lebogang was anxious now about how her youngest sister would take their conversation. It was for Sedilame's benefit that Lebogang had still not broached the subject of their gathering, why she searched, picking and abandoning, for more palatable ways to say what needed to be said. What she wanted to say was ugly and direct: Since the break-in at their childhood home in Serowe, their mother could no longer live on her own, but neither could Lebogang keep her in her home. The burned pot was proof, a minor disaster that could have been much worse. Surely Lebogang had done her part. It was those words—"doing her part"—that she balked at. She was the oldest and knew her obligations as a daughter, obligations that mirrored those she had taken on as a wife and those that had come with being a mother. Her enduring dutifulness was her love. But her duty had reached its limit.

Lebogang glanced at Sedilame, who was gazing dreamily out the kitchen window, her face childlike, absorbed in whatever phantoms Lebogang was too sensible to see.

"Sedi," Lebogang said gently to her sister, "are we together?"

Sedi turned from the window and looked at her phone. "I am here, aren't I?"

"Ah, I haven't seen Rraagwe-Pako all day," their mother said from the living room. "Where is your father, is he at work?"

"Yes, he is in Kampala," Leruo said. "I just now told you. Don't you remember?"

"You told me?" their mother said. "You are lying. Naare o hapaane? Don't lie to your grandmother. Look at me when I am talking to you! Don't you know it's wrong to lie to your elders? Marete a gago!"

Boitumelo could only stare in shock. When did their mother start using profanity? It was disorienting that the woman who looked and sounded like their mother could act in ways so foreign to her. Over Christmastime in Serowe, she had startled them when she had asked for their uncle, her brother, who had died two years before. *Mme, Uncle Modise is not here*, Sedi had said. *Old woman, you were there when we buried him*, Boitumelo had said. Their mother had laughed away her embarrassment.

Now Boitumelo watched her older sister as she twisted the wedding ring that pinched her heat-swollen finger. Lebogang spoke, her words hemmed in by a hesitant formality.

She said, "Though I am tall, I will keep my words today short. We are women now. We have sight. We do not need a prophet to reveal to us that the woman in there, who raised us, is no longer the woman she used to be. We all know what happened in Serowe in July—the break-in and now, last night, as you can see, the meat forgotten on the stove. It's only with God's mercy that my oldest boy came downstairs and turned the stove off. We could be talking something different. Those are my words. I think you hear me."

"I think we can all agree that Mme can no longer live by herself," Boitumelo said. "She is at risk of criminals who know she lives alone. And she is a danger to herself. One of us has to take her. Somebody who can take good care of her. We can't just leave her. My mother is not going to be one of those old women wandering the village muttering to herself. She is not going to be accused of witchcraft."

The older sisters nodded at each other.

"What does *she* want to do?" Sedilame asked.

"What do you mean?" Boitumelo asked.

"Have you asked her what she wants to do?"

Boitumelo was incensed. "You *know* what she is going to say. She is going to want to live in her own house, where she can go to her church and see people she has known her whole life. But we can't just let her. Did you hear what Lebo just said? She almost burned the house down."

"We are talking about my children here," Lebogang said, her voice breaking.

"Are you listening?" Boitumelo said to Sedilame.

"In Serowe, she lost her bag," Lebogang said, "all her documents in there. She went to the bank and forgot her handbag in the taxi."

"You know I can't take her," Boitumelo said, addressing only Lebogang. "I am always at work. And I don't even have the space." Her house was her house, and it reflected back the treasured ethos of her life: her daily striving, goals met, days slayed from her first swallow of an apple cider vinegar shot in her unlit kitchen, kickboxing on an empty stomach, even surreptitious Kegels at her work desk, all ways to reassure the body of its aliveness.

"Sedi—" Lebogang began.

"She has three roommates," Boitumelo interrupted.

"Come on," Lebogang pleaded. "I don't think it would be fair on Rraagwe-Pako. What would he even say about my mother living here full-time? She has been here for months. And his sisters, who knows what else they would accuse me of?"

"Why do you care what those witches think about you?" Boitumelo asked.

"I have to come right out and say it," Lebogang said. "She has to be out of my house by the time Rraagwe-Pako returns from his trip. She cannot be here when he learns his house almost burned down with his children in it. She can't be here. I want her out."

Now the words were in the open. The sisters fell quiet. Sedilame was angry that her sister would expel her own mother, like a street dog. Boitumelo wished an old-age home was an option, like she'd seen on TV; how clean and efficient that could be.

"Maybe we should just hire a maid for her," Lebogang said. "For the house in Serowe."

"Are we *all* going to pay for it?" Boitumelo said. "I know some of you would always be crying about the money."

"Boitumelo—" Lebogang started.

"Am I lying? Besides, I don't know if we could trust a maid so far away, unsupervised. That would be as good as throwing Mme away. You hear all these stories, these maids feeding the elders in their care pus from their wounds or menstrual blood. Or! Or they become violent toward them. I just don't know if we can trust them."

As she spoke, Boitumelo became aware of the convulsions of Sedilame's shoulders, her head dipped into her chest. "She is crying. Are you crying? Why are you crying?"

"I just meant that you shouldn't treat Mme like a child," Sedilame said. But really, she had just remembered when she was young and her mother used to bathe her. In the bathtub, she would tuck her hands into her armpits, flare her arms into wings, and her mother would press her fingers down the curve of her spine, counting her vertebrae to predict the number of children Sedilame would have. Some days it was nine, some days thirteen.

"Sedi, nobody is treating her like a child," Lebogang said. She looked at Boitumelo, who was chugging from her water bottle and shooting daggers at Sedilame, who was still sobbing.

"Remember your watermelon in that combi?" Boitumelo asked.

The older sisters laughed. Their lives were different now, but they shared a repository of childhood memories—of carrying firewood and little mesh bags of concrete to school, of buying half loaves on credit from Reka-Reka tuckshop, of buying groceries with stamps from the cooperative, of splitting a watermelon while carrying it home in a combi. All that humiliation was in the rearview, and they could laugh about it, as an ordeal they had escaped.

OUTSIDE, the air hung heavy and still. It was one of those days that stretched on and on: the sun early to rise, by midday lulling everything catatonic, slow to set. The jacaranda tree in the backyard had shed all over the pool. Its light-purple flowers stuck to Lebogang's oldest son as he dipped his body in and out of the water. None of the sisters could swim. The pool was mostly for the benefit of Lebogang's sons and their friends, who had taken swimming lessons at the private schools they went to.

The sisters' mother lay prone on the patio. Her feet were bare, her head too. Her blouse was open and fanned out on either side of her. She pressed the flesh of her stomach and chest into the coolness of the tiles. Sedilame lay next to her, gazing at the wisps of clouds above. She wanted to lie out on the lawn and feel the sun on her face. But it was the kind of brutally hot day where the sun shone with a blinding brightness, its rays razors, a certain pressure in the atmosphere that usually portended rain, but the rains had been scant that season.

"Mme, I need you to help me undo my hair," Sedilame said.

Her mother pushed Sedilame's head away from her. "It's too hot."

She had this tendency, Sedilame did, of needing her mother's hands on her. To undo her braids or oil her scalp. Even on that day, when she arrived at the house, she had playfully sat on their mother's lap and laughed at her nephews' consternation. She knew the embarrassment her family felt on her behalf, that her life had not turned out as her performance at school had led them all to believe. The thick of that shame never left her; she waded in it every day, when she had to tell her mother that she had quit yet another job. She avoided her primary school friends, her relatives from Serowe, the group of students she'd left with for England (most returned, working for Debswana). She avoided her sisters too. It was only because Lebogang had coerced their mother into making the call herself that Sedilame had shown up today.

"Let your sisters do it," her mother said.

Lebogang sat on a patio chair across from them. She was balancing a tray on her knees, slicing a watermelon, her face knitted in concentration. Boitumelo paced on the brim of the pool, laughing into her cell phone, toe dipped into the water.

"You have the sweetest hands," Sedilame said. She poked her mother in the stomach. "Mme, I am asking. I am begging you."

Her mother sat up. "What's wrong with this girl?"

Boitumelo walked up to the patio and bent down to pull the flaps of her mother's blouse closed. "Button your shirt, old woman," she said gently.

"Maybe what we need is someone with some kind of medical

training," Boitumelo said to Lebogang. "Not quite a nurse, but something like that. A professional."

"Mme is sitting right here," Sedilame said, staring up at her sister.

"Sedi, I can't be here the whole day," Boitumelo said.

"Go, then."

"And waste the day?"

Sedilame blinked slowly. "We don't have to decide today."

"When do you propose we decide?" Boitumelo asked. "Seriously, Sedi, when are you going to stop crying so we can make a decision? You are not a child."

Sedilame stared up at her sister. From where had she inherited such unpleasantness?

"Sedi, you are making this difficult. We don't have time." Boitumelo saw her sister flinch. "Maybe you should move to Serowe. What are you really doing in Gabs? Like, really? What are you doing here?"

Some months, when she could not cobble together enough money from her piece jobs, Sedilame fantasized about escaping to Serowe. She dreamt about waking up in her childhood bed, a daily breakfast of sour porridge and milk, gossiping with her mother in the cool breeze beneath the mulberry tree. But her mother was no longer her mother, so home was no longer home. Their mother was seventy-seven. She had never been married. There was a time Sedilame admired her for it, found her an unwitting feminist model, one who had decentered men from her life once she had exhausted their uses. Now she dreaded her mother's loneliness and her disappointments. Days as wide and silent as the sky. Sedilame was repulsed by her mother's new mysteries, her manner of bending over a plate with singular focus, eating with the intensity of a child, her guileless blinking as she emerged from whatever crevices of her mind to ask the same question she had posed minutes before; her retreat into some unearthly place to which Sedilame could not follow.

"I would have been shocked," Sedilame said, "if Boitumelo, our boss, had not shown up to decide everybody's life."

Once, Sedilame had thought about going to spend time in Serowe, to learn about the expansive and disparate seasons of her mother's life. She had thought she could study her mother with anthropological seriousness, absorb her stories by osmosis, discover the cosmology for her own life. That had been when she, childishly, thought her mother would always be around. But her collage of Tupperware and dinnerware, sets of *Encyclopaedia Britannica*, the old hand-wound Singer sewing machine, photos and academic certificates, the large enamel bowls, shoes and berets, dresses, doeks, winter coats, raincoats, duvets, and satin pillowcases were losing the weight of their meaning by the day.

"Sedi, just answer that one question for me," Boitumelo said. "What are you doing in Gaborone?"

"Everybody calm down," Lebogang said. "Here is some watermelon." She passed the tray of watermelon around and they each took a slice. Lebogang waved the tray in the general direction of the pool and called to her nine-year-old, who was still playing whatever games kept him so occupied.

THE WATERMELON WAS BEAUTIFUL: pink, firm, and sweet.

She devoured one cooling slice and reached for another. In her time they drank watermelon. In her childhood, she and her brother Modise dipped their hands into a cut half, tore at the flesh, then shared the shell to slurp up the juice. Once in a while, she was stunned at how much of life had changed. With tender affection she remembered the girl she had been, who had been fierce and loud at all the games of batho-safe and skontiball, dress tucked into her panties. Days spent outside, undeterred by the heat. Her grandsons were indoor creatures, scuttling over phones and television games. Now and then she tried to trace the meaning of her life. She had spent most of it working, fifty years as a teacher. In Serowe, still today, wherever she went, her students rushed to greet her and talked wistfully about the sharp sting of her stick on their shins. But it wasn't just Serowe. All over the country, she had worked. She had left Makalamabedi after ten years, a wealthy woman, gifted cattle and goats by the villagers. In Mmadinare, in Francistown, in Maun, she had met the fathers of her girls. Twice she had been fervently in love with the men. Only once had she immediately fallen in love with the swaddled baby the nurse handed her. Once she fantasized about leaving the baby on the hospital bed and disappearing. Some days she remembered the boys who had broken into the house, their loud spurts of breath in the lonesome silence of her bedroom. Had she not been so frightened she might have recognized them; she might have connected faces to mothers. These days, she got mired in her thoughts. Images and sensations and sounds from a long-ago time overcame her: the trickle of warm urine down her leg as she stood in place watching a python slither across the road, the quality of the nightly silence in the first VDC room she ever lived in by herself, the tart sweetness of the moretologa she sucked on so much her teeth hurt. Her memories were like the known forests of her girlhood, in the summer months they spent harvesting phane in the bush. Then, all the girls knew not to call one another's names out loud; the forest could echo an unfortunate girl's name, drawing her deeper and deeper into its recesses. So many of those girls of her youth were gone now. Those surviving were scattered all over the country, in the meager care of their children. Some days she could remember the survivors only by their ailments: Boitshoko with the swollen knees, Kesolofetse bedridden somewhere in this same Gaborone, Bakgobi with the trembling hands and fainting spells when she missed her pills, Kgomotsego with her lost eyesight, confined to the darkness of her yard, shouting eager greetings to any voices passing by. There was something she needed to do, something she needed to tell her son-in-law. Her girls talked about her, often, as though she were not sitting right next to them. On the phone she had heard her oldest girl lie about her, telling someone on the other end that she had almost burned her house down. She seemed to remember the meat on the stove, the smoke billowing in the kitchen. Routine for a woman such as herself who had never enjoyed cooking. In all the days of her life, she had never enjoyed cooking. In all the days of her life, she had never worn a pair of trousers. In all the days of her life, she had never ridden a train, even though she used to dream of it, of embarking in Palapye at night and waking in an entirely new town. She hadn't seen her daughter's husband all weekend, and there was something that she needed to tell him. She needed to say . . . she wanted to say . . . Mostly, she was embarrassed. The world was moving on without her. Sometimes her girls talked about her as though she were not there. With her oldest she would have family around her, her impatient grandsons, a chasm separating them from her, their cell phones and violent games and the maid they preferred to talk to. With her middle daughter, there would be shouting, fights every night, just like when she was a teenager, impatient for the world. With her youngest she would feel most like a burden, the end of her days written plainly in the sorrow on her youngest's face, and it might fortify her, that palpable script of her ending, to face it with dignity. *I wonder if it will rain before winter*, she heard her daughter saying, her youngest, her light.

When Mrs. Kennekae
Dreamt of Snakes

E very winter, Mrs. Botho Kennekae's husband took time off from his driving job in the city and spent three weeks at the cattle-post, where he did whatever men did there—presumably offer the softness they withheld from everyone to their cattle, for the cattle were the great loves of their lives, so beloved the men called them wet-nosed gods, so beloved the men agreed: without cattle, a man pined and lost his sleep; still, having cattle, a man fretted and lost his sleep.

To be loved like that, Mrs. Kennekae thought, to be longed for and fretted over, it would make her heart ache with happiness. It could certainly abate this loneliness eating her already, even now, even here, a part of the gathering of early afternoon shoppers at the feed store in the Gaborone West industrial area. A cavernous ware-house, underlit and dank smelling, crisscrossing planks up above her in place of a ceiling. Around her, more men than she could count, laughing and loud talking, even the Afrikaner men in shorts though it was July and the winter had moved past its clemency into biting cold. Men in dustcoats wheeled past in their carts. She looked around, hoping to be noticed, but she might as well have been an apparition wandering before the unseeing. Pushing her trolley, she prowled the aisles, looking from the message on her phone to the bags upon bags stuffed onto the shelves and stacked on the floor. Coming upon a young man in a dustcoat inscribed with the name of the store, she asked, "What kind of people get help here?"

The man turned around to look at her. He was a tall, skeletal sort. Skin tight over his face, giving him a put-upon look. "Mma?" he asked.

"I am just saying," she said and giggled a little in a show of lightness, friendliness. "I have been walking around the store and I can't find anyone to help me."

"What are you looking for, mma?"

She consulted her phone. "Wheat bran."

"Follow me," the man said. Mrs. Kennekae glanced at the product labels plastered on the shelves as they walked past: LABLAB (for protein and fiber), LUCERNE (valuable source of vitamins A and E), MOLASSES POWDER (energy source—survival feeding), SUNFLOWER SEED MEAL (protein), SORGHUM BRAN, MAIZE BRAN, and ehe, WHEAT BRAN.

"How many bags?" the man asked.

Mrs. Kennekae squinted at the price.

"Maybe two bags."

"Just two bags? Are you sure? This is a new kind of feed, government recommended."

"Who can afford more than two? And still have money to buy food for the herdboys?" Mrs. Kennekae leaned in. "You know how they are, *those* kinds of people, they complain and complain, they are like children, so we have to spend our last thebe on them. What can we do? They have your whole life in their hands! All of your cattle. If you don't bring them their Lucky Star and their cigarettes and their Chibuku, who knows what would happen? *They* are our kings."

The man's face tightened further in a grimace, but he did not say anything.

"No, no, they are like my own children," Mrs. Kennekae said, waving away the man's discomfort. "Kennekae, my husband, he loves them too. He will be there for three weeks, living with them, eating with them. Three weeks. I always say at least I will have the house to myself."

"Do you need anything else, mma?"

"Go, go," Mrs. Kennekae said. "Don't let me squander your day."

Mrs. Kennekae watched his peculiar side-to-side swaying gait as he walked away from her. She pushed her trolley past all the men and their products: DAIRY BOOSTER ONE-NINE (milk production booster), CATTLE BOOSTER PELLETS (weaning shock preventative), cattle dewormers and dips to spray over cattle hide. Mrs. Kennekae was staggered at the myriad trappings they had come up with to care for cows, mere animals. To be cared for in that way, she thought again, then felt an echo of guilt that she had let one of her desires slip into the world like a dark spell.

She had awoken, that morning, from a dream in which snakes slithered at her feet. Countless of them, their scales glittering in the sun, for it was summer, and her feet were bare in the white spray of water gushing from the outside standpipe. In the bewilderment of waking from the dream, she had felt the beating of her foolish, hopeful heart, still refusing to cede its monthly hopes to the inevitability of her age. Despite her ongoing impasse against her mother, Mrs. Kennekae had never let go of her mother's warnings about the heart. A heart was a witch, Mma-Marea said; what it desired it could conjure into the world. Left untended, the heart would turn covetous, Mma-Marea said, and what was a covetous heart but an abyss, always wanting, wanting, never satisfied with what it had.

Mrs. Kennekae *worked* to guard her heart—against its desires, against its lapses. She never complained about the winter weeks of her abandonment. Instead, early in her marriage, she had luxuriated in the solitude, the unfamiliar girlish feelings of pining for a man who was her own. She had spent her nights sprawled on the couch, her body naked under a blanket, watching omnibuses of all the soapies she and her sisters had loved. She ate leftovers straight from the pot, standing in the kitchen, looking out the window to observe her neighbors' goings-on, to observe her vivid dream of a child, a little girl, stumbling and playing in the front yard. Seven years into her marriage, much had changed. Lately, on the days her husband left, the solitude of the house pressed against her and in the silence she was compelled to weigh the inadequacies of her life: their inability to move alongside their old friends to better neighborhoods, the improvements to the house that she still hoped for, the failures of her body: of her womb to carry a child, of her heart to cultivate virtue.

Pushing her trolley toward the tills, she fished out her ringing phone from her handbag. Her oldest sister, Marea. Mrs. Kennekae braced herself.

"Are you at work?" her sister said, without a greeting. She sounded out of breath, as though she had just run inside from unexpected rains.

"What do you want, Marea?"

As a girl, Mrs. Kennekae had followed her sisters Marea and Ketsile to choir practice when she was considered too young to go. As a girl, she had begged for the same dresses as theirs, itching to outgrow the frilly ones her mother insisted on. As a girl, she had run after her sisters to link her arms to theirs, to fall in step with them as they walked to the mobile library parked at the Botalaote kgotla. It had been years since they had buried Ketsile, and Marea had taken it upon herself to run everybody's life.

"What do you want?" Mrs. Kennekae asked. She was not in a mood to be lectured to about the risks of leaving before her shift at the clinic ended, even if she was just a cleaner.

"I JUST SPOKE TO MME," Marea said. "Lorato kept her up again. Crying, crying, crying, the whole night."

"Marea, I already told you," Mrs. Kennekae said. "If I could, I would help."

"This is Ketsile's child."

"You think I don't know?" Mrs. Kennekae said. "But a teenage girl?"

"She could help out when you are at work."

Mrs. Kennekae knew she should do what was good and virtuous. Lorato, her niece, she could come spend some time in the city, away from the severities of her grandmother; she could apply for government sponsorship for school, perhaps look for any kind of pitiable job, even if it was in the Chinese-owned shops. Mrs. Kennekae could usher her into a new life.

"Does Mme know," she asked Marea, "that you are asking me to do this?"

"I would bring her with me to Toromoja," Marea said, "but there is nothing for her to do here. And Mme is old, Botho. She doesn't know what to do with her."

Perhaps Lorato could help thaw their mother's heart toward Mrs. Kennekae. Surely there was plenty they could do together: resuscitate the backyard garden with spinach and tomato seedlings, go to the malls on their free afternoons to admire the expensive clothes and the perfumes, sing together while cooking as she and her sisters had done. They could tackle Kennekae's reticence with their chatter and laughter. Yet Mrs. Kennekae was reluctant to bring a child that was not hers into her household, even if that child was her deceased sister's. It could rupture something about the life she still wanted with her husband; it could erase the hopefulness of their early years of marriage, when they spent Sunday mornings in bed, satiated, planning the work on the house, determined toward the revenge of a happy life.

"Kennekae would never agree," she said to Marea. "Never. I could talk to him. I will try. We will see."

IT WAS TRUE that maybe she had embellished a little to her family about her life in the city. She had needed to. She had needed her family to think, despite everything, that she had at least done well for herself. So, in those early days, after her whiplash ceremony, she had told her sisters about Kennekae's house, which he owned and had paid for, about which size she let slip many exaggerations. The house was in Ginger, yes, but she had trusted she had the facilities to convince Kennekae to sell it for a BHC low-cost in a more orderly neighborhood, New Canada or Maru-a-Pula. Or to at least construct a stop-nonsense wall around the yard or renew the house with a fresh lick of paint. None of those things had come to pass, and her family had never really forgiven her the parsimony of her wedding, depriving them of their joy at her joy. Hadn't her mother, enthroned in her honor, called her hard-hearted, and hadn't she called her marriage a disgrace that tarred the whole family with her ruthlessness? Her mother, buoyed by her old customs, had said the absence of cattle from Kennekae's family was a boulder in her eye, obscuring her recognition of the man her daughter was introducing as a husband. And hadn't she, Mrs. Kennekae, nurtured hope that the imminent arrival of grandchildren would remove that boulder? The years had glided past, keeping intact the emptiness of her womb and her mother's silence. But apparently her family had not forgotten her talk of the house. Her sister's repeated request gnawed at her as she hailed the taxi-special, as the driver hauled the sacks of feed into the car boot.

"A woman who cares about livestock," the taxi driver said as they drove off. "I am impressed."

"Owai, my husband sent me," Mrs. Kennekae said. "Last-minute additions. He leaves for the cattlepost at dawn."

"And you? You are not going with him?"

"Kennekae is very old-fashioned, a real Motswana man," she said, her preening instant. "My father was the same. I don't think my mother has ever been to the cattlepost."

"Cattle are man's work," the taxi driver said. "Where about is your cattlepost?"

"It's around Pilikwe."

"That's where you are from?"

"I am married there," she said. "My family is from Serowe."

"I can tell," the taxi driver said, looking sideways at her. "A woman from Serowe, you can see right away."

Mrs. Kennekae bristled instantly. She knew that the man was referring to her wide hips and her heavy buttocks. "I am a married woman," she hissed.

And although the man apologized, she kept the rest of their conversation curt, sticking only to giving directions: *second turn left after the circle, right turn by the driving school, straight toward the Coca-Cola-red tuckshop.* There they were, the young people who always congregated at the benches outside the tuckshop, drinking even during the day, playing music and exuberant games of mhele and dice. The car inched past them, past her old neighbors' houses, now occupied by people who played obscenity-filled music and made wood-fires in the corners of the yards. Some of the houses were unpainted, the shade of the gray cement of their plaster only deepening when it rained. It hadn't rained in weeks, months. In all the yards, plastic buckets had already been fitted under the outside water taps in wait of the water being turned back on for the day.

"It's the house with the bricks," Mrs. Kennekae said, and the man brought the car to a shuddering stop outside her yard. Mrs. Kenne-kae's yard did not have a fence; all day people walked across, past the house toward the alleyway leading to the combi stop. By her tap, a stack of hollow block was bricks piled up. They were meant for the boundary wall, but she and her husband had still not been able to buy enough. Somebody had left a pair of freshly washed white sneak-ers on the bricks, gaping tongues out, like two panting dogs. The taxi driver unloaded the cattle feed and propped the bags by the bricks.

The house had once been painted yellow, way before she was Mrs. Kennekae, but the color had faded, bleached away by the ele-ments. This house; it was a far cry from the house of her childhood in Serowe. A four-bedroom house at the foot of the Botalaote hil-lock, with five treacherous steps leading to a high veranda. Her fa-ther, Rra-Marea, himself had selected the different tiles for each of the bedrooms, and had circled the furniture he wanted from the catalogues mailed to them. Mrs. Kennekae remembered the red and white checkerboard tiles in the sitting room, the plush buttercream couches she and her sisters were not allowed to sit on for years, each of the sisters graduating to sitting on them as they moved to senior secondary school. Before, they had sat on the floor, beside the three-seater couch facing the windows, Marea and Ketsile exchanging incredulous glances and laughing into their palms as their father, who had, once upon a time, worked in the gold mines in Johannesburg and claimed fluency in Zulu and Xhosa and English and Afrikaans, butchered his translations of the nightly soapies for their mother.

In Mrs. Kennekae's own sitting room, sacks of cattle feed loomed in the corner, against the room-divider unit she had just finished paying off. She hauled the two bags she was bringing with her inside. The room smelled vaguely like fermenting sorghum, as if a drum of khadi were brewing somewhere in the house.

White plastic buckets crowded the kitchen floor, dregs of water in each. The breakfast plates were in a bowl on the kitchen unit, unwashed. Mrs. Kennekae opened the tap; the pipes gurgled and released a single errant drop. Her heart sank. She always felt freshly, singularly betrayed by this, as though it were just from her the city was withholding its water. In her disappointment, the slick frenzy of her desires churned inside her, slinking into the world. She didn't just want a house with no plastic buckets on the floor, nor just hot water gushing from the shower, nor a paved yard, a stop-nonsense, a garden in which she planted only flowers, a life with not a worry of money. What she wanted was to be immersed in a particular kind of dream, of the stories she watched on TV, of the men who went to extraordinary lengths to charm the women they loved, filling entire rooms with roses, rejecting the lives they had lived before. What she wanted was to be inside the enchantment of the story of the two lovers who had renounced their families' disapproval and made their ascent up Baratani Hill, which was not even too far from the city in which Mrs. Kennekae was standing. Mma-Marea had always told the story as a cautionary tale, pointing out that the lovers' heedlessness and disobedience had doomed them, had driven them to disappear somewhere up there, never to be seen again. But for Mrs. Kennekae, there was something alluring in their love of each other, so outsized and overpowering that it had compelled them to leave everything behind to consecrate a piece of the hill with it, to live happily there, forever, without the meddling of their families.

The handle of the plastic bucket had clamped onto her finger, and the pain traveled its length, awakening Mrs. Kennekae to the realities of her kitchen. Perhaps she should call her sister, Mrs. Kennekae thought as she emptied all the water into one bucket. Bringing Lorato was the right thing to do. She carried the empty buckets outside. The sun was just setting, its orange rays softening the harsh edges of the day. Already some of her neighbors had switched on their outside lights, to combat the darkness that would soon come. As she approached the tap, Mrs. Kennekae saw a frog leap away and disappear somewhere behind the bricks. She stopped and gasped softly. As young women, whenever she and her sisters saw a frog they tormented each other, asking, *Is it you? Is it you who has had her leg broken? Is it you who is expecting?* Pregnancy had been their worst terror back then. Mrs. Kennekae queued the buckets in front of the tap and peered into the dusk. She could not see the frog anywhere. She stood outside for a while, quieting her longing to follow the frog into the darkness of the world beyond her house.

In the house, Mrs. Kennekae put the meat on the stove. She dusted the room divider. She swept the rug with the grass broom. She mopped the floor. She watched the clock. She used the remnants of water to boil rice. She checked the time on her phone. She packed her husband's suitcase. She removed his big coat from the wardrobe and draped it over the suitcase. She packed cans of pilchards, cans of corned beef, packets of snuff, and other small luxuries to buy the herdboys' loyalty. She sliced an onion into the pot of meat. She checked the water. She checked the time on her phone again. She tried to locate, in her mind, the exact street her husband was driving on at that moment, wanting to believe something about the pair of them, that they had been dreamt up together and that, due to that dream, she could intuit his whereabouts.

Yet there was a time before Kennekae was her husband. A time when he was just a name on another woman's mouth, the mouth of a friend of hers, in fact, that she had been in the church choir with. The two of them had become close in Mrs. Kennekae's first year in Gaborone, when she had needed a new church home, having fled Serowe because of how she had lost her bank teller job (all she had done was borrow a little off a customer's account, with the full intention of paying it back at month's end, but her manager hadn't seen it that way). During their choir practice breaks, when they sat on the steps off the stage for a sip of water and to check their phones, the woman would often grumble about him, *He was gone again this week. He causes me so much loneliness. He was working late this week, but at least he will be paid his overtime.* Mrs. Kennekae had rolled her eyes at the woman's flaunting of a life filled with security and happiness, but she had been able to corral her heart. For months. At least until the two got engaged and Kennekae started attending services regularly in preparation for their church wedding. In her memory, Mrs. Kennekae erased the woman altogether and focused instead on what Kennekae had looked like then, in those dark manly suits he wore those Sundays. He had had a certain dignity, a mystery she couldn't puzzle out due to his quietness. Also, strength; his quietness had given him mystery and an aura of strength, hadn't it, and she had thought, hadn't she, that these two qualities were sufficient. A lifetime of discovering him, and his strength to rely on. He was meant for her. The notion had taken root in her heart, and once there had intoxicated her so she would have done anything. She had asked

Kennekae and the woman for rides home after choir practice; she had squeezed next to them in the front of his van, their knees all squished together, the wind billowing her scarf and draping it onto his face.

The particular roar of that van had lodged itself in her head, and even now, she recognized it above the voices on the TV and the music from her neighbors' houses. She followed the van in her head, trailing it to the morula tree to the right of their house, heard its coming to rest. She heard the clank of the door as he shut it, his footsteps as he walked up to the house, the thud of something heavy, the thump at the stoep as he shook the dust off his feet. In a minute he would enter their home, sighing with relief. She heard him, the clink of his keys on the coffee table.

"We are going to die of thirst this year," she said to him from the kitchen. He came to the door, looking mournful in the gray trousers, the pale blue shirt, the black tie and cardigan she had picked out for him. He looked largely the same as when they had first met, although he had, again, lost some weight, as he always did before his trip, the weight falling off him with no effort at all, which rankled her; his thinness an admonition, she thought, against her as a wife, for weren't married men supposed to have the dignified potbellies, the rounded faces announcing how harmonious their homes, how well fed they were?

"Even now, no water?" he asked.

"These Water Utilities people," she said, "we are children to them. We leave for work, no water. We come back home, still no water. We might as well still be living in the village, rising before the sun is out to fetch water at the public standpipe."

"The water will come," he said. He would pick up the weight at the cattlepost, from the daily fresh cow's milk. And at the cattlepost, he would slough off the exhaustion palpable about him, returning to her with sour milk and biltong and monkey oranges and dried wild berries and his body, restored from doing God knows what. She studied his face as she always did before he left, taking in his heavy-lidded eyes that made him seem indolent, his wide splat of a nose, the closed-off quality of his face, never quite vulnerable except in bed.

"Le thotse jang?" she addressed him formally, in the plural.

"Owai, we are here," he said. "Putting one foot in front of the other."

In a moment, he would go into their bedroom to change into tracksuit pants.

She followed him out of the kitchen, almost tripping over a forty-kilo bag of cattle feed.

"What is this?" she asked. "Lucerne?"

From the bedroom door, she watched as he bent to drape his cardigan over a chair.

"You bought more cattle feed?" she asked.

"Yes."

"You sent me that message. I brought two bags."

"I am going to take all of them with me." His voice was always steady, such that she could never tell when he was exasperated or excited.

He pulled his trousers off, his movements slow and assured. His legs and arms were unveiled before her, dark and thick and muscular, and she thought, with new pleasure, of how she was the only one who ever saw him like this. Opinion was divided on how exactly she had pried him from that other woman. Some even said that the only explanation was that she must have given him medicine, the kind that promised that a lover would *see* no other woman except the giver of medicine. Not that any of those rumors had mattered to her. What had mattered at the end was the ring on her finger.

"How much money did you spend?" she asked.

"Botho," he said. "It hasn't rained all year."

She entered the room, opening a drawer in their wardrobe, searching for a warm sweater.

"Have you heard what they have been saying on the radio?" he asked. "There is no grazing grass. Cattle are underweight. Dying. Who knows what I am going to find?"

"I am not refusing that. All I am saying is that maybe you should have told me. Maybe I had plans for that money."

"What could be more important than this?"

She walked over to him, his sweater in hand. She swept her eyes over his impenetrable face, like a torchlight helpless over the vast velvet of night. She felt a familiar stab of fear, that she did not know him at all, even after all these years. She *had* known him for only six months when they got married. The haste had been necessary, of course, because of her age, thirty-eight then. She had no longer had any uses for youthful meekness. She had not wanted to go through the long process of consultation, his uncles and her uncles calculating how much she was worth. Of course, none of the uncles were available to her now, nor her aunts, nor her mother, to consult on any marital troubles.

"I was thinking," she said, looking away from the nakedness of his body, "maybe we could sell some—"

"Sell? Botho, that is my inheritance, from my father."

"Just one or two . . ."

"All these years of me building up this herd and you want me to sell?" he asked. He always talked about the cattle as a herd, so solid, so collective, against little old her.

"Just to help us out, maybe we could start on the wall. Hmm, Papa, what do you think?" she asked, placing her hand on his thigh.

"No," he said. "My father gave me my start. The wall, it can wait. The wall is not going anywhere." She handed him the sweater and watched him put it on, his face first obscured inside the sweater, then revealed.

THEY ATE THEIR SUPPER in front of the TV, watching another of her soapies. In his silence, she felt the weight of their argument. You can learn your way around a forest, but never around a person, her mother used to say. Mrs. Kennekae considered broaching the subject of her niece, but she imagined Lorato sitting next to them, wrapped in the silence of their household. She could tell him about her dream, the snakes that had slithered at her feet, or the frog, what they portended, but she would not be able to survive his cynical rationality.

"In the taxi today," she said instead, "the driver asked me if I was going with you to the cattlepost."

He was sucking the marrow from the bone of the meat he was chewing, and he stopped to look at her then, incredulous, an oily ring around his lips.

"Maybe I could go, one day," she said. "With you."

"Botho, be serious. There is work at the cattlepost. Serious work. I can't work and watch over you too."

"Watch over me?" Botho asked, making her words light as a feather. "What do you mean by that, my husband? Huh? What is there at the cattlepost that I would need to be watched over?"

He turned to look at her and she dropped her gaze onto her plate. "I work hard," she said. "You should see me at the clinic."

"You wouldn't like it there," he said, as though he knew everything about her.

When he went to bed, she stayed on in the sitting room, filling her head with the images that fueled her longings—men humbled before the allure of their wives' bodies, the looks of devotion the men gave the women they were in love with. Intermittently, she walked to the kitchen to check whether the water had come. Finally she switched the TV off and the noises from the neighborhood invited themselves in.

In the darkness of the bedroom, Mrs. Kennekae shivered as she pulled her nightdress over her body and climbed into the warmth of their bed. She had been surprised, when they first got married, at how tender he became in the blankets. She had reveled in her abilities to transform him, instinctively raising her bottom to receive him and wait for the first gasp of his breath, which came each time, as if the mysteries of her body were ceaseless. Now she settled herself and waited for him to reach for her, knowing how she would soon control his body with her legs, and knowing that wherever he went, he would have her all over him, the wet heat of her lips on his neck after he stilled. Always, she fell into a deep sleep after, and always, when she awoke, she felt fondly for him, her heart expansive, wanting to give him everything. When he didn't reach for her, she turned and touched his shoulder. She touched his shoulder again.

"I am tired," he said. "And I have a long journey tomorrow."

"Good night," he said, when she did not respond. She could tell when he fell asleep, promptly. Her, sleep eluded. Her stomach grumbled; she was suddenly famished. Mrs. Kennekae never could sleep well on the nights before her husband left for the cattlepost, rearranging in her head all the things that she still needed to pack for him. Food for the road; a flask of Five Roses tea, milky and too sweet, just the way he liked it; bottles of water; all the things that she knew, without her, he could never remember to take.

In her head, she pictured her husband's van driving the A1 out of Gaborone, past Pilane, past Mochudi, past the dryness and the drab uniformity of all those other villages. Stopping for diesel at Dibete, then taking the turnoff at Palapye into a narrow dirt road, and here she imagined the truck swaying on the bad road dotted with potholes to a place that she had never been to. She thought about his cattle—hers too, she supposed, but she never could think of them as her own. She could never remember the herd count no matter how many updates her husband gave her, nor which bull had been loaned out, which heifer had given birth, which seemed sickly. No, when Mrs. Kennekae thought about the cattle, all she could come up with was a mass of writhing animals whose coy lowing her husband sought out, sneaking off for a weekend whenever he could, animals whose pet names he chanted softly under his breath, clucking his tongue as he rubbed his hands over their lustrous hides. The three weeks at the end of winter were what he looked forward to the most, and Mrs. Kennekae was always afraid that he might not return to her, that he might be swallowed by that unknown place, oblivious to the demands of time and bosses, answering only to his beloveds.

AT THREE A.M., she put her slippers and coat on and walked to the kitchen. The water was back, finally, its pressure firm. She filled a big pot and heated the water on the stove. She filled all the buckets in the kitchen and multiple bottles for her husband to take in his van. Outside, the yard was awash in the opalescent light of the full moon. The bucket she had left outside had overfilled and the water had spilled everywhere. There it was, the frog, by the tap, and it leaped away as she walked up to it. Another frog? The same frog? Nobody but she had seen it. With a sudden childish conviction, she was plunged into a delirious belief, that this particular frog was an emissary sent to her, with news her heart had been awaiting. She peered behind the bricks, walked into the alleyway leading to the combi stop. In the distance, from another yard, she heard the hard hit of water on the bottom of a zinc bucket. She turned back, afraid she would be mistaken for a witch.

Inside, she carried a bucket of hot water into the bathroom and stood it in the zinc tub. She went into the bedroom. She was shaken by the reappearance of the frog and stared down at her sleeping husband, wondering if she could tell him.

"Tirelo, Tirelo," she whispered.

"Tirelo, Tirelo," she called to him, leaning over him.

He opened his eyes and sat up. "Is my water ready?" he asked, and she stepped back to escape his foul breath.

He whistled as he bathed, and in the kitchen, the kettle whistled as it boiled. Mrs. Kennekae stood at the door, peering out into the dark, wanting to believe her new conviction. Maybe she could call Marea about this development, she thought; maybe they wouldn't even have room for Lorato. But Mrs. Kennekae knew what her sister would say: She would say, *Grow up.* She would say, *We are no longer girls.* She would say, *You still believe in those old things?* When she turned around, her husband was standing behind her, wearing an old navy coat over khaki trousers and a sweater.

"I will make your tea," she told him. Meanwhile, he loaded the van. Her body felt strange, perhaps already changing and declaring its demands. Her breasts were heavy and tender. The dumplings she was making reeked of yeast; her mouth flooded with sour saliva. She escaped outside for a breath of air and watched him heave the heavy bags into the van. She carried the dumplings out to him, under the morula tree. In the early morning, the city, lit up by the moon, was yet blue and quiet, like it was only to the pair of them that it belonged. She looked up at the sky, silently wishing her husband would also crane his neck so that the two of them could share in this moment, a gaze at the immodesty of the moon. But he kept on heaving bag after bag into the back of the van.

For her, the moon surfaced the pull of long-ago feelings, when she was just a girl and much was possible. *New moon, new moon,* she used to shout, as did her sisters, at the bright, full orb. Her sisters had asked for new clothes, another pair of leather shoes, better grades at school. But she had been unable to name what, precisely, she desired. Inchoate, outsized feelings secreted from her chest, unknown, but out there, she was sure of it. And so she had shouted: *New moon, new moon, bring me! Bring me!*

She wanted to hear those same words echoed by her husband. *New moon, new moon,* she wanted to hear him say it, to hear him name his desires about their life, but now he was wiping off the dust of feed on the back of his trousers, rubbing his hands on his buttocks. Something about his posture, his half-squat in the dark, the pathetic movement of his arms, was a disappointment to her, an affront to the extravagance of the moon.

"Let me go," he said, smiling gently at her. For a moment she could see the tender face he would bring back from the cattlepost.

Under the enigmatic lunar light, she arrived with a solemn certainty to a knowing of those long-ago desires: love and happiness. She was full of it, the terrible knowledge that she would never, ever have them to her satisfaction.

"Drive carefully," she told her husband grimly. "The road has killed many."

That sounded like a curse, she thought, a dark desire named.

"Look out for those uncared-for cattle on the road," she tried again.

"Be careful," she said. "Be careful."

She watched him drive away from her, the rear lights of the van, and when she could no longer see their bobbing she went back into the house. Soon it would be day, noise returned to the world, and she wanted to call her sister before the clamor of it was too loud for her to do the right thing.

Early Life and Education

ONE

Back in 1971, when Lerako was three, his grandmother was seventy-something and weary and, in her weariness, newly fallible to lapses in propriety; she gossiped to Lerako as though he were not just a boy but a peer, a woman of her age regiment. The two, Lerako and Nkuku Mma-Remmonye, had their set habits. From the moment Mma-Remmonye woke before dawn into a world still veiled blue-black and noiseless to the close of day, when she lay prone on the floor and Lerako walked her back, his toes digging into the loose pleats of her skin, the two moved through their hours with certainty, with little anticipation of the day's inevitable ending.

Lerako woke much later than his grandmother one morning, roused from his sleep by the rattle of the grass broom she used to sweep the yard. He went outside and stood at the stoep, watching her figure, suppliant, bent double, enveloped in the haze of dust rising from the ground. He watched her, certain that she would feel his presence and know that it was time for his bath. But this morning, she did not turn around. Consumed by her chore, she swept farther and farther away, her movements wide and loping. Lerako was suddenly afraid, gripped with the irrational notion that she was very far, and that there, where she was, she could not find her way back to him.

—Nkuku! he called to her. Nkuku!

Still she did not turn around. He crossed the stoep, his bare feet leaving tiny prints on the floor, which smelled of melted candles and paraffin and was yet sticky with that morning's polish. He walked up to her in silence, his feet sullying the clean wide tracks the broom had left on the ground.

—Nkuku, he said, his voice tremulous.

She turned around, presenting a glimpse of her face, blank and terrifying and sweaty—yet familiar the instant she smiled and threw her broom down.

His grandmother had clocked it all, by then: Mma-Dikhumo's oldest boy leaving Mma-Tumediso's yard through the concealed back entrance, Mma-Ruta and Rra-Ruta arguing again for all of Botalaote Ward to hear, and Karabo arriving home after sun-out, dropped off by that new nurse from Tutume. She reported all this to Lerako when she bathed him in the plastic tub outside, at a corner of the two-room brickhouse where the merciful rays of the morning sun could reach his body as the water cooled.

—And as for that girl called your mother, Mma-Remmonye added, there is no woman there, kala ya me. Sleeping, still. At this time? I have seen no movement from her rondavel this morning. That heart of hers is not in anything, is it, my boy?

Lerako closed his eyes and settled his butt more into the plastic tub. Mma-Remmonye scrubbed his entire body and stuttered her fingers through his hair, lamenting all the while the misfortune of his face, which, she said, was the face of an ox, square and large, nostrils too big for a boy his age.

—Were God to remember you, let us pray that He does, then you might grow into your face, Mma-Remmonye said.

—Nkuku, Lerako responded, his eyes shut against the soapy water. Nkuku, you are wounding the baby's heart.

He had a formal and old-fashioned manner of speaking, which he couldn't help, after the hours spent with a woman her age.

—Nxa, he, kala ya me, his grandmother murmured her words of consternation. She deployed a pumice stone on his neck and down his spine, causing him to sway front to back. She slipped her hand between his buttocks and washed there.

—Show your grandmother your watermelon, she asked. A blatant attempt to return to his good graces.

He pushed his stomach into a tight globe. Knock, knock, knock, she used her knuckles on the distended belly, testing the ripeness of the watermelon. He only smiled. She cupped his crotch, then brought her hand to her nose and pretended an ostentatious sneeze— eeeeeethiyaaaaaa!—as though reeling from the strongest snuff, and now he laughed, a pure gurgle of laughter that made her heart brim full and white.

The sound lessened the residual guilt Mma-Remmonye lived with, over the insults she had hurled upon her daughter the day she had slinked back home shamefaced and pregnant a year after leaving Serowe for work. A waste of the money they had scraped together to put her through school, Mma-Remmonye had said. What kind of woman opened her thighs for any Bashi walking past, she had asked. And now look, she had said to her daughter, now your breasts have fallen. Mma-Remmonye had still not spoken words of apology to her daughter, but she had prostrated herself, in her duty and devotion after the baby was born.

Such devotion: in the vigilance of her prayers for the health of the baby and the mother; in her preparations of the hut for the new mother's confinement. She had placed a log across the threshold of the hut, thus barring women of menstruation age, women recently miscarried, and all men, who, owing to the heat of their feet, you never could tell where they had been and what they had picked up there. She had been vigilant in keeping the baby's belly button tucked in, in applying the ash and the root of the makgonatsotlhe herb to the baby's delicate, pulsating fontanelle. She had insisted, hadn't she, on separate utensils, separate food, separate cooking fire for the new mother, so her milk wouldn't be sullied by whatever maladies lurked within the rest of the household. She had had the discernment to accept with one hand and throw out with the other the gifts of sour milk and cuts of meat from women who only pretended to be on good terms with her family.

Her vigilance had paid off. Here was the boy, healthy and shiny and bigheaded, sitting down to a breakfast of soft sorghum porridge and Five Roses tea. An obedient boy. She needed only ask once, With which mouth are you eating, and with which are you speaking? and he would fall silent as a rock and finish his soft porridge.

In a minute he would grab a branch off the pepper tree and follow behind her, so they could finish the morning's sweeping together. And he would be right behind her as she filled all the buckets in the household with water, balancing a little cup on his head with the posture and grace of a woman who had been going to the standpipe for years. Early afternoon, they would break for another cup of tea, to quiet the buzzing of the withdrawals from the first one. Even when other boys came by wanting to play, he would refuse and sit with her in the hut they used as a kitchen, braving the choking woodsmoke while she made their lunch. In the ebbing heat of the day, they would sit under the mulberry tree, where she would read from her

Bible, clumsily tracing the words with her fingers, for her education was wanting, and he would lie beside her, studying the wide blue sky through the mulberry leaves.

A perfect boy, she thought. His only fault: nightly, when she opened her eyes after her prayers, he was always asleep, which gnawed at her, his slumber a suggestion, perhaps, that the boy had already taken after the heathenism of his mother, or, perhaps, that her nightly prayers were just a beat too long. But no prayer to the Lord, the God of the Israelites, He who Provides for us, the Sustainer, the Noble One who desires for us to live, could ever be found too long.

TWO

Mma-Remmonye had been married to Ponatshego Mminapelo, a Motalaote like herself, who had just been a year old in 1902, when Kgosi Khama established Serowe as a capital, following the years of thirst that led to the abandonment of the old capital at Palapye. She had had fifteen pregnancies, some of which were spoiled before she could even show. She had given birth to three boys, only one of whom was still in life, the Remmonye who had caused her youthful breasts to sag, who had given her her name and the dignity befitting a person. Of the four girls that Mma-Remmonye had given birth to, only two had been alive at birth, and of those two, only one, Dikeledi, Lerako's mother, had survived to adulthood.

This fact did not make Mma-Remmonye any easier on her daughter, for she was from the generation whose love was shrouded in fear and bewilderment at the whims of a God who took just as easily as He gave. Her love was hard and bitter and cautious. She was suspicious of her daughter's habits, her oblivion to the heft and lift of life, her delusion that days could be squandered, that a woman could be too lazy to do the work that would prove the value of her hands. Her daughter did not seem to understand that her hands were her armor—against poverty, against an inevitably bad marriage, against the elements— the deficiencies or excesses of rain, against a face this side of beautiful, against the ill luck of being found unlovable. With the work of her own two hands, a woman could slink past some certain calamities of this world and fashion her own kind of life. But her daughter did not want to hear any of that. Dikeledi's real talent seemed to lie in frittering away her money and her days on her frivolities: her monthly relaxer crème; new dresses in every impractical hue and fabric; handheld mirrors slipped into the most delicate plastic frames; fragrant body lotions that she dabbed onto her throat and the small of her back; store-bought bedcovers; floral sheets, which *were* beautiful; woven baskets that her daughter convinced the old women of Botalaote to sell to her just because she liked the look of them. So, all day, on all days, Mma-Remmonye absently reprimanded her daughter.

—As for this mother of yours, kala ya me, she would say to Lerako, she must see me as her own kitchen girl. Spending all day at that small job of hers. As if I ever see any money from her. Do we ever see money from her, my boy? We never see any money from her. She is just hunting for one thing, isn't she, boy-boy? I know what she is hunting for is another baby.

After having Lerako, Dikeledi had briefly returned to Francistown to seek more work, but she had since been in Serowe full time, working as a teacher of adult learners. It was a job that shouldn't have taken all day. Her students were mostly women, mothers who had to steal a couple of hours between finishing their own chores and hurrying home before their husbands arrived to empty houses. Yet Dikeledi left mornings and stayed away all day, arriving home as the sun set.

—Did she forget that she is a mother, kala ya me? Nobody told her to hurry into being a mother. Motherhood is not a playground, is it, my boy?

Lerako never responded to his grandmother's questions, which she asked out of habit and affection, out of a reassurance that she was still with him. The questions made a funny feeling settle in Lerako's stomach. He caught glimpses, in the questions, of his mother's negligence of him, her indolence and miserliness, devoted more to her own life than to his.

Not that it mattered what his grandmother said. Come evening, when his mother walked through the gate, Lerako forgot all that. He launched at Dikeledi, laughing, arms extended high in a demand to be picked up. Sometimes she buoyed him into the air and perched him on her hip. Sometimes she refused, claiming exhaustion. That evening, when her son barreled toward her, she said, This white dress that I am wearing, do you not see it?

—A man of your age, crying to be carried, Dikeledi said to her son. You know what you need? What you need is a sister, or a brother, right, boy?

—People, are you listening? Mma-Remmonye said, seemingly addressing the skirt in her lap, whose hem she was mending.

—A sister? Mma-Remmonye continued. And I wonder who is going to take care of that sister. Me, as you can see, people. I am an old woman. These bones of mine are tired and ready to return to their owners.

—And as for me, Dikeledi said, I am just standing here, talking to my son. I didn't ask anybody anything.

—Ijo, Mma-Remmonye said. We will hear all about it if this baby some people leave here all day falls into a fire.

—What I am asking myself is, when I leave my son here, am I leaving him with people or just trees?

They spoke casually, not even facing each other, but Lerako sensed that they were arguing. He stood between them with a furrowed brow, trying to follow the contours of their argument, but it was beyond any knowledge he had yet accumulated.

—Maybe the trees are tired, Mma-Remmonye said. Maybe some people should put their shoes on, gather their burdens, and take themselves back to Francistown.

—Mme? Mme? Lerako asked, tugging at his mother's arm. Where is Francistown?

—Francistown is very far from here.

—And did we used to live there?

—No, my boy. Only I did, his mother said. You weren't even here.

—Where was I?

—You weren't born yet.

—Where was I?

—You were . . . She waved her hands around. You were not here. You . . . I hadn't even thought of you yet. I had not even imagined you yet.

A vast white blankness pushed up against Lerako's thoughts. He retreated into his mind, plodding over his mother's words. He was little, he understood that. He was a baby. He was younger than all his cousins and younger than his mother, and his uncle and aunt, and his grandmother, but he could not comprehend that once he had not even existed.

THREE

—Please, Ma-Lontone! Dikeledi yelled. Pray for me!

She was standing in the doorway of her rondavel, an olive-green towel tied around her chest, calling to Lerako and Mma-Remmonye.

Lerako was sweating already, even as he stepped out of the two-rooms. The air was cooler outside, but it could not penetrate the thick smear of Vaseline his grandmother had applied to his face, nor could it penetrate the itchy sweater she had knitted for him, nor the long black trousers he wore only on Sundays.

—Will you put me in your prayers, Ma-Lontone!

Lerako stopped to look at his mother. She was smiling, her face still swollen with sleep; baiting them, he saw. Lerako was four now and knew that Lontone was the name of the church he and his grandmother attended, an hour's walk from home, which his mother never visited no matter how many times she idly talked about going. Maybe I will go with you to church, she said sometimes when Mma-Remmonye hummed a church song and his grandmother would look up hopefully. In a decade, studying for a test, Lerako would learn the genesis of the name Lontone. London Missionary Society, the text-book would say, and at the epiphany, Lerako would exclaim out loud to himself, in the quiet of afternoon study, startling his fellow students out of their heat-induced stupor. The truth of what his teach ers said reached him and struck him for the first time as real. That missionaries had thought his people's ways evil and savage; that missionaries had sailed across the world to save his people from their ways. The vestiges of that sojourn lay around him, permeating everything. Lerako would be stunned by the arbitrariness of it all, in that moment of raising his head from his book, that men could set off with the idea to rescue his people from darkness, that a church could be built, and that almost a century later he would be sitting in his classroom, reading about it. Just what other knowledge lay concealed before his unseeing eyes, he would wonder then and many times after. But that awe and frustration were many years in the future.

That morning, Lerako was concerned with the sweat beaded on

his face, the itch and heat of his sweater, the emptiness of his stomach. Winter was coming to a close; sweltering heat was imminent. He wanted to stay home with his mother, knowing it would be a day of listening to music on the radio, basking in the rays of the sun.

—Send some prayers my way, Dikeledi said.

—Thoba-thoba, kala ya me, his grandmother hurried him along, ignoring her daughter.

His grandmother was a small woman, rough of fingers, straight of back, the sternness of her face thwarted by wrinkles. Lerako liked it when she too put on her Sunday uniform. For her, a long black skirt over black stockings, flat leather shoes. Her heavy white blouse was long-sleeved, buttoned all the way up to her throat. On her head was a little starched white hat that would assume, when Lerako dreamt about her, years later, a touching ordinary holiness.

The walk ahead of them was long, all the way to the interior of the village. They wended through the circular maze of yards and dusty footpaths, through corridors of tharesetala hedge and new chain-link fences, all of which were bewildering for Lerako but seemed as transparent to his grandmother as the palm of her hand. The two always arrived late to church, for Mma-Remmonye could not walk past anybody without stopping to greet and pushing him in front of her so he could also greet. In Botalaote Ward, she exchanged sprawling greetings with the people she knew, who asked after her family, whether she had heard about Rra-Nkopa over in Basimane who was just as good as gone, and whether she would be able to make it to the wedding of Mma-Tshiamiso's granddaughter, who had decided to get married in Mochudi, these young children these days, going all the way to the south, forcing old women such as themselves to bite their mouths with this new *tla, tla, tla* tongue they must now speak, and had Mma-Remmonye . . .

—Tshipi ya re bitsa, Mma-Remmonye would say, to cut off the peregrinations of greetings.

The gospel has been diluted, she told Lerako, ever since other denominations were allowed to set foot in this Serowe of Khama. Since then, all these faith-healing churches had sprouted everywhere, and their congregants did not understand the value of time.

—Their services go on and on, for hours, kala ya me, Mma-Remmonye would say. The churches of laborers and maids.

In other parts of Serowe, her greetings were quick and perfunctory, her stops momentary.

Lerako was relieved when he saw the steeple of the church, high above the otherwise flat landscape of the village. Even the reddish-brown sandstones of the church were more colorful than the nearby yards, which were full of huts and squat brickhouses. For years Lerako believed that the metal cross on the roof of the church was what his grandmother referred to when she called the church "tshipi." Tshipi e a bitsa. Re a tshiping. Only much later did he learn that what she referred to was the bell that, in the early days, summoned all the villagers to service, back when Lontone was the only church sanctioned to practice in the village and its attendance was compulsory. But this was something that Lerako would not know for years.

What he did know, in that moment, was that he and his grandmother would step into the cool, darkened interior of the church, which was already alive with the coughs of the congregation and the sonorous voice of the preacher, and his grandmother would curve her back and tiptoe toward the only available seats, where she would fit in with the other women, wearing the same white shirts and the same white hats, and he would sit beside her so she could watch him and arrest his squirming with a look. On this Sunday, Lerako was taken with the electricity inside the church, the air charged with a kind of intense attention, bodies listening and poised toward the preacher. Throughout the service, Lerako watched his grandmother, the improbable pink dart of her tongue as she wet her finger before turning the pages of the Bible. The quiet thud of her fist on the hymnal as she opened her chest to sing, at the very top of her voice, her favorite song, which went:

God's forgiveness
That, I do seek
Let me feel it
In this heart that cries for it

After church, back home, Dikeledi had made lunch.

—At least we will taste your hands today, Mma-Remmonye said when Dikeledi knelt before her to wash the older woman's hands, outside, in the shade of the mulberry tree. Halfway through the meal, a van parked by the gate of the yard. In the back were Lerako's four cousins, all girls, aged nine to thirteen, in tiered, ruffled dresses. The younger three hopped out of the van, squealing and running into the yard to fight over lifting him. His cousins made a big fuss of him, kissing his cheeks, and Lerako covered his face with his hands.

Remmonye and his wife, Mma-Esther, followed at a more leisurely pace. Mma-Esther shouted her greetings from the gate. They lived within the same ward, and Remmonye stopped by several times a week to inquire after his mother's health. Sometimes he brought a bunch of too-ripe bananas or oranges stayed too long on the shelves at his general dealer.

—Is there any more food? Mma-Remmonye asked Dikeledi.

—There might be some porridge, but no spinach, Dikeledi responded, turning taciturn at the sight of her brother.

Mma-Remmonye looked down at her plate, which was almost empty.

—Go on and empty the pots for them, she said to Dikeledi.

She paused in her eating, licking the crust of porridge from the tips of each finger. With Remmonye, Mma-Remmonye was open with the largesse of her love.

—Mme, maybe they already ate, Dikeledi said.

Mma-Esther came to sit on the mat beside her mother-in-law and touched Mma-Remmonye's wrist in greeting. Dikeledi stood up and bent her knees in her greetings to her brother and her sister-in-law.

—We are eating, Mma-Remmonye said to Mma-Esther.

—Owai, we are just emerging from lunch ourselves, Remmonye's wife said.

Dikeledi shot a triumphant look at her mother, and then escaped into her rondavel.

—Hello, boy, Mma-Esther said to Lerako, and Lerako dipped his face into his open hands. He was terrified of her, of her face, which seemed, always, shuttered and aggrieved; later, older, he would think that she was withholding something of herself behind the rigidity of that face and he would wonder if the restraining was a kind of punishment of those around her.

—Hello, boy, Mma-Esther said again, without a smile.

Lerako wiggled out of his cousin's arms to follow after his uncle, who was walking around the yard, arms folded on his back, examining the houses, pointing at the sections of the roof that would need rethatching soon, the windowpane that might need replacing, kicking at the wooden pillars around the rondavel.

—Where is Dikeledi? Remmonye asked. She sees us and she disappears. Is she a thief?

—You know how she is, your younger sister, Mma-Remmonye said.

—She should be watering these plants, Remmonye said. She should be applying grease to these poles, so the termites don't get at them.

—Owai, your sister, there is no person there, Mma-Remmonye said.

—Motlogolo! Remmonye called to Lerako.

That was all he ever called him. Nephew. As though the evocation of what bound them was talismanic and could seal them tighter together. He was a short man, already balding, his shiny dome prone to sweat even in winters, so he always kept a handkerchief on his person.

—Uncle? Lerako answered.

—How is it that you can see your uncle and just stand there, without hurrying to make me tea?

—But, Uncle, I am a baby, Lerako said.

Everybody laughed. This happened often, that he uttered some words and people would burst out in surprised laughter. He was startled now, trying to figure out what was funny. But his uncle took his hand, and when he sat down, he placed Lerako on his lap. Lerako knew, without the ability to put it into words, that his uncle's love for him was true and absolute. The boy had heard often the stories of his uncle's immediate infatuation with him when they first met, three months after Lerako's birth, when he was first let out into the world from the room of his seclusion. But Lerako had not yet heard what people said about Remmonye's devotion to him, which was that it was a displaced love, love meant for his daughters, or the sons he believed his daughters should have been.

—You coming with me to church today? Remmonye asked Lerako.

Lerako shrugged, understanding the question to be meant for his grandmother.

Sometimes Mma-Remmonye allowed him to go to his uncle's

church. And upon his return, Lerako would spin around, mimicking the way the congregation danced, clapping his hands and playing pretend handbells. Mma-Remmonye had been raised to respect men and she always gave her son the respect owed to him. But the truth was she didn't trust the church her son went to; it was one of the new faith-healing churches, prideful of its undignified handbells and the whirl of the multicolored ankle-length robes worn by everyone, men and women. Something there was about the church that frightened Mma-Remmonye, something troubling in the riotous singing and hand clapping, perhaps the ecstatic dancing, in the midst of which the congregation surrendered to a force beyond them, which they called the holy spirit. It frightened her. It reminded her of the ancestral intercessions that she had attended with her sister as a girl, sneaking off there after dark, lit up with an illicit joy and thrill, to witness the nighttime liturgies, the chants and prayers and songs and dances, ordinary adults overtaken with the frenzy of skirting between this world and the next.

—Tell your uncle we have just come from church, kala ya me, she said. Tell him we have just returned from Khama's church, and we had a beautiful service, didn't we?

FOUR

The adults in Lerako's life read the sky. Every morning they tilted their faces up to the immensity of the sky to deduce the measure of the day in store for them.

—Today the sun is so hot it's as if it is screaming, they said on the days the sun rose white-hot and fierce.

Sometimes they saw the dark gather of rain clouds and were hopeful, but the clouds were only taunting and dispersed before their eyes.

They asked visitors: Where is the rain where you are coming from? The guests would say, sometimes: We have not seen any.

Other times: We have seen it in Molepolole or Moshupa. We will eat this year. We will drink watermelon and bite into some mealies.

One October morning in 1974, Lerako was woken by the deafening pops of raindrops on the corrugated iron roof. His grandmother was not in bed beside him but was standing by the open door of the house in her nightdress, just watching the white curtain of water.

—It's raining, Mma-Remmonye said to Lerako when he walked up to her, in a voice he would later remember as reverent. He did not respond. He stood next to her. In a moment, Dikeledi came in from her rondavel, exultant, wet and vivified by her dash through the rain. She lifted Lerako and kissed his face.

—Are the buckets out? she asked, and seeing that they were not, she ran to put two buckets in the yard to harvest the sweet rainwater.

—It's pouring, Mma-Remmonye said to her when she came back in.

—It is pouring, Dikeledi said. At least. At least.

It's pouring. At least. At least. Lerako held the words in his head, turning them this way and that way, trying to understand the strange, emotional intonation he heard in both his mother's and his grandmother's words. The words coming out of his grandmother's mouth were trembling, as though she was on the verge of tears. *It's pouring. It is pouring.* It would take Lerako at least twenty-five years to understand the tremor of those words, the comprehension arriving while he is in London, in his college library, reading about the drought that had ravaged his country just years into independence. Four hundred thousand head of cattle dead, he would read. But that morning in 1974, he turned the words round and round in his head, wondering at what held his grandmother and his mother both spellbound, why they watched the rain with a proprietary air, sighing their happiness now and then, as though the rain were a spectacle brought down solely for their enjoyment.

His mother grabbed his arm and dragged him out into the yard, telling him to skip, skip, skip! He laughed and he skipped!

—Come on, sing! his mother shouted at him. Pula nkgodisa!

—Rain, rain, make me grow, Lerako sang, after his mother. Oh, when will I grow!

By afternoon, the sun was out, the sky denuded and blue again, the muddy ground the only sign of the morning's precipitation. The yard was fragrant with the scent of the earth after the rains, and here and there white butterflies fluttered and gallivanted through the air. Remmonye stopped by, gingerly stepping around the puddles in the yard, holding up the trousers of his suit. He beat his shoes against each other at the door, wiping his massive head with a spotless white handkerchief.

—It rained, he said to his mother, after their greetings.

—We have seen rain, she said. This was rain.

—It will be a female year, he said.

—Let's hope so, Mma-Remmonye said. Let's hope God remembers us.

The rain seemed to animate the adults in his life as much as it did the earth. His grandmother put out the seeds and grains that she had saved from the last ploughing season—sorghum and maize and millet and beans and watermelon and sweet melon and sweet reed.

Weeks passed, more days of rain; water seeped enough into the ground to soften it. The Selemela glinted nightly in the sky. The kgosi declared the ploughing season could begin. Most of Botalaote Ward packed up and loaded their vans and their oxcarts and their donkeys and made their ways to their respective ploughing lands.

Mma-Remmonye and her son and his wife and Lerako headed to Tshethong, where they had six hectares of farmland.

Dikeledi was the only one who refused to go. She had a job, she said. Mma-Remmonye pointed out that her students would probably go to the lands as well. But Dikeledi was adamant. Mma-Remmonye lamented her daughter's laziness, an illness, she called it, a sign of rot, but still they abandoned Dikeledi, just as other families abandoned their infirm, to the emptiness of the ward and the village at large.

LERAKO AND MMA-REMMONYE shared the older hut, which was also the hut where they made the fire when it rained, and the one where they stored some of the farming implements. Their first morning at the lands, Mma-Remmonye rose from her bed before daybreak and turned to make sure Lerako was still asleep.

Outside, the moon lit up the whole yard. Waiting for her was Remmonye, a cow horn and a hoe in his hands. Together, they walked in silence to the field, careful not to rouse any sound. Their ankles grew wet from the dew on the grass. Mma-Remmonye had a peculiar sensation, walking behind her son into the farm that had been left to her by her husband, who had himself inherited it from his grandmother. The sensation she had was an inundation of fatigue, at the work that lay ahead, of growing food from this land. Her heart was a hardened little kernel in her chest, and she strove to soften it toward the work with memories of the scent of freshly upturned earth, the juice of new maize on the cob, the satisfaction of a difficult job done well.

They walked first to one corner of the field, and Remmonye dug a quick, shallow hole. Mma-Remmonye dipped her two fingers into the horn and brought out a bolus of medicine, black and held to-gether with animal fat. She flicked the mixture from her fingers into the hole, and Remmonye kicked the topsoil back. They did the same at the other three corners of the field. The work of ploughing could begin.

Every daybreak, Lerako straggled after his grandmother as she walked the land. Basket in hand, she broadcast the mix of seeds over the unturned earth, as far as her arm could throw, a profound act of faith. In a week, Remmonye turned the soil with a mold-board plough pulled by a tractor, which would need to go to a neighbor next. After that, Remmonye's job was done and he went back to Serowe to take care of his general dealer. In January, when weeds grew alongside the awaited crops, the women entered the field with their hoes and removed the weeds to leave the crops room to flour-ish. And as the crops grew, the women returned to the fields at sun-rise, banging bowls together to chase away the quelea birds that settled upon the soft sorghum grain in numbers and the porcupines that chomped on the sprawling watermelon crops, leaving spiteful little bites on the unripe melons. They examined the leaves of the maize and the sorghum to wipe away the eggs of the stalk borer. Some days, the women went into the bush nearby to harvest phane. How his grandmother suffered! Putting a tentative hand into the leaves of the mophane tree, grimacing and giggling at the wriggle of the phane in her hands, disgusted as she squeezed the intestines out. Here her work was slow; by the end of the day, only a handful of phane in her bucket.

In late April, winter on the horizon, the women harvested what they had been able to salvage. They stayed all day in the fields, pausing only at midday to make a fire under a mophane tree to cook a simple meal of porridge and dried bean-leaf morogo. They pummeled the sorghum and millet grain heads and boiled some of the sweet maize to dry. They cooked the sweet bean leaves with melon seeds and left the beans out in the sun. They peeled some of the sweet reed to dry in bite-size sticks. At the end they counted their harvest—ten sackfuls of sorghum, three of millet, five bags of maize, ten bundles of sweet reed, five wheelbarrows of watermelon, only one wheelbarrow of sweet melon, six bags of beans, two bags of dried bean-leaf morogo.

—At least, they said to one another when everything was done, proud of the work of their hands. We will not starve this year. We will eat porridge. God has remembered us.

There was always next year, they reminded one another. Next year they would be more ambitious. They would plant different kinds of sorghum. Perhaps more melons, more maize, more millet. If the rains came.

FIVE

They arrived in Serowe to a clean yard: the weeds cleared, thepe gathered, clear wide sweeps from an early morning broom. It was as though Dikeledi had been expecting them. Here she was, radiant in a sun-yellow dress, her hair dark and slick in a pushback, her skin gleaming. Here she was full of giggles and bite-kisses for her son's cheeks, bothering her mother about how much darker her skin had become in the sun. Here she was unloading the sacks of sorghum and beans without being asked, without complaint, at that.

—Some people must have missed us, Mma-Remmonye said, clicking her tongue.

Before the week was out, Mma-Remmonye had discovered the source of her daughter's new good nature. There were whispers, from those who had stayed, about a man who had come around, some-times even spending the night. Mma-Remmonye was furious and ashamed, but did not wish for a return of those ugly words she had uttered when her daughter had arrived home pregnant.

As they were having supper one Sunday, Mma-Remmonye asked, Did we have any visitors while we were away?

—Visitors? No. Was Mme expecting visitors? Dikeledi asked.

—Ao? Am I not allowed to ask? Mma-Remmonye said pleasantly, balling up some porridge to dip into her gravy. We were gone for so long that I thought maybe some people might have stopped by.

—No, old woman, nobody stopped by.

—Hmm, maybe these old ears deceived me, Mma-Remmonye said. I caught some whispers that a car parked here every day. Forgive me, I heard wrong.

—This is why I don't like living in the village, Dikeledi said. Everybody's eyes stuck on you. And, Mme, what if a man came around? Don't you want me to get married?

Marriage? Marriage was a different matter. Mma-Remmonye was afraid to look at her daughter, afraid she would be met with a familiar, sardonic smile.

—Married? Mma-Remmonye asked.

—He wants to pay magadi for me. He is a good man, mma. He has a job. A police officer. He is a boy from Serowe too, from Manna-thoko.

—Such words, Mma-Remmonye said, looking at her daughter.

Dikeledi kept her face down, earnest and afraid, her mother saw. Mma-Remmonye was relieved. Then a thread of sadness unfurled through her. Her very last child. Her daughter. Heading into the wilderness of a married life.

—If he intends to marry you, this boy from Mannathoko, why

would he speak these words to you, out there at the playground? Does he not know that you have parents? What does he think, he thinks you fell off a tree?

A CHORUS of voices coming from the kitchen reached Lerako where he lay in his bed. It was early morning, still dark, and sleep beckoned him back, but in the next room the women's voices kept him awake.

—Dikeledi is a person now, the women said. You have done your work, Mma-Remmonye.

Lerako got up and opened the door. It had been weeks since their return from Tshethong. The gathered women were uniform in their blue German-print dresses and matching headscarves, their blankets tied around their waists. Their talk was swift and loud, as nimble as their hands as they assembled trays of the best teacups and saucers. Mma-Esther sat aside, her smiles like grimaces, and when she saw Lerako by the door, she said:

—Did we wake you, boy-boy? Come here!

Her voice was deep and raspy, as though from lack of use. Dikeledi turned around and walked to him and rubbed his hair. She too was wearing a long traditional dress, a slick wave of her relaxed hair peeking out from under her headscarf. Some of the women snuck glances through the window at the kgotla assembled outside Mma-Remmonye's yard, where the men of Botalaote Ward sat in a half-moon, bedecked in their best formal jackets: plaid, navy, houndstooth. Some wore the heavy coats they brought out only in deference to the coldest period of winter. Before them sat a group of the men from Mannathoko, and the women, in the kitchen, laughed at their obsequious postures, obvious even from where they watched the men. In the kitchen, the talk continued unfettered.

—Will the calf be taken alongside its mother? one of the women asked.

—We have heard that he cannot take the calf with its mother, Mma-Remmonye said.

—These young men these days, the women said.

—Maybe it's better this way, Mma-Remmonye, the women said.

Mma-Remmonye looked at Lerako and said, Bomma, women's stories are never-ending. We are here for a reason. Aren't the men finished?

The women from Mannathoko Ward approached the house. Their German-print dresses were a bright red. The Botalaote women emptied out of the kitchen and met the women out in the yard. Lerako remained in the kitchen with his mother, who shushed his questions, and together they listened to the murmur of the women's voices, their tale about their son's trek in the sun, his fortunate meeting with a beautiful maiden who had quenched his thirst with the sweetest, coldest water, whose delicate footsteps they had followed to this yard. The women from Botalaote agreeing that indeed they had a beautiful maiden for a daughter, who was as precious to them as gold, as fragile as glass. By seven a.m., one of the women came to fetch Dikeledi, to meet for the first time the people who would become her new family.

FROM THAT DAY FORWARD, Lerako's cousins Esther and Ruth and the other girls and boys of Botalaote Ward gathered, evenings, in front of Mma-Remmonye's yard to practice the songs they would sing at the wedding. They sang:

Hey, mother-in-law
Leave those pots alone
Here comes their rightful owner

And they sang:

As I glide along
With these familiars
For whom am I leaving my mother's home

And from that day forward, the older women of Botalaote gathered at Mma-Remmonye's yard every morning to touch the soil.
They mixed red clay and cow dung and water to plaster the walls of
the huts. They applied white clay and ocher and drew designs on the
exteriors of the huts. They built a new lapa in front of the two-
rooms. Mma-Esther, the most skilled and talented among them, applied cow dung to the floor of the lapa, and then traced ditema and
lekgapho onto the floor. She was quiet and drawn, almost as though
she weren't there at all, as though the shapes she was leaving in her
wake were created by a phantom. She didn't seem to hear as the
other women stopped their work to stand behind her, to admire the
elegance of her hands, the daintiness of the lines, the uniformity of
the curves of the shapes.

All day, the women talked about the upcoming wedding. They
burst into spontaneous ululations at the sight of Dikeledi. Mma-
Remmonye especially would stand and grind her arms into her chest
and let loose a flutter of melodic ululations, so beautiful that the
other women fell quiet in deference. And Dikeledi moved her body
for the women, dancing gracefully and laughing easily. Lerako had

turned weepy, hovering around his grandmother. The women called him Mma-Remmonye's purse.

—Here is your purse, Mma-Remmonye, come to do women's work again.

WITH THE DELIVERY of cattle to her family, Dikeledi was, by custom, married. She remained at her mother's house, in wait of the modern white wedding, but now her husband could enter freely, in the light of day. The man's name was Pusoetsile Pinagare, tall and dark, enamored of tight-fitting short-sleeved T-shirts. Around him, Dikeledi was decorous, modest of dress, her only concession to her earlier cheekiness her insistence on calling him PP. He had a mole on the side of his nose, which seemed to grow large and sinister whenever the man crouched down to talk to Lerako.

—Do you know who I am? he asked Lerako when they first met.

—A man, Lerako said, and the gathering of women laughed.

—Just a man? Dikeledi asked, turning to PP in laughter.

Lerako looked away, hiding his face in his hands, a new kind of heat washing over his body at the sight of his mother laughing with the man. He trailed after her that whole day, following her—and him—into her rondavel, staying right by the door when Dikeledi told him to go to his grandmother.

ONE AFTERNOON, Mma-Remmonye and Remmonye took Lerako to a tailor at the Serowe mall. He was afraid of everything in that crowded stall, with bolts of fabric stacked on wooden shelves against the walls; he was nervous about the way the fabric unrolled and hung down, as though it could tumble down onto him at any moment. He was afraid of the two men who sat behind the sewing machines, who never straightened their backs or took their eyes from what they were doing. Lerako was even afraid of the owner of the stall, a tall and heavy-faced Zambian woman, head wrapped in colorful scarves, who smiled and forced her broken Setswana into full sentences, punctuating, where she faltered, with, Akere, my friend?

Remmonye was in his element, unhooking suits hanging from the walls and holding them up to his body before the full-length mirror.

—Very, very nice, my friend, the Zambian woman said.

DAYS, weeks passed. On every evening of those weeks, young men and women sang at Mma-Remmonye's gate. And as they sang, the sweltering evenings turned cool and dark, the sky far off and loosening more and more of the distant glitter of its stars. As the evening turned into night, and the night turned a dark the thickness of velvet, the voices of the young men and women turned hoarse and distracted. They groped for one another's hands. The girls suffered from a sudden onset of shivers and retreated into the arms of the boys. The boys rested their chins against the girls' shoulders, and the bass that emanated from the boys' chests vibrated against the girls' bare necks. And as they sang, they imagined that maybe, in another couple of years, they themselves would be sitting inside, listening to their peers sing songs in preparation for their own weddings.

HIS MOTHER was nowhere to be seen. His grandmother was nowhere to be seen. Yet their yard was full of people that morning. Men who

waved him away as he watched them put up a tent. Women ululat-
ing as they arranged chairs and tables inside the tent. Old women
who rubbed his head sympathetically when he asked where his
mother was.

—You will never be an orphan, boy-boy, an old woman said to him.

Lerako's mind plodded over the comment, trying to understand
why the woman had said what she had said. Just then Mma-Esther
gathered Lerako and other small boys behind the two-rooms, checking specifically that they had not bathed before giving them plates
of white samp and meat. The good boys who had had an early morning bath skulked away unrewarded. Just as Lerako was trying to understand why they were being permitted to eat unwashed, Mma-Esther
sent the boys with the inscrutable instruction to find an axe and
place it with the blade facing the sky.

His older cousins ran Lerako a bath and only then, as he was
bathing, did Mma-Remmonye materialize, soaping his neck and his
back in silence. She put him in the new suit made for him by the
Zambian woman at the mall.

—Be a big boy today, kala ya me. I don't want to hear about any
tears.

The sad tenderness of his grandmother's smile held the key to
whatever it was he was missing.

He sat between his uncle and his aunt in their van. They were
the last in a six-car procession to Lontone. There, they entered into
a room he had never before seen in the back of the church. His
mother was back there too, in a white dress, standing still in the
nervous chaos of Mma-Esther adjusting the veil covering Dikeledi's
face. Lerako heard the quiet hubbub of voices from the main church.
He followed behind his uncle, who walked his mother out into the

church. Pusoetsile was standing at the front, on the stage, and a burst of ululations frothed from the women in the church as his mother walked up to stand in front of Pusoetsile.

Driving back to Botalaote, the cars hooted the entire time. Wherever there were people, on the roadside, in their yards, they stopped to pump their arms in the air and to ululate. Remmonye allowed Lerako to press his fist onto the hooter, Lerako laughing so much that by the time he arrived in Botalaote, he was empty and buoyant. He escaped from the tent, where he was supposed to be sitting next to his mother, to join the other boys in the daring game of running up to an elder, slapping their shoulder, and darting away to laugh helplessly. The boys were plied with food and fizzy drinks, tiny glass bowls trembling with jelly and custard, peach slices swimming in clear syrup. Whatever woman brought them food would cluck over Lerako sympathetically. In the afternoon, the choir of the older boys and girls who had gathered nightly at the gate danced and sang into the center of the yard.

In the evening, the procession of cars, still bedecked with balloons, drove and hooted all the way to Mannathoko. There, Lerako joined a procession of men who sang and walked into the yard, an old man at the front holding the hoof of a cow. Then Lerako sat with his uncle at the kgotla, where the men gave Dikeledi's new husband instructions for marriage.

—You are no longer our son, those people from Botalaote are now your parents. You have to respect them and take care of them, as you would the parents who raised you.

—We are giving you our daughter Dikeledi, who is precious to us. Lerako was startled hearing that word, "giving."

—This woman, Dikeledi, whom we are giving you, has parents, who love her. She is still our child, even as we are giving her away to you. We have taken care of her her whole life, and now that responsibility falls to you.

—A wife is to be taken care of. The kind of man you are will show in your ability to take care of your wife. A wife needs food to eat and soap to bathe. A wife needs love to be happy.

—A wife is not a mule to be whipped whenever you are unhappy. We would rather have our child back than a body to put into the ground.

—Treat her like glass, the way she has been accustomed to.

—Our child is cherished, she is just like treasure to us.

—She did not fall from a tree, she has parents, who have taken care of her from the time she entered into the world.

When Dikeledi and PP were brought together, she was wearing a sky-blue shawl around her shoulders and a blue headscarf. People stood up to shake his mother's and PP's hands. Remmonye stood up too, holding Lerako's hand in his.

—Ee, nnya, the work is done, Remmonye said. We have brought you home.

—Ee, rra, Dikeledi said.

—We should head back, Remmonye said.

Mma-Esther came up behind them, fastening her shawl closed.

—The sun has set, Rra-Esther, she said to Remmonye. We should go back and see how they are doing over there. There is still lots of work to do.

—Woman, Mma-Esther said cheerfully to Dikeledi. You are home now. Time for us to go back to our own home.

—Time to go home now, boy-boy, Mma-Esther said, looking down at Lerako.

They walked away among the swirl of the crowd and the dust rising with the dusk.

ONLY A FEW STRAGGLERS remained in Botalaote. Some of the women were still in the house, dividing the cuts of meat that would be given away to relatives based on their rank and marriage status.

Although tired, Lerako found it impossible to fall asleep that night.

He found that something large and painful was lodged in his chest. But he did not want to cry. He did not want to. His grandmother was asleep and his tears would wake her.

—She is probably falling asleep right now, Mma-Remmonye said. It has been a long day, akere, kala ya me? I hope she is able to wake up early tomorrow and show the kind of wife she will be.

Lerako lay still and quiet.

—She is probably going to sleep now, his grandmother said again, after a while. I hope she is sleeping well. I hope those Mannathoko people have blankets for her.

And now Lerako cried.

—What you think, kala ya me, she said. You think crying will bring her back? We should be grateful that she had enough luck to find someone to marry her. We have to thank God for that.

Still, Lerako kept crying.

—Come on, let's find something to eat, she said.

Although the kitchen was full of bread and meat and samp and salads, his grandmother poured them a cup of motsena. Lerako sipped it down slowly; he merely tolerated it, hating the texture, the weird lumps and mix of flavors, but decades later, in the freezing lonely years of his studies in England, he would sometimes wake yearning for its tart comforts. He would send emails to friends, asking them to mail him even just a one-kilo bag of A1 Super maize meal that he could ferment on his own.

SIX

Only twice since the wedding had Lerako seen his mother. Once in early December, when she brought his new Christmas clothes. The second time was Christmas day, when she and PP arrived in the after-noon, bearing a two-liter Coke and a box of Choice Assorted biscuits. The adults gossiped outside, in the shade of the mulberry tree. Before they left, Dikeledi got into the car and showed her mother how she could drive forward, and in reverse. Mma-Remmonye watched with a quiet intensity, turning now and then to Dikeledi's husband as though wishing to quiet him from his shouted instruction at Dikeledi. Dikeledi alighted from the car with a wide smile, asking her mother, Did you see me? Mma-Remmonye was stunned at what the changing times had made possible for her daughter to do.

In mid-January of 1976, Dikeledi arrived in Botalaote, in the driver's seat, all the way from Mannathoko, her husband in the car with her. The two had driven over to bring Lerako's school uniform: gray shorts, gray trousers, white shirts, two pairs of socks, and a pair of black leather shoes. Lerako was eight years old.

—You look so smart, kala ya me, his grandmother said to him a week later. I know you will grow up to be a teacher.

Mma-Remmonye was walking him to his classroom on the morn-ing of his first day of school. He was stiff in his crisp and immaculate uniform, his polished black shoes that pinched his toes.

His heart beat loudly inside him, but Lerako did not cry when his grandmother left, unlike the other kids. He entered the class-room curiously, looking around at the tiny chairs and desks, at the blackboard, at their teacher, who wore no headscarf and had her hair cut as short as a man's.

All day at school, he was lonely for his grandmother. His head buzzed, wanting his cup of Five Roses, and his teacher's voice was loud, as was her chalk as she wrote on the board, sounding out the words.

—N-na-na, the teacher wrote on the board.

—Bo-na n-na-na.

—Bo-na n-na-na o a le-la.

Lerako struggled to hold his pencil.

At the end of the day, his grandmother was waiting for him at the school gate. But the following day, as she walked him to school, she pointed out the landmarks for him.

—See, remember to turn at this morula tree.

—Once you pass by this Water Affairs building, then you know you are close.

—See, it's not the first tuckshop which is your turn, but the second one.

—You are a big boy now, his grandmother said, and you will have to find your own way.

He was relieved at the end of every day when he could go home. At first, he would run home directly, reminding himself of his grandmother's words—tuckshop, Water Affairs, morula tree—and in the distance, he would see his grandmother standing by the gate to her yard, her hand shielding her eyes against the sun, and he would sprint the rest of the way. Three weeks in, he had made friends with the other boys. They mocked him for his square face, asking him whether it was too heavy for his neck. He laughed along with them. They pestered him about his long eyelashes, which fluttered as he slow-blinked and thought everything through. Because of the proximity of his name to a certain anatomical part, they called him

La Nnana. After school, they turned into a band of adventurers, dedicating each afternoon to a different quest: they went seeking the hot golden fatcakes Dodola was famous for, and loitered outside the store begging for money; they went to the butchery to observe the viscous trails of blood on the ground, the swinging carcasses idolized by flies; they hunted for empty Coke bottles in the dumpster behind the Bottle Store that they could barter for more Coke. Every day they went farther and farther away: they sprinted to the Maphatshwa Grounds to watch a football team practice on the dusty pitch; they took a morbid walk past the mortuary, where they knelt and cast curious eyes at the black cars driving in and out; they hiked to Thataganyane and slid down the rock formations there; they traveled to the tuckshop in Sekao Ward to witness the man who could make a chicken cluck from the recesses of his belly.

Lerako arrived home filthy and exhausted, the thrills of the afternoon receding into apprehension at the sight of his grandmother, who would inevitably be awaiting his arrival at the gate. It hurt her too, Mma-Remmonye said, twisting his ears while he begged for mercy. It hurt her that she had to discipline him. But it was her duty to bend him toward the light while he was still a green, yielding sapling.

He was relieved, one evening, returning from a day of baiting the stray dogs living up Palamaokue to find the gate gaping open, his grandmother absent from her usual spot. He would slip in unnoticed and change his uniform, he thought. The house was unlocked, but there was nobody inside.

—Nkuku! Nkuku! he shouted, but there was no answer. The rondavel was locked. He pushed open the kitchen door, which was never locked, and stared at the soot-coated walls, as though his grandmother might be camouflaged there. A tin of hot water was still on the three-legged stand over the fire, but the fire itself was out.

—Nkuku! he shouted.

He walked around the yard, even looking up the mulberry tree. He sat on the stoep of the two-rooms. He waited. He was hungry but had never fed himself. When it started to get dark, he walked over to his uncle's house. His two youngest cousins, Hannah and Mary-Magdalene, were oiling each other's hair under the mokoba tree at the bottom of the yard. Lerako did not stop to talk to them; he continued walking on to the main house.

—Lerako! his oldest cousin, Esther, exclaimed when she saw him.

She was in senior secondary school now, and was sprawled on the couch still in her school uniform, the bottoms of her stockings dirty.

—Shame, Lerako, Esther said. We forgot about you.

Lerako looked down. His face felt strange; pinpricks pulsed on his skin, over the thin film of cold sweat. Hannah and Mary-Magdalene had come in behind him and were now lingering at the door, watching him with wide, curious eyes. He was quiet, standing in the middle of the room. He wanted to tell them that he couldn't find his grandmother but was too shy.

—Nkuku is in the hospital, Esther said, as if she had read his mind.

—Don't look so scared, she said. She is fine. Mme and Ntate went to see her. She is fine. I don't know what happened. She was cooking, maybe it was too hot or maybe there was too much smoke in the house, but she collapsed. She is lucky Ntate went to see her today. She is fine. Don't cry. Didn't you hear me say she is fine? She will be back soon. Don't cry.

—Don't just stare at him, Esther said to her younger sisters, find him something to eat.

Over the two nights Mma-Remmonye was hospitalized, Lerako

slept at his uncle's house. It was a different world, unfolding in ways unknown to him. His cousins spent the light-drenched hours of the afternoons splayed on the couches in the sitting room, laughing and telling their mother stories. Their mother was transformed in those hours, her face radiant with her laughter. At dusk, when Remmonye's van made its way up the yard, the girls darted into their shared bedroom and disappeared behind its closed door. Then Mma-Esther would have to summon them to bring their father food, and they would troop from the bedroom, greet their father in a melancholy chorus, and disappear into the kitchen. The girls themselves were an astonishment. They were jolly and duplicitous. In the sitting room, they knelt to wash the adults' hands with serious faces, but in the kitchen, where they ate around a blue plywood-top table, they whispered and gossiped and shook with noiseless laughter. The two oldest girls imitated the frenzied way their father hit his teaspoon against the cup when he stirred sugar into his tea. The clink of the spoon against the enamel cup carried, the girls complained, a siren summoning passersby who would drop in announcing their great thirst. Lerako was shocked by the amount of food his uncle ate—a heap of porridge on one plate, the beef stew on another. When it came to night prayers, the girls were left to their own devices, to pray in their own room, a pair sitting on each of the beds they shared. To start, their prayer was loud and legible:

> Ke sale ngwana bokoeng,
> Ga kena thata epe,
> Mmoloki o nthusang . . .

Then the prayer devolved into any kind of nonsense, and the girls would fall into fits of giggles. Lerako slept on a mattress on the floor between the two beds. The girls volleyed their laughter and their whispers from bed to bed. Once in a while, their mother came into the room to tell them to keep quiet, and they hushed for a moment. Inevitably, their whispers, like meerkats, would stick their heads out, would swivel this way and then that way, their gossip meaningless to him, for it was about people at their church, people he did not know. It went this way all night and before he knew it, Lerako was being shaken awake by his aunt.

Mma-Remmonye was embarrassed by all the attention lavished on her upon her return from the hospital.

—I just haven't been listening to my body, she told the stream of visitors.

Her cups of tea trembled in her hands. No longer could she withstand the heat and smoke of a wood fire. No longer could she lose herself in the simple act of sweeping her yard. No longer could she walk all the way to Lontone. Remmonye bought her a Primus stove. A deacon from the church came to her every first Sunday of the month. How it upset Lerako, the sight of the deacon's tiny white car wagging its way toward their yard, parking outside their gate. At its sight, Lerako knew that he would have to turn off the radio and lose track of whatever football game he was listening to. Still, he would bring the coffee table and the teacups and saucers outside to the mulberry tree, where his grandmother would be waiting in her church uniform. His grandmother and the deacon sang their hymns; they prayed and partook of the flesh and blood of Christ.

SEVEN

—Bagaetsho, I have roused myself from my sickbed to come bid farewell to this woman lying here, my friend Sekgele Mminapelo, the mother of Remmonye and Dikeledi. She raised these children that God gave her. We were girls together, me and Sekgele, and we were in the same regiment of Makgasa. We sang together at the Christmas concerts. My friend Sekgele, Mma-Remmonye, had a beautiful heart, full to the brim with love. She was also one of the most stubborn people I have ever met. I think those of you who remember the trouble at the lands, with the people from Mokwena Ward, then you know what I mean by stubbornness. The stubbornness of an ox, that was my friend Sekgele. I don't know a woman who kept a cleaner house than Mma-Remmonye; she truly believed that cleanliness is next to godliness. And she was a believer, who came a little late to the faith. But didn't Christ himself say, bring me all your lost? She had been lost. A brewer of alcohol, which was how she raised her children. But she threw all that away after she found God, and was a most devoted Christian. She never missed a Sunday of church until these past years when she became too ill. Mma-Remmonye was one of those women gifted with the best, most melodious ululations. People used to say, when she didn't go to weddings, and she didn't go for a while, after her daughter died from food poisoning from eating at a wedding, people used to say, It was a good wedding, but Mma-Remmonye wasn't there. So, that is the caliber of person these children have lost today. My friend is gone. She is gone to join her husband. And I want to ask her, if she can hear me there, where she sleeps, I want to ask you, Sekgele, to prepare the path for me. I too am tired and would like to rest these bones.

Sitting in the darkened tent, among those who had gathered for the vigil, Lerako jerked his head up. He was surprised at the words coming from the old woman's mouth. He had never before heard that his own grandmother had been a brewer of alcohol. For sale? He did not know a world where his grandmother came into contact with alcohol. Lerako thought he was the only one hearing the woman's words, hearing the tear in what he had stitched together of his grandmother, her likes and dislikes, her beliefs; and this tear was letting in diffuse light, exposing the invisible seams of her life. The old woman who was speaking must have made a mistake, Lerako thought, but even his own mother, Nkuku's daughter, sitting beside him, had not reacted with any surprise. His uncle was sitting up there somewhere, red eyed and closed in, and wouldn't he have intervened? His uncle was sitting up there, and behind him, behind the door, just inside the house, was the coffin that held her body, and Lerako knew that, were he so inclined, he could, the following morning, gaze upon her body for the last time. And Nkuku had had another child? He was dizzied by the strange information. His chest was constricted and his throat sore, and his face was wet with tears.

His mother, sitting next to him, murmured something unintelligible and pulled him down toward her. Her fingers were swollen and hot against his neck and he jerked his head back up again.

—Shh, baby, shh, she said to him.

She sat with one hand on her heavily pregnant belly, and with the other she tried again to pull Lerako's head onto her shoulder, but he refused to yield his neck. His face was pinched close, and she felt hurt for him, wishing she could shelter him from his sorrow. He was ten already but appeared much younger; he had yet to cultivate the facility to conceal his sorrow and his anger, even as he kept his face closed against her. He seemed afraid of her. Even when she said to him, Come here, baby. He couldn't look her in the face.

In Lerako's face, Dikeledi sometimes saw his father, and she was reminded of that brief glimmer of time when she had thought she had left her childhood behind. She had been swept up in the romance of him, Lerako's father, his exoticness and his righteousness, a South African who had escaped Johannesburg in the dead of night, and who had stalled in Francistown, waiting for word to move on to Zambia, and after that, Tanzania. She had never been certain if he had made it, or if he had died. She had thought about him in the final months of her pregnancy, when she had been ashamed in the face of her mother's fury. She had thought about him at the hospital, when those nurses at Sekgoma Memorial scolded her when she cried at the pain roiling inside her. We were not there when you were opening your legs, they had said. Yet they had turned tender as soon as the baby slid out of her, cooing at his face, showing her how to line up her nipple with the pucker of his lips. And in the three months of her seclusion, she had dreamt, sometimes, that Lerako's father would appear to claim his son, and her. After those three months, Dikeledi had emerged to the world, thick with her love, her cheeks full and glowing. She had put aside her fantasies, and the only possession of his that she had given to her son was his name. She had wondered often about how easily her mother and brother had forgotten their anger. Perhaps it was better that way. Perhaps that is what would happen with Lerako, that one day all this sorrow, all this crying would be a distant memory.

EIGHT

Early in the morning, exactly two years after her funeral, Lerako dreamt of his grandmother. In the dream, the two of them were seated in a patch of thepe growing wild and abundant in her yard. A big sky-blue enamel bowl separated the two of them and contained the leaves they were harvesting. About them was the pungent smell of greenness; even his fingertips were stained with green juice. You are pinching the leaves, aren't you, kala ya me, his grandmother said.

They will turn bitter. In the distance, Lerako heard a thud . . . thud . . . thud . . . , and he knew immediately, even within the cocoon of his dream state, that it was the sound of his uncle's axe chopping wood. Lerako slipped into wakefulness and stared up, for a moment, at the ceiling of his bedroom. He sat up in his bed and extended his arms, believing still that his hands would be tainted green.

His fingers were clean, except for the row of calluses on his palm, which he peeled in moments of deep thought or anxiety.

—Men work, his uncle had told him when Lerako moved into his household.

He had put him to work. Chopping firewood, weeding the yard with his older cousins. He cooked the cow lungs and kidneys that his uncle brought home for the dogs. He was responsible for filling up the black plastic drum in the kitchen with water. His uncle's new sand-mining business had quickly turned successful, and on some weekends, when his uncle's laborers quit, Lerako had to fill in. They would drive in from the edges of the village, lying on the mound of sand like lizards basking in the sun. The work left his whole body sore, his shoulders pulsating with a radiant pain. Radiant too was the stink of him, of heat and sweat, of a sharp and metallic matter coating his skin. There was still much work to do on the extension of the house, and Lerako helped put in the floor tiles in the kitchen, worked on the plumbing and painted the outside walls another weekend. During the week, he and his cousins fulfilled their unending quota of chores.

Sundays were for church. His uncle drove the entire family; the children rattled in the back of the seven-ton sand-mining truck, the adults up front in the cab.

—Look at him, Esther would say about her father, with a disgust that always shocked Lerako. Esther now worked at a furniture store in town. She was still mad that her father refused to allow the girls to wear trousers. Lerako happened to know that Esther sometimes folded a pair into her handbag before leaving for work in a modest knee-length dress.

—I wish he could just go somewhere for a month and leave us alone, Ruth responded.

And yet, at church, Esther and her sisters were perfectly courteous, bending their knees and smiling, speaking well of their father to anybody who asked.

But on this morning, exactly two years after his grandmother's funeral, Lerako got dressed slowly, feeling the pain congealed on his shoulder blades, which ached pleasantly as he dressed. Outside, he stood for a moment at the veranda, staring at his uncle, there, down by the corner of the yard where they kept the stack of firewood. The stack was so big that he only saw, once in a while, the sharp glint of the axe blade slicing the air, just before he heard its thud as it split the wood. Lerako was tired, his body steeped in some fatigue that rendered him melancholic. Lonely too. Loneliness had become a faithful companion, even here in his uncle's household, with its many and loud inhabitants. He walked down slowly, squeezing the pimples on his face, grimacing at the needle of pain as he pinched. The thud of the axe was louder, as was his uncle's groan, which he emitted in concert with the thud. His uncle's neck and back glistened with sweat.

Remmonye stopped and raised his white vest to wipe the sweat off his face.

—Motlogolo, he said.

—Dumelang, Lerako responded.

—You finally got out of bed, boy?

Lerako laughed uneasily. His laughter was careful, restrained.

Now that he was older, Lerako was wary around Remmonye. He had seen the quick turns of his uncle's anger, sometimes directed at his employees, often directed at his daughters. He could never be sure what side he was going to get, the raging beast or the tender man who called him nephew.

—You ready, boy? his uncle asked. For tonight?

The warmth in Remmonye's voice urged Lerako to tell him about the dream he'd had, of his grandmother. It was childish, perhaps, unmanly. He was certain his uncle would dismiss him with a mocking laugh. Lerako wished to look into his uncle's face, the face of a man, and understand him, to know the deep thoughts he had when he was alone. He wanted to ask his uncle about his grandmother. He wanted to know if Remmonye ever thought of her. But under his uncle's stare, Lerako looked down, scuffing his shoe against a rock stuck in the ground.

—I think I am, Uncle, Lerako said.

—Good. I am proud of you, his uncle said, handing him the axe.

—I have honor because of you, his uncle said.

THAT NIGHT, the light of the moon washed over the compound of the church. A chilly breeze, befitting a May night, a harbinger of the severity of the coming winter, swept through. The shadows of the mokoba tree and of the half-finished church buildings loomed, and Lerako imagined he heard the rustle of some creatures in the shadows. Lerako was standing to the side of a pond the church had dug and filled with water. He would not be the only one baptized; there was a pair of twin girls who held each other's hands; an older man, his hair white already, whom everybody had known as a drunkard; and there was a girl slightly older than Lerako. All needing salvation from their wayward lives. All those who would be baptized stood aside. Each of them wore a simple cream robe that even Lerako understood as symbolic, the exchange of this simple robe for the purer, whiter robe that would then become their church uniform. He understood it, he thought. The washing away of sin; emerging from the water as pure and sin-free, committed to living a life of virtue, his every thought flooded with light. He thought, in those moments, as the bells and the music clanked around him, of his sins. Maybe his sins were not too bad. He never stole, except for a piece of meat once in a while from one of his cousins' plates. He tried to be kind, except there were times he and his friends had not always been kind to some kids at school. He tried to keep his heart and thoughts pristine, except he sometimes wished his mother's husband ill, for no reason at all. His mother too; sometimes he conjured a picture of her in his head, although in these scenarios, she was never Mme but just Dikeledi, and in his imaginings, she would be crying, full of some unfathomable pain, except she couldn't be injured, she couldn't have been beaten up, she couldn't be at the risk of death. But pain, she would be in pain. He tried not to be covetous or prideful, although he realized that school was easy for him; he did well with no effort at all, and based on that, he knew with a pragmatic certainty that he was destined for a life better than his friends'.

Around him, the congregation sang and clapped their hands. Lerako clenched his jaw against the cold, against the furious beating of his heart. The second of the twin girls had just emerged from the water and a joyous wall of women had formed around her as she changed from the dripping robe. Lerako walked toward the pond and dipped his feet into the cold water. The water came to just about his waist and he struggled toward the priest, whose exertions thus far had left him breathing loudly. The pressure of the man's hand was heavy against his head, and Lerako could not decipher the enigma of muttered words issuing from the man's mouth. Then the man pushed Lerako's head under the water, and leveraged his arm under Lerako's back to jerk him upward, above the water, where the loudness of the music met his face with the intensity of a slap, then he dunked him under again, once, twice, the music and bells dulled under the water. Then as he approached the rim of the pond, two men hauled him out of the water onto the solidity of earth. He emptied his ears of water and inhaled quick spurts of the cold and holy air. The men surrounded him. His uncle, in the middle of a song, handed him a towel, slapping him on the shoulders.

CAMEL THORN BUSHES and acacia trees and shepherd's trees abounded. They were everywhere and bordered the narrow dirt road Remmonye's car swayed cautiously on. The branches of the trees reached out and scratched the sides of the van. Remmonye squinted into the dark, stopping now and then to allow a lone impala or duiker to dart across the road. Lerako kept his eyes on the night, with its dark and its dangers outside the closed window of the vehicle. He was on the lookout for snakes that could droop off the tree branches onto the windshield.

　—Motlogolo, I can't believe this is the first time you are going to the cattlepost. A boy of your age? Aren't you almost a man? In a couple of years, you will be bringing a wife home, and how do you think you will manage that with no cattle? We are getting there, motlogolo, with the few beasts we have. Perhaps one day, we too will be one of those that can eat rice. That last drought nearly finished us. But what am I talking about? You were just a baby then, still without sight, smelling of mother's milk. Heh? Isn't it that way, boy? You young boys of today, you grew up in such softness. You Independence

children. You see, me? I grew up at the cattlepost. I have been herding my father's cattle since I was a little boy, since before I could talk.
I am telling you! I know cattle, boy. I know that cattlepost like the
back of my hand. I know the lay of that land. We used to go hunting,
just us boys, for rabbits and monitor lizards, tortoises. But you boys
these days are so soft. If you want to know the truth, boy, I wish I
could just live at the cattlepost. Drink milk, spend the day herding
my cattle, playing my segaba. Heh? Are you laughing, boy? I can play
the segaba like I had it clasped in these hands when I emerged from the
womb. I could grow so fat if I could live at the cattlepost. But, this
life, these days of modernity. I have to be in Serowe to watch out for
my laborers. My business would collapse in a day if I left any of them
in charge, and then what would we eat? This beast called a belly, my
boy, is a demanding master. That's what we toil for, our stomachs, so
that even we, whose blankets only reach our shoulders, can eat. That
is why I have no choice but to leave my cattle to Masarwa.

His uncle rolled down his window and spat into the swift, darkened air.

—Now, listen to me, boy. Let me tell you something about Masarwa. They are not like us. They are shifty. They are thieves. You
can see it in their eyes. When they see you, there they go kneeling,
and calling you their White. But as soon as your back is turned, they
will steal from you. They are like rats; they will bite into your finger
and blow cool air into the wound. Don't trust them, motlogolo. Are
you listening to me? They are not a God-fearing people like us. Have
you seen how they live? They live like animals!

The only Basarwa Lerako knew were the Basarwa children who
attended his school. At least, a dark rumor about their provenance
had coiled its way around the school. But the kids looked nothing
like the pictures of Basarwa he had seen in the books from which

they read social studies, in which the Basarwa were always half-naked, holding ostrich eggs with the veneration owed to a god, kneeling to conjure fire from two sticks and dry grass, appearing as though from a remote and miraculous age. To Lerako, the pictures seemed to show the inadequacy of the men's smiling yellow faces against the savagery of the sun; their squinting eyes were mere slits amid the wrinkles of their faces; their hair was just tiny little coils on the arid landscape of their scalps. His schoolmates were nothing like that. They arrived at school with hair oiled and combed just like his and did not have the stupid, placid smiles of the men in the pictures. They seemed no different from him. But he and his friends taunted them all the time; even following his baptism, after he had sworn to keep his deeds kind and good, still, after school, he joined his friends and shouted to the kids: Mosarwa! Mosarwa ke yoo!

The new day still held the darkness of night when Lerako and his uncle arrived at the cattlepost, though light was seeping in at the low edges of the sky.

—We are here, boy, Remmonye said as he turned the engine off. He stepped out of the van and looked skyward, his face pure, a boy's face. He breathed the air in deeply, and Lerako mimicked him, but to him the air was heavy with the scent of cow dung and the heat of animal bodies. Lerako followed his uncle down a narrow path bordered by knee-high grass. To the kraal they went, and through the remnant of dark, all Lerako could see were the tips of the horns of the cattle. From Remmonye's chest issued a low clucking, warm and mollifying, targeted toward the stilled beasts. Hearing the coaxing, the cows stirred and lowed gently in response. A surge of excitement radiating from Remmonye reached Lerako and he perked up, longing to be swept up in it. His uncle pointed this way and that way at the lowing, gently masticating beasts.

—There, his uncle said softly, that over there is Thokwanampe. He has been with us for years. The thamaga one over there, no, where my finger is pointed, that is Tshunyanante. There goes Banthoi, look at how shiny and beautiful his hide looks now; we had to nurse him back to health. Banthoi, Banthoi! Ah, over there, that's Thokwanantle, who has birthed for us plenty of beautiful calves, a miraculous cow; we thought she had reached her end last year, and she brought forth Ephatshwa. Over there, the bull that has captured my heart, the bull that has made everything possible, we are talking about vitality, boy, no weakness here, that is Bobojane.

Lerako was uncertain whether this soliloquy of arcane colors and descriptions was really meant for him, for his uncle seemed quite immersed in a world of his own creation, communing with his beasts, which stirred and lowed and raised a veil of dung-scented dust and a remarkable heat that was suffocating to Lerako but to which his uncle seemed immune.

Remmonye now entered the kraal, the clucking vibrating from his chest, his posture cautious although his face still wore an expression like a sunbeam. He tenderly slapped some of the cows' hides until he reached an ordinary brown cow. His uncle knelt reverently before the cow, then thrust his face upward, between the cow's hind legs. He ground his nose into the cow's teat before latching his mouth on to it. Lerako watched from outside the kraal, yet heard the messy grunts, sounds to which he had never before been privy. His uncle came away from the cow with a dazed look and motioned for Lerako to join him in the kraal.

Into the kraal and its heat and its stink, into the heave of the great bodies of cattle, Lerako entered. He had not realized how big the cattle would appear up close. He felt minuscule next to them. He averted his boyish eyes from the animals' large faces, the nostrils flaring with heat, the heavy engorged teats. Lerako was only thirteen, an excruciating age; his face was aflame with his embarrassment.

—Kneel, his uncle commanded, and Lerako knelt.

—Touch it, his uncle said.

Lerako reached gingerly for the teat, through the cow's stomping legs, and pressed at the surprising rough warmth with his fingertips. His uncle bent down to speak quite close to Lerako's ear.

—Nothing else you eat in your lifetime will ever taste as sweet as this, his uncle said. Nothing else will satiate your appetite like this. Do you hear me?

—Yes, Uncle.

—Good, now open your mouth, closer!

The heat and odor of the teat overwhelmed Lerako's face. He kneaded, his eyes shut.

—What is this boy doing? his uncle wondered. Motlogolo, squeeze, squeeze!

Lerako's eyes followed his uncle's hands, and Lerako imitated the downward squeezing motion, his mouth open below the heavy teat. An arc of warm milk, sweet and pungent, squirted onto his gumline, into his mouth. He stood up then, wiping his mouth. He avoided his uncle's zealous look and stared instead at where they had come from, at the compound, which was revealed as the dark of night waned.

He saw two dilapidated huts, half-finished, which had not seen any fresh soil in years, a tarp hung over the side of one of the huts. As Lerako studied them, a man appeared from the vast darkness of the hut, squinting into the light, then across the distance between the compound and the kraal. Upon seeing Remmonye, the man removed his woolen hat and jogged over to them. Lerako tried not to stare at the little coils of hair on the man's head, at his face, which immediately became placid and dumb. He was embarrassed at the state of the man's clothes, which were tattered and potent with the stench of sweat and dirt.

—Lekgoa la me, the man greeted Remmonye, twisting and bending his body so he was shorter even than Lerako.

—Matshwenyego! Remmonye called to the man, maneuvering between the cattle and exiting the kraal, Lerako behind him.

—Just waking up? Remmonye continued, his tone jocular. When do you milk the cows? You let them out to graze at a time of your own liking, when the sun is already high in the sky?

—Ah, no, my master, I was just coming to let them out, the man said. We let them out early, lekgoa la me.

—And how is everything? Remmonye asked, spreading his arms expansively.

—Everything is how it always is, lekgoa la me, Matshwenyego said. We ran into some trouble. But it was nothing much, mong' ame. You are here now, lekgoa la me, and we are hoping that because you have come to see us, maybe we will get some tobacco.

Remmonye laughed.

—Always tobacco this. Tobacco that. You know how expensive tobacco is?

—Owai, how would I know? Me, a lizard like myself, who can only live in a cattlepost?

—Don't worry about it, Matshwenyego, I brought some tobacco for you.

—Thank you, master. Thank you, lekgoa la me. You have made me very happy.

—And I brought some extra feed for the cattle, in the back of the van.

Lerako watched his uncle, how he smiled down at the man, how he seemed to grow taller, fuller in the presence of this man's servile manner. He liked it, Lerako realized. His uncle liked that this man called him "my White," and that he prostrated himself so before him.

Lerako was still marveling at this when he heard a sudden loud crack. In the stunned silence, and from the man's sunburned hand rubbing his cheek, Lerako realized that his uncle had slapped Matshwenyego on the face. He was furious, suddenly, Remmonye, his chest heaving with angry breath, his finger stabbing the air toward a long string of meat hung out to dry on a wire between two trees. The length of meat buzzed with the green sheen of flies.

—My master, we had to do it, Matshwenyego said, his voice on the verge of tears. Forgive me, my master.

Lerako did not know where to look. He had never before heard a grown man sound so childlike.

—After those drops of rain in November, Matshwenyego said. One of the heifers, the brown one with the white spots, was stuck in the mud, my master—

—Spot of rain? What rain? Mud? What are you talking about? Remmonye asked.

—We took the cattle to graze, my lord, maybe some of them were thirsty and they wandered over to the pond that used to be at Maminalegwete, and that cow got stuck in the mud. We tried everything we could to rescue it, my master. Everything we could. We couldn't just have left it to the vultures. My master knows that would have been waste. We had to rescue it.

Matshwenyego kept his head low, his right knee bent and hovering above the ground, but he trained a wary eye on Remmonye. Lerako heard the clink of his uncle's belt unbuckling.

—Stealing from me? his uncle roared. Eating my cattle?

The belt whistled as it whipped through the air, and thwacked as it landed on Matshwenyego's back.

—Forgive me, lekgoa la me, Matshwenyego cried.

Lerako edged toward his uncle, then, thinking better of it, edged toward the van, putting it between himself and the altercation. His heart was thunderous in his ears, seeing the red welts rising immediate and angry on the man's arms and face.

WHICH OF THE CATTLE had the boy taken a liking to? If he could prove himself by identifying just two cows by name and color, Remmonye told Lerako, then he would give him two calves. Just like that. Here, thank you. From one man to another. Not many people got their starts that easily.

They were heading back to Serowe at the end of the weekend.

Did Lerako know how hard it was to start a herd of cattle? Remmonye continued.

But the boy had encased himself in a reproachful silence. Remmonye fell silent too. Lerako was still just a boy, he thought, far from grasping the ways of the world. A herd of cattle was life itself. More precious than anything. It was his legacy, it was. It was dignity. His herd of cattle carried him aloft as a man. Nothing, certainly not a dog of a Mosarwa, would take that from him.

NINE

Owing to his age, fourteen, and his gender, male, Lerako could no longer share a bedroom with his two youngest cousins. He had to displace Esther from her room into Ruth's. Still, the wardrobe in the room was full of Esther's clothes. Still, the girls used the room as a de facto salon; it always smelled of Blue Magic and burned hair. Some mornings Lerako woke to stinging eyes from the sulfuric smell of the relaxer crème Esther had applied to her hair; other days he watched her teasing her hair out with an Afro comb, a vision that, in the early morning light, reminded him of his mother.

This was in 1982, when, all over the country, government officials were holding meetings, urging men to contribute to a fund to build their own university. *One man, one beast* was the rallying cry. The perennial ethos of duty and self-sufficiency compelled men and women: cattle rearers, the newly educated class of teachers and nurses and social workers, traders, farmers, even those without a single cat or dog to call their own contributed bags of beans or sorghum. The country was theirs, a gift from God and their forefathers, and they, the people, had never been afraid of building new worlds. It was a time heady with optimism, a time of idealism despite the disheartening news of atrocities happening in nearby countries. It was in keeping with the heady elated atmosphere that Remmonye gave two of his beasts to the cause. In the excitement of all this possibility, of these new beginnings, Remmonye decided too that this was a time ripe for opening a church of his own.

He was called to do it, he explained to his wife late at night, as she rubbed his back.

God chooses his servants, shepherds well suited to leading a flock of sinners to the light, he explained to the children the next morning, as they sat with bowed heads before him.

One Saturday in March, soon after their father's announcement, the girls gathered in Lerako's room. Esther was sitting on a chair by the open window, a mirror in her hands, as she watched Ruth put her hair in rollers.

—Has that one even said what the name of the church is? Esther asked. In her looks, Esther took after her mother. She had the same square face, given to appearing stern. But in her personality, she was more like her father, her speech quick and full of mischief.

—New Babylon Church of Jerusalem, Mary-Magdalene piped up. The two youngest sisters were sprawled on Lerako's bed, watching with reverence their sisters' dexterous and knowing habits.

—Full Gospel of Christ, Hannah piped up too, not wanting to be left out of the fun.

—No, St. Anna's True Gospel of Christ, Ruth said. That's what bo-Mme told me.

Ruth was the second oldest, and the favorite of their mother's, similar to her in reticence and seriousness.

—I am asking myself if we have a choice, Ruth continued. Can we choose to still go to our old church?

—You think you can make a decision of your own in Rra-Esther's house? Esther asked. In this, Remmonye Mminapcló's house? In Rex's house? You must be new.

The youngest girls laughed, thrilled by their oldest sister's evocation of their father's naked name.

—That's why I can't wait for, you know, to get serious, Esther said. Then maybe I can finally leave this house.

Every once in a while, the two oldest sisters spoke to each other in this private manner, a solid door shut against the younger sisters. They became remote, the older sisters, giggling together, their resolute secrecy exquisite and torturous to the younger sisters, who continued asking their futile questions. But Lerako knew that Esther had a boyfriend. He had come upon them kissing once on his way back from school.

—What is he doing? Ruth asked suddenly. He couldn't have had us go to a different church? Who starts a church?

—Hey, you, Esther said to Lerako, has he said anything to you?

—No, Lerako said. But what's wrong with starting a church?

He retained his loyalty to his uncle. Cattleposts, he had decided, were far-off places, necessarily sequestered from the eyes of good, decent people, where battles of good and evil, far above his comprehension, were fought. Cattleposts had little to do with a boy like himself; they needed be left to the efforts of men like his uncle, men who fought for goodness and decency. He had thought about it, now that he was distanced by time and space from the cattlepost.

—What's wrong with starting a church? Esther asked, raising her head to look at him. What's wrong is that it's embarrassing—

—Keep your head still, Ruth said.

—Sometimes I wish a shovel would fly from one of the laborers' hands onto his head!

The girls giggled and Lerako felt fury building in his chest.

—Stop saying such things about him! He is your father! he yelled.

In the brief stunned silence, Lerako was embarrassed by his outburst.

—Only a mother knows a child's true totem, Esther murmured.

She and Ruth giggled again in their private way.

—Let's tell the truth, Esther said. Have you noticed how Ntate never looks at us?

—He is ashamed of us, Ruth said.

—That's not true, Lerako said, but even as he said it, he was racking his brain fruitlessly for an occasion he could use to prove them wrong.

—He scares me, Mary-Magdalene said and then covered her face and slid down on the bed.

—He scares me too, Esther said. Seriously, which one of you has been alone with him in a room, without BoMme there? Mary? No. Hannah? See? She cut her eyes at Lerako.

—Yes, Lerako, we know you are his favorite, Ruth said.

—No, I am not, he said, then thinking about it, he conceded.

—It's only because I respect him, he said. I do everything he tells me to. I don't say these things behind his back. I listen to him.

—You think we are ill-mannered?

—No, Lerako said, flustered. He liked his cousins, and he knew their father liked them too—he worried himself about their futures— but they *were* girls. They did not know what it was like to be a man. What could a man, like his uncle, discuss with girls? If his uncle showed him any favoritism, it was only because Lerako was a boy, who would one day become a man, acquainted with the burden and the duties. His cousins, no matter what they did, would always remain women.

—I am finished, Ruth said. You owe me. The way your head is as big as that hill!

Esther's head was abloom with multicolored rollers and white pins sticking from them. Her face was so tight she couldn't even laugh without grimacing in pain. The girls went outside, where they basked in the sun as they waited for Esther's hair to dry. In his room, listening to their floaty girlish talk, Lerako was weighed down with the certain difficulty of the path before him, the burden of making his own way in life, as a fatherless boy.

HE WAS shaken awake that night by his uncle, who summoned him out of bed. Lerako followed Remmonye to the sitting room. Improbably, his aunt and his cousins sat there, on the floor, in the near dark, their faces illuminated only by the flame of a candle on the coffee table. Was he in a dream? Lerako wondered. Sit down, boy, his uncle said, and Lerako groped among the tangle of legs and sat where there was space. We are all here, his uncle said. Lerako wondered to whom he was speaking. Then he noticed a figure wearing all white, a woman, also sitting on the floor. Who was this woman? Was this the person to whom his uncle was speaking? Who was this woman and why was she here? He looked around him at his cousins, at Mma-Esther, at his uncle. All around him was quiet, even his two youngest cousins looking down. Lerako felt afraid all of a sudden. What was this that they were doing? The woman started to pray, or uttered something akin to prayer; Lerako couldn't understand the words she was saying. She had started speaking in a language that he did not know but that he understood as legible, *Nkulunkulu* the woman said at some point, *Ezwilini* the woman said, then the woman's language started to fall apart, none of the words holding together, but as the words broke down, her voice rose and her body started to tremble, as though quite outside of her control. Lerako looked at his uncle again and saw that his face was down, suppliant, receiving whatever it was that was coming forth from the woman. A torrent of something beyond language, something approaching the texture of a wail, and Lerako felt his stomach clenching in fear. He felt sure that he was going to cry. He felt sure of it, then the woman's voice reached its apex, and Lerako was afraid that the neighbors would hear. But just like that, the woman's Babel cut off. Her body kept its tremors and its mutterings, like the relieved sighs of a child after the intensity of a good cry. Mma-Esther stood up and silently delivered a full cup to the figure, and she drank deeply from the water. The woman was returned to her body and to the silent room. She wiped her sweaty face with the corner of her white scarf. She talked pleasantly with Remmonye. She got up and went outside, to use the pit latrine, Lerako thought, but after a while she returned with a bowl against the rim of which lapped a viscous liquid. Then Lerako saw that he was not released from whatever this was. His uncle told them one by one to get up and go to the woman, first Esther, then Ruth, then Hannah, then Mary-Magdalene. Lerako didn't want to do it. He kept trying to catch his uncle's eye or, failing that, to catch Esther's. Esther looked quietly furious but knelt obediently before the woman. The woman cut incisions onto the inside of Esther's wrists and pressed some kind of herb or root into the cut. Then she patted the surface of the liquid in the bowl—some kind of animal blood, Lerako saw—and patted it all over Esther's head, her face, her neck. This was wrong. Surely this was wrong. They had all been baptized, all the people in this house. They had pledged to worship no false gods, no idols. Hadn't the Lord said— And his uncle signaled for him to go. It's okay, his uncle said when he hesitated, and then Lerako was extending his trembling arms to the woman, and he felt the delicate pain, two swift cuts on each wrist, and the sting of whatever she was grinding in there. The scent of the blood was metallic and thick and filled his nose; he felt the blood on his head, sticky on his neck. He might never be able to wash the stench away.

He stayed outside on the veranda watching the distant sun rising from somewhere beyond Swaneng Hill. He couldn't bear to face the others, who had made him party to some pact that nobody had fully revealed to him. When he started to shiver from the early morning cold, he went indoors. Coming out of the bathroom was his cousin Esther, her washed hair wrapped in a damp towel, her face filled with her own discreet sorrow. Washed again, he thought, his heart breaking for her. He grasped for words to say to her, jocular words, to dismiss as trivial whatever it was they had just participated in. But the words eluded him. He stepped into his room and closed the door behind him.

In the morning, only two other people, aside from his uncle's family, were in attendance at the new church, a couple whose half—the husband—Remmonye employed in his sand-mining business. The place of worship was the hut the family sometimes used as the kitchen. His uncle was valiant that afternoon, singing louder and longer than everyone, sweaty and preaching a ferocious sermon, dancing around the fireless hearth, but it was no use. St. Anna's True Gospel of Christ worshipped only that one Sunday. Two months from that Sunday, Remmonye and his family returned to the fold, the forgiving bosom of their old church.

TEN

The temptations of the flesh were everywhere. A boy like himself, fifteen, nearly a man, needed to be vigilant. Lerako had grown into his face; something about its squareness had morphed into a chiseled handsomeness, despite the constellation of pimples cluttered across his skin. He examined the pimples at length every night, squeezing, then applying a dot of toothpaste to the protrusions. He had grown taller too, taller than his uncle and his aunt, than all his cousins. His long, feminine eyelashes soothed girls into confiding in him, and his earnestness made them feel safe. Yet when they came to him as a group, he trembled in front of them, shaken by the alien feelings they inspired in him. At school, the girls congregated around him, especially when he got off the field after football practice. They whispered into their clusters. They shouted: Hi, Lerako! Lerako, come here! And he went to them, with some trepidation, holding a football in his hands, for something to do, having a troubling idea of what they desired from him. Every night, to remind himself of what was at stake, he read from the Bible, from the book of Revelation. *And they sang a new song before the throne and before the four living creatures and the elders. No one could learn the song except the 144,000 who had been redeemed from the earth. These are those who did not defile themselves with women, for they remained virgins. They follow the Lamb wherever he goes. They were purchased from among mankind and offered as first-fruits to God and the Lamb. No lie was found in their mouths; they are blameless.* He guarded his feelings, corralled them, so that he sometimes came off as cold. He was terrified of sexual sin in particular, and of the punishment that awaited sinners, as laid out in Revelation. *The lake of fire is the second death. Anyone whose name was not found written in the book of life was thrown into the lake of fire.* His friends goaded him: What kind of man was he that he wouldn't take what was freely offered him? Man must eat, they said. Man must taste the sweetness of flesh. His boys bragged of their own adventures: sex in the classroom after school, sex in their fathers' cars, quiet sex in the girls' houses and the early morning sneaking out before the household awoke. Lerako absorbed their badgering, laughing easily. He was better than them, he knew, superior in his ability to control himself, to resist giving in to those earthly raptures. Eventually he became contemptuous of the girls and their persistence, their looks betraying a hunger harbored in their bodies. It angered him, that hunger in their eye, for it exposed them as women with no self-respect.

But there was one girl he was drawn to. Dimpho was her name; she had the disconcerting habit of chewing her Bic pens, so her lips were constantly streaked with blue and black ink by the end of any school day. Around the other girls, she behaved much the same as they did. But she turned inward during class, quiet and focused as a monument. On study break, when the other students threw drawings of one another across the room, she sat quietly, flipping through her notes as though she were far away, somewhere else entirely. She did better than he did on every test. Finally he swallowed his pride and asked only that they study together. They stayed behind in the classroom and talked about Shaka Zulu's army formation and the properties of loamy soil. She would sometimes surprise him by slipping her shoes off, with no embarrassment. She liked to place her hand on her neck, as though to cool the heat of her throat. She looked him in the eye whenever she pointed out any answer he had gotten wrong, to see how he would react.

After their study sessions, they headed to Newtown. In the dusk, he walked beside her, in the wake of the slightly medicinal scent of her hair. Dazed and quiet. She talked ceaselessly, about all the events taking place in South Africa and Zimbabwe, and about the bioscopes that she and her friends went to see sometimes, about their neighbors who fought every month end, about the world-famous writer who lived not too far from their school. She never minded his own reticence, and never allowed the conversation to lapse into silence. You should read more, she told him sometimes, plucking a book from the depths of her schoolbag and placing it in his hands. The books were always novels by American writers—John Grisham and Danielle Steel and Sidney Sheldon—and she would explain their plots to him. She would stop talking only when they reached Nelgo General Dealer, which was as close to her house as he would go, and then she would shift her schoolbag to her other shoulder and wave to him.

Only then would he come awake. Only then would he notice the old women carrying buckets of water on their heads, homeward. He saw boys pushing gas cylinders in creaky wheelbarrows. Only then would he notice the little girls playing their last games of the night, their shrill voices accompanying the dusk:

—Lee le le bodileng!

—Nna 'a ke a bola!

In the future, he would try to recall the exact sensations that enveloped him on those evenings. Everything seemed good and beautiful. The sun setting with its many improbable hues, the sky appearing somehow distant yet very close, so that he felt, sometimes, that something was out there, something that looked out for him. It made him feel one minute lonely and small, peculiar, tender with tears, and another minute cheerful and invigorated, the secret of Dimpho's books radiating from his backpack. Those evenings, he was compelled to walk past his grandmother's yard. Since the absence of any occupants, the yard had been corralled off with a thorn bush. He barely recognized the house in which he had spent those early venerated days, the rondavel fallen in after years of neglect, the paint peeling off the walls of the two-rooms.

Nights, as he read, Lerako was fascinated by the world of the books—Hollywood and American courtrooms where ordinary people could decide the fate of a man on trial. There were always descriptions, in the books, of creamy throats and heaving breasts and silken parts between a woman's legs. Lerako was scandalized by these passages, though he wouldn't stop reading, even as his blood roiled inside him and his penis stiffened in his underwear. At night, when he was by himself, he thought about Dimpho, how her hands had seemed to awaken fireworks under his skin, and his hands would go to his penis, and he would touch himself until he came with a shudder, and then he would feel guilty, praying desperately.

He was embarrassed to face her when he handed her the books

back, afraid that, somehow, she would gaze at him and see beyond him as he stood before her, into the person he was at night, his hands quick and hot on his penis, his face agonized in ecstasy, moaning low and ashamed.

After a couple of weeks, Dimpho suggested that they just study at her home.

—I have to keep an eye on my grandmother, she said.

He couldn't say no.

Her grandmother was sitting outside in the yard, drinking from a gourd, when they arrived.

—Nkuku, Dimpho yelled from the gate, you said you would stop drinking khadi.

Lerako was shocked at the idea of a drinking grandmother.

—We are going to do our schoolwork, Dimpho said, without greeting her grandmother.

—Your mother will be here soon, her grandmother said to her.

—We are just doing our schoolwork, Dimpho said.

—Okay, Mmasekoponyana.

A burst of surprised laughter escaped from Lerako and he turned to look at Dimpho. She did have a big forehead, he realized, and he saw too, in the way her hand instinctively went to obscure it, that she was ashamed of it. A feeling of tender pity came over him. She was alive to him in a new way then, as one who had a whole other life unknown to him, one with nicknames and other mysteries.

Outside, her grandmother sat drinking and picking out weevils from a basket of beans, and inside, Dimpho tried to kiss him.

—Stop, Lerako said, I am here to study.

—All you want to do is study! Dimpho said. You can't know everything, no matter how much you study.

—Wena kana you don't need to study. You are a woman. Somebody is going to marry you and take care of you.

—How can you say that? Dimpho cried. You think just because I am a girl it doesn't matter whether I pass or fail?

He was quiet, taken aback by her anger.

—I am smart, she said. I am going to be a doctor.

—No one in my family has ever gone to university. Or even completed form five. I have to make sure that I pass my form five. And, wena Dimpho, you know I am saving myself for marriage.

—You want to tell me that you are never going to kiss a girl until what, until you get married?

—I am saving myself for marriage, he said. It is the will of God that you abstain from sexual immorality . . . it says that in the Bible.

She looked at him, then smiled coquettishly.

—Yes. But you are my boyfriend.

The word immobilized him.

Aren't you? Dimpho asked. Everybody thinks you are.

The heat and scent of her body next to him seemed to blot everything out. His eyes shut, his stillness betraying none of the exhilaration coursing through his body, he allowed her to cup his face in the soft coolness of her palms. His body was willful in its reactions to her hands, which were now tilting his face up, and though his eyes were closed, he felt her over him, he felt how close she was, her soft sweet breath on his face; he felt betrayed by his heart, beating thunderously, and the tiny fireworks that were coming alight under his skin, the groan he emitted when he felt her lips on his.

That evening, walking home by himself, he was in a delirium. To puncture it, to bring himself back down to earth, he thought of all the solid things he was: A son. A nephew. A grandson. *Kala ya me.*

A believer, born again. He grasped for what was still shimmering ahead of him: a university student, a graduate, a car owner, a home-owner. He would become a person, a man worthy of respect.

ELEVEN

A Brief Compendium of Everything Lerako Mminapelo Learned in University (1989–1993)

He learned to speak up, to show up as a man, not a boy, and give a firm handshake in his introductions of himself to his new classmates and professors; the former young men and women his age, from all over the country; the latter men, mostly, from all over the African continent, who had studied in America and the United Kingdom and the Soviet Union. They intimidated him, his professors; righteous and radiant in their erudition, they prowled the campus halls debating in their pristine English matters Lerako did not yet understand—the souring of the post-colonial ideals, the exhaustive and endless protractions of the struggles for liberation, the tentacles of the feudal system even in this new age, the latest raids on Botswana soil by the South African police, the meeting between Mandela and de Klerk, which Mandela really should be careful about, he would do well, Mandela, to remember Machel and the Nkomati Accord.

He learned to navigate the bewildering maze that was Gaborone. How quickly the city had grown impenetrable; in the just over twenty years of its existence it had sprouted sweltering pockets of informal settle-ments, sagging heavy with masses of people and shacks, far from the or-derliness of the garden city principles that had governed its design, Lerako had learned, just two years before Independence. In his early innocent months in the city, he learned what combis—Broadhurst Route 2, Broad-hurst Route 5, Tlokweng Route 4—to take from the bus station past the government enclave, past the Parliament, past the Main Mall and the city council building, past the national museum and Princess Marina Hospital to the University of Botswana campus. He learned what combis—Broadhurst Route 5—to take to Tsholofelo for church. Later, the city deboned before him, he learned the shortcuts to the bus rank; to church; to the Gaborone Dam, where he could watch the fishermen; and to the African Mall and Main Mall, where he could watch films starring Chuck Norris and Cynthia Rothrock and eat at restaurants, learning how to eat with a knife and fork without the cutlery clattering onto the table. It took the four years he was at UB for the city to open before him, and even more years, two of them spent abroad, for him to gaze at it with a dispassionate eye and have it cower before him, revealed for what it really was, a giant village masquerading as a city. How small it was! But even then, its true face did not arouse disappointment or contempt in him, but rather a tender fondness for the boy he had been, who once had found the city so impenetrable.

In his dorm room, Lerako heard his roommate, a boy named Patimile, talk to his friends in Kalanga. In their leaning together and laughing and speaking in that unknown language, Lerako had the sensation of being cast aside, ridiculed the way he had ridiculed those Basarwa boys in school. *Speak Setswana*, Lerako hissed at the group. Patimile was instantly incensed. These are not the old days, Patimile said. You think we are your serfs just because you are a Mongwato? Lerako learned thus that people assumed he was a Mongwato just because he was from Serowe. When he said, Actually, I am a Motalaote, people often asked: Which ones are those? It was easier to just let people assume that he was a Mongwato, he realized. There was a certain prestige in it too, being a Mongwato; just the name conjured all the greatness and history of the dominion of that nation. Lerako saw himself plainly. Here in university, his intelligence was not exceptional. He possessed neither the wealth nor the sophistication of city living. What he had was his origins from that famed Serowe, a borrowed superiority, which nonetheless elevated him in the eyes of many.

He learned to fuel himself with cupfuls of Five Roses and Ricoffy through the night to study for his classes: Introduction to the Study of History; Introduction to Information Communication Technology; African Cultures and Civilizations to C. 1500; The Rise of Europe to World Domination; Mfecane and the Settler Scramble for Southern Africa; Religious, Political, and Economic Aspects of Imperialism.

People laughed at Lerako when he left his dorm wearing his church robes. His fellow students laughed at him, their laughter contemptuous and embarrassed; people in the combis looked at him as though he were vermin. His robes, he realized, broadcast ideas about him, revealed about him a paucity of wealth, of sophistication, of education. These assumptions shamed Lerako and, he thought, no longer suited who he was, or who he was attempting to be: a young man at a place of higher learning, seeking knowledge, for whom the aperture of the world was opening up, letting in a glimmer of discernment. Lerako started folding his robes into a plastic bag and putting them on at church, but before long, he felt a low thrum of shame every time he folded his robes, and abandoned them altogether, showing up to church in his chinos and long-sleeved shirts. Then he was ashamed of where the church was, Tsholofelo, a low-income, high-density area, and he was ashamed of the inadequacies of the church building, which was just a small unplastered room with corrugated iron roofing, and of the other churchgoers, exactly the kind of undereducated people he was unwilling to be mistaken for. Then he stopped going to church altogether, preferring instead to meet with the university Christian Union, which held weekly meetings on Tuesday nights, the services and Bible readings in English.

When walking girls to their dorm rooms, Lerako learned to walk slightly behind, so he could admire the curves of their bottoms through their dresses. An innocent pastime, for eyes could do no harm. He learned to sit at the study desks in their dorm and talk and learned the right hour to leave without inviting trouble. He learned to allow girls into his own dorm, and the exact angle at which to leave the door open, which would simultaneously grant them privacy and the transparency to show passersby that nothing untoward was taking place in the room.

Were it that quinine had never been discovered, his professor said in class. This professor was a bearded and bespectacled man from Malawi, with a large, craggy face given to flashes of mischief, which now glimmered across his face as he asked, *What kind of world would we be living in had quinine not been discovered?* He paused after his question and swept his gaze across the class. That gaze and the studied casualness with which he leaned against his desk made Lerako sit up and pause his hands from pinching his pimples. *When ground up, the professor said, the bark of the cinchona tree produces this bitter-tasting potion, from which quinine was distilled. There are schools of thought that believe that without that discovery, Europeans would not have been able to penetrate the interior of the African continent.* The professor smiled slightly, again sweeping his eyes over the class, as though to assess the impact of his revelations on his students. *Before this discovery, British explorers and traders called Africa the white man's grave. Any attempts to penetrate the interior resulted in death. From yellow fever. From malaria, especially. But quinine! Quinine made it possible for explorers, traders, missionaries to survive malaria, and to enter into our world.* Sitting in the now darkened room, at the front of which his professor had lowered a white screen, Lerako was again frustrated and overwhelmed by the seeming arbitrariness of history, that the bark of a plant could allow for the images his professor was now zapping through—calloused hands hacked off by the Belgians in the Congo; the stacked skulls of the Herero in Namibia; generations massacred by the Germans; the emaciated, defiant bodies of the Kikuyu Mau Mau in Kenya, mauled to death by dogs at the instruction of the British.

He learned to parcel out his student allowance and he learned the name of the street vendor who would give him meals on credit, which of her food to avoid (the coleslaw) if he did not want to spend the night in the toilet, which of her food would fill him up all day (the samp and beans).

Lerako learned what football games he could attend for free at the national stadium nearby. What security guards to befriend for illegal free entry into paid games.

When his roommate sent him into exile, Lerako was forced into a program of nocturnal walks, sometimes past the Village into Tlokweng, sometimes into the heart of the city, past the government enclave. He walked unseeingly, frustrated by how much he had yet to learn, the world still an impossible puzzle invented by a trickster. Unsolvable. On his walks, he thought he felt the hum of all the world's knowledges, and all of its truth, hovering out of reach. Some matters Lerako knew instinctively, matters whose origins he had never sought to question. There was knowledge that had always seemed intractable and deep-seated, cellular inside him, that was now dislodged by the new ideas. Lerako agonized over what else he believed which would be proven false. Upon his morning return to the room, tired and exasperated and delirious, eyes red rimmed, he was cowed by the sight of his roommate's girlfriend, her numinous and warm body, the sacred murmur of their goodbyes, forehead to forehead. But all that was shattered when the woman left, and his roommate stretched languidly and said, Where did you go, monna, Lerako?

Could colonialism ever be justified? his professor asked. *Could we ever say, well, our colonial masters brought modern science and modern medicine and Western education and so we can forgive them their colonial-era atrocities? Western religion! Which most of us subscribe to, right? How many people in the room are Christians? See? Can we then say our colonial masters brought us Christianity, a doctrine, after all, which preaches forgiveness, and humility, and turning the other cheek and all that, how to withstand our earthly suffering—the loss of our land, of our cultures, of our ways of being— to withstand all that with the knowledge that some messiah would come and deliver us to eternal salvation and other eschatological nonsense? Fairy tales!* The professor slapped his hand on his desk and removed his glasses, wiping them with a handkerchief and expelling angry spurts of air. Lerako heard his fast-beating heart. He was dismayed with his professor for calling the gospel a fairy tale. Not that Lerako could vouch for the veracity of all the stories in the Bible, but he believed. He believed in Christ the same way he believed in the sun's steady rise every morning. It was true that some of the stories did not make any intellectual sense. But the professor seemed angry and strangely emotional and he had used that word, "eschatological," which Lerako had never heard. Before he could raise his hand to ask for clarity, which was a term all the smart boys in the class used, his professor continued. *What did they get in return? Because it was certainly not out of altruism that they set sail for our shores. Empires are rapacious entities; they are violent entities. They exist because of violent conquest and plunder. Their hunger for raw materials, labor, and territories to dominate predicated on their cultural superiority, their beliefs that they are the master race, that the people within the territories they dominate are not equally human and do not have legitimate cultures and systems of knowledge.* Lerako bit back his question; he felt nervous and slightly queasy at the professor's rage, and for the rest of his life, that slight queasy nervous feeling would return whenever people talked about building business empires.

Within the scope of his academic world, intellectually, theoretically, Lerako accepted the possibility that women were as good as men. That they might indeed be equal to men. He had come to learn, in fact, of some exceptional women, women such as Manthatisi of the Batlokwa, and Gagoangwe, the One-Eyed Queen of the Bangwaketse. Yet, in his real life, faced with their smiles and the endless industry of their daily habits, he could not recognize himself in them, and in their strangeness, he thought, lay their inferiority.

On his nocturnal walks, he turned over all the new knowledge he had acquired. He had known, of course, from those social studies books he had had to read as a primary school student, the same ones that had shown Basarwa conjuring fire, that they, Basarwa, were the first inhabitants of Botswana. But now his professor had asked: *If they were the first people, are they not the rightful owners of this land, and if they are the rightful owners of this land, why are they the most economically disadvantaged, living in the poorest villages with the least amount of resources and infrastructure?* Lerako could not put what his professor had said about empires out of his head. Conquest, plunder, violence. If the Bangwato had come upon the territory they now lay claim to through conquest and cattle rustling, was that not imperialism? He thought sometimes about how he and his friends had chased after those Basarwa children, screaming at them their own name as though the name itself were an insult. If the Basarwa were the first people in this land, was it not true that the land belonged to them?

At the invitation of one of the girls from the Christian Union, Lerako had joined the UB Dance Sport club. Over three months, he attempted to learn the cha-cha and the salsa. What he learned was his feet's lack of facility with rhythm. He watched the other dancers glide around the floor. Never had he felt so big and so clumsy, like an elephant attempting to tiptoe. He kept in closed position to his partner, Mositi, who had recently renamed herself Mercy. Arm styling, Mercy whispered to him when his large and disobedient arms encircled her tiny waist, and he retreated, his fingers grazing only the small of her back, his other arm hovering behind her shoulder. Footwork, footwork, she whispered when his feet rammed over her toes. Lead your partners, the dance instructor shouted above the music, and Lerako felt sure it was to him he was shouting. He was aware of everything about his partner, the daintiness of her waist and the precise movement of her feet. His body was at odds with the music, but Mercy's body felt right at home in his arms. The heat and scent of her perfume in his nose. When she disengaged herself and danced away, holding to him by only the tips of her fingers, then hurtling back into his arms before smiling up at him, he understood then why men risked everlasting salvation to be with women.

Lerako learned his ABCs: abstain, be Faithful, condomize.

Of course, Lerako had, in primary school, learned the story of the Three Kings who had taken the epic journey to England, back in 1895, to beg Queen Victoria for protection against the encroaching Boers and Cecil Rhodes. Who hadn't learned that story? Every Motswana had, whether educated or uneducated; a story confirming to the people their humility and resourcefulness and pacifism, their enduring philosophy that the greatest victory lay in dialogue. In class, his professor asked: *What are we saying here? Are we saying we ran to the British and said, Please, Master Race, please colonize us, please make us your ever-grateful subjects? What then do we make of these questions from Sechele in 1885, which is when this whole story of protection started? What did Sechele ask? He asked: Why is our country to be taken from us? What are we protected from? What is the matter? What do you mean by protection? That was Sechele in 1885. Ten years before the kings traveled to England.* Who was it, Lerako wondered that night as he did his reading, who was it that had benefited from spreading that palatable myth? Who had sought to conceal what really happened, the courage of the kings' journey, their humane appeal to be recognized as equally human, as people deserving of their own land.

Lerako learned how to unbutton a woman's shirt and how to unclasp a brassiere. He learned the weight of a woman's breasts in his hands, smoother and softer than a cow's teats. How to lean over and flick a tongue over her nipples.

Lerako learned how to sniff out on-campus events where one could get free food. Symposiums, readings, club meetings, consciousness-rising meetings. Cucumber and tuna sandwiches, bread rolls and cold meats, fatcakes and tea. Finally he found a regular meeting, every Wednesday in the auditorium in the Social Sciences block—you had to sit through lectures and demonstrations on HIV/AIDS awareness, but afterward, they handed you a coupon for a free lunch and a fizzy drink. Thus he learned to slip a condom over a banana in under a minute.

Esther sent a letter, filled with the gossip of home and church, in which the most important news he learned was the pregnancy of his mother, Dikeledi.

He learned to confess his love to a girl, his confession a deceit. To say, I am unable to think of anything but you. He learned how to tell a woman, with a straight face, that all he wanted was to study with her in his room. Later, he learned to beg: just the tip. And afterward, he learned to say: See what you made me do, you felt too good.

TWELVE

Ministry of Education Headquarters
Private Bag 0045
Gaborone
12th March 1993

Mr. Lerako Mminapelo
Post Office Box 0026
Serowe

Dear Sir,

I am pleased to inform you that you have been offered a position of Teacher—Social Studies Department at C3 salary. You will be appointed to Letlhakane Community Junior School in the Boteti Sub-District, under the supervision of Miss Teko Botshameko, principal therein. You are expected to report for duty on 1st May 1993, post the anticipated completion of your studies.

Please contact the Boteti Sub-District Education Office to make accommodation and transportation arrangements.

Yours sincerely
Bonno Ntlale (Mr.)
Principal Education Officer

THIRTEEN

He was the first of the Mminapelos to graduate from university. He was a government employee, permanent and pensionable. He arrived in Serowe laden with gifts. For Remmonye: a suit, brand new, purchased from Woodford's in Letlhakane. For Mma-Esther, a going-out dress, light green, elbow-length sleeves, square neck, and to go with it a chiffon scarf in a deep green color. He left a similar scarf to be taken to his mother. For his cousins, a top each, bought from an enterprising Zimbabwean woman who appeared once in a while in Letlhakane with a bag stacked full of clothes and seat covers. For Esther's daughter he bought shorts and a T-shirt with a watermelon print on it.

—What did we ever do to deserve our own White? Remmonye cried, his shiny eyes full of laughter.

Mma-Esther clapped her hands once, twice, in gratitude. She trailed the scarf around her neck with obvious pleasure.

—You will be blessed, cousin, Ruth said, spending your first paycheck on us like this.

—Let me look at you, Esther said. You are a real lekgoa. All you are missing is a narrow nose. If that nose was just a little narrower, and that hair a little longer . . .

Lerako only laughed. It rankled him, this exasperating title they foisted upon him. Perhaps he should talk to them about it, he thought, now that he understood its nefarious genesis, that proximity to whiteness was what was strived for. But how embedded it was, within their language and their history. It felt simultaneously too trivial and too grand to tackle. So he laughed his discomfort away. Yet deep down, some part of him, a part that hadn't caught up with his intellect, that still ascribed whiteness to all that was good and aspirational, that desired to be put on a pedestal, to be considered better than his cousins and his peers, that part of him flickered in pleasure.

LERAKO had been working for a year when he felt secure enough to take out a bank loan and buy himself a simple Toyota Corolla. Immersed in the scent of newness still around its interior, he drove the car home to Serowe to show it off.

—Our White, Remmonye said, as Lerako expected. His uncle was older, shoulders bent forward, his old vigor all seeped out of his body. He puttered around the car, his white handkerchief flapping like a flag from his back pocket. His uncle kicked at the wheels of the car, peered into the engine, whistled his admiration. Remmonye pressed his hands to the body of the car and prayed over it, sweat running down his face. Then he went up to his bedroom and returned from there with an old dirty cow horn, from which his fingers procured black fat that he applied to the back of each of the wheels.

—The world is full of people with ugly hearts, motlogolo, he explained. You can never be too careful. Even those who flash their white teeth at you in laughter can kill.

Lerako was filled with pity. Watching his uncle, Lerako told himself that he was performing an act of generosity, letting his uncle near the car with his prayers and his medicines. It was for his uncle's peace of mind. As for Lerako himself, he no longer believed. He could no longer overlook the lapses of logic.

He could admit to himself that there were times he missed the certainty of faith. Though he was learned, and learning still, the world, to him, seemed abstruse, obscured beneath some shadow he could not penetrate. There were times he wanted the mysteries and secrets of the world laid bare before him. Those times, he rebuked himself. What was the end point of his rapacious appetite? It recalled, for him, the impulses of the colonizers, who had been fired up by the notion that everything in the world should be within their grasp, with their desire to penetrate and excavate and lay bare every mystery for their use. They lacked reverence for the mystery of life. They refused the humility to submit to that enigma, to perceive themselves as nothing but a speck of sand, insignificant. There was no place in the world where they were satisfied to be mere guests. They had contrived it so, by sheer brute force. The torment of unknowing was still with him, but he met it with disgust when it reared its head, and he had resolved to be satisfied with his life, to view as noble his humble surrender into uncertainty and mystery.

———

FOR A COUPLE OF YEARS, Lerako endured, as all must, the quiet, obstinate piling on of days. Every year a new batch of students arrived who asserted themselves by taunting him: Teacher No Mistake! Teacher Don't Teach Me Nonsense! And every term he learned new student names, and watched their eyes glaze over as he taught them about the Mfecane Wars and about Mzilikazi. In the staff room the teachers had the same perennial complaints about the meagerness of their salaries. And in the staff room, there surfaced the same gossip about who was hunted by debt collectors and who had slept with whose wife, and once in a while the teachers would be upset about some political scandal, but the anger would be forgotten in the fog of everyday living. Lerako spent most evenings reading in the quiet privacy of his home, on the cheap brown couches that belonged to the education ministry. Some evenings he socialized with the other teachers, having suppers at his or their quarters, or drinking on the weekends. Other evenings he spent at his home with a woman, pleading his incompetence in the kitchen, and the women—nurses, teachers, social workers, all—were happy to fuss over him and make him meals he had never before eaten: spaghetti Bolognese, malva puddings, lamb chops, and mashed potatoes. The women dropped in to clean his house and do his laundry, and woke early after spending the night to make him breakfast. Always, a couple of months of this and he would feel himself suffocated by their quiet and eager hunger to be married, to have his children, and he would replace the woman with another. And every couple of months he received a phone call from his uncle Remmonye, asking for money for diesel or medicine for the cattle, and always asking if Lerako had not yet found a bearer of water to give Remmonye grandchildren; a maiden without too much physical beauty, for such beauty can be deceitful. And some months he received a phone call from his mother, Dikeledi, who asked for money to finish paying off her lay-by. And sometimes Esther called asking for money for school uniforms or shoes for her daughter. And it seemed that all his days passed in the same way, that sometimes he would look up bewildered that six months had gone by. And he would be stunned anew when another six months had passed in the blink of an eye. Or another year. In the future, he would struggle to remember anything about the passage of that time, all the days piling onto one another.

There was only one incident, during those years, that stuck with him, that rattled him so much that he never confessed it to anybody. He had dreamt about his grandmother while napping on his couch, and to clear his head had decided to take a walk, with the vague idea of getting himself fried chicken at a small café in the town. He was caught in a brief and intense flash of rain on an afternoon in February, in his third year in the village. He had tried to outrun the rain, but it stopped as suddenly as it had started, and his clothes were soaked. He walked on toward the town. The rain had driven people inside, and so he walked alone, water sloshing in his shoes. In the gloomy cloudiness, all the leaves of the trees were vivid and jewel green, all the yellow walls of the homes vibrant.

Up ahead of him, an old man was using a large bright-red umbrella as a walking cane, carefully avoiding the puddles on the ground. Lerako's heart sank, for he had been enjoying the solitude. The old man looked backward and slowed down for Lerako, who walked up to him reluctantly.

—Dumelang, Lerako greeted the man.

—Rra, the man said in response.

They talked about the rain and commiserated about being caught in the downpour. They talked about how the rain was a blessing, even so late in the ploughing year. The man studied Lerako's face as they talked.

—O mosimane wa mono, monna? the man asked eventually.

—No, sir, Lerako said. I am not from here. I am a visitor here. I am from Serowe.

—Serowe. Yes, our masters. Where in Serowe are you from?

—I am from Botalaote, Lerako said.

—O, pelo, pelo, the man said, and Lerako smiled at the evocation of his totem.

—Whose son are you? the man asked.

Lerako was taken aback by the question. He could not speak. He cleared his throat. The old man stopped to look at him, awaiting his answer, but by then they were by the main road and a black hearse was driving past, and the old man bent his knees in respect, but Lerako jetted across the road and into the café.

The talk among his colleagues, in his fifth year of teaching, was of increasing oneself. At the bar, at the Sunday football games, at the dam outside the village, where they took their girlfriends for picnics and braais and to listen to the latest music, everybody talked about increasing themselves. The government needed the human resource, to replace the manpower that had died during the height of the epidemic, human capital, men and women with graduate degrees. The country needed biologists and physicians, more mining and construction and electrical engineers. The country needed more and more nurses; the hospitals were full to bursting, the hospitals needed cardiologists and oncologists.

Lerako was not interested in any of that. He thought of how noble it could be, to teach at the single university in the country. All the best possible minds could pass through his hands; he could grab hold of those minds while they were still steeped in the confusion and ignorance of youth, and he could steer them in the right illuminated direction. They would come in green and leave as citizens. His old torment about living in the unknown world had never fully left him, and he thought that learning more history and philosophy could lead to some revelations about all matters noumenal—the best way to love, the dead, faith, and other phenomena.

FOURTEEN

Later, he would avoid all thoughts and all mention of his two years in England. Whenever it came up in conversation with his colleagues, he recalled a bone-chilling cold, his body always clenched. He recalled the maddening frenzy of the city, the buildings too tall, giving him the feeling, sometimes, that they were cutting off air. He missed the wide-open spaces of home, to which he had never before given any thought, and he missed the relentless beat of the sun on his neck, which, now that it was so far away and missed, he thought of fondly, the sun no longer a menace but a life source. What he would recall too of his time in England: shame. At the tables he gathered around with his classmates and new friends for dinners and potlucks, he couldn't understand anybody's accent, nor could they understand his. His mind plodded as he attempted to follow the quick turns of the debates and the conversation about postcolonialism and Negritude and the new millennium coming. He would find himself thinking, fondly and bitterly, of his grandmother's admonishment—*With which mouth are you speaking, and with which are you eating?*

Once, at an Independence Day celebration at the Botswana embassy in London, a white man named Nigel learned that Lerako was from Serowe. The man let loose a flurry of Setswana. He was one of the old Swaneng crowd, he said, when it was still a privately run school, when, for teachers, it depended on expatriates from England and Sweden and Norway and Canada and the USA. He asked about Lerako's studies, seemed interested in Lerako's research into the political and historical influence of Serowe on contemporary Botswana politics. Nigel talked about his Serowe, the music concerts the expatriates used to attend, the ballroom dance competitions, the multicultural feasts they had cobbled together from provisions that arrived once a month. He too missed that humble village on the other side of the world, Nigel mused.

By then Lerako had already come upon his theory about white men who professed to love the African continent, who reminisced about it with misty eyes. It wasn't the place they missed, nor the people. Their nostalgia was solely for the status of their lives there, people deferentially allowing them to go to the front of any queue, children running after them, screaming *Lekgoa! Lekgoa!*, the most desirable women throwing themselves at them. So he was instantly contemptuous. He was angry too that his village had made this man feel welcome, whereas he, in Nigel's world, was treated as less than human. But that night, falling asleep, Lerako wished he had talked to the man more, to understand better how the two of them, such different people, coming from such different worlds, could love the same place.

IN EARLY 2000, when fears of the Y2K bug were proven false, Lerako bought a ticket to return home. He was thirty-two, and he had been made an uncle four times over. For the first time, he had a nephew. The boy, Mary-Magdalene's, had been given the solid name of Kgosietsile. What did he know to teach the boy?

—Motlogolo, he said over and over again, lifting the boy, whose diapers perpetually hung heavy with their foul contents.

One day, Lerako might lead the party seeking a wife for his nephew, he thought. The boy would look to him for ways to live in the world as a man.

His cousins, now that they were all mothers, seemed better equipped to handle that existential question. They all seemed solid somehow, with some special knowledge conferred upon them by parenthood. The mischievous, laughing, two-faced girls he had once upon a time shared a room with were present in there, though, their mischief glinting in their faces in the way they asked him what he had brought them from overseas. In the way they asked him if he had gone all the way to Abroad and returned without a white wife.

He was home now, where the nights were studded with distant stars and the mornings were filled with work. He had responsibilities to attend to, and the morning after his arrival his cousins took him to see his uncle Remmonye, who had been hospitalized for months. Their father had just been moved from the TB ward into one of the regular male wards.

—You are just in time, Esther told him.

The girls were self-assured and unflappable; undeterred by illness and their confrontation with mortality. There they walked in a file, among the beds, to the back of the ward, talking and laughing in the loud whispers of their childhoods; there they pushed the curtains around their father's bed. They scattered around the bed, opening drawers, wiping surfaces, checking the greeting cards left on the bedside table, talking all the while over their father's still body.

—He looks a little better today.

—I think he looks just the same.

—But at least he is out of TB.

—Oh, that was bad. Bad!

—For a while there, I had given up.

Lerako was scandalized, at their implacable fussing, at his uncle, lying prone and useless on the bed. He did not even look like himself; his face was dry, not a smidgen of sweat anywhere. Lerako's eyes moved quickly and guiltily over the altered face, dark and emaciated and dull. But now it was the person on the bed who turned his eyes on Lerako, looking at him, first with no discernible recognition. Then he opened his mouth to speak, but all that came out was the gargle amplified by the tubes in his mouth, going down his throat. Was it an attempt to bid him welcome, or an attempt to bid him farewell? Lerako was wounded at his inability to understand; he stormed out of the ward, all the way out of the hospital, and waited for his cousins. The day was overcast, cloudy and windy, not cold, not really, but everybody, all the people coming in and out, were bedecked in boots and leather jackets, layers of woolen sweaters. How endearing, how moving that they thought this was cold! Lerako smiled to himself. He was home.

BEFORE HIM, solitary as he, the road stretched endlessly. Though it was afternoon, the road seemed to be carrying him into a darkness. Lerako had not been on this road for years, perhaps in longer than a decade, certainly never by himself. Always, in those long-ago days, when he idolized and was terrified and was baffled by him, he had taken the drive with his uncle Remmonye, and the front of the van was crowded by the sheer breadth of his uncle and his uncle's stories. Lerako thought he smelled now the unmistakable scent of his uncle's white handkerchief, drenched with the sweat of his body and his head. Lerako's throat hurt. It had been a month since Remmonye's funeral, and still Lerako could not think of him without a knot in his throat.

—You are the man here now, his aunt Mma-Esther had told him. You are the head of this family.

Lerako had tried to wiggle his way out, remembering his old ideas, that the cattlepost was a place he did not need to be, a place where elemental battles were staged, grand standoffs between good and evil, between civility and depravity.

—This responsibility falls on you, his aunt had insisted.

This time he arrived at the cattlepost in the early evening, just as the sun was sinking into the horizon. All around, a haze of dust in the air. It was beautiful, Lerako thought, getting out of the van. In the distance he heard the lowing of the cattle and the heavy toll of their bells. Lerako heard the high-pitched voices of boys calling after the cattle, Matshwenyego's sons. Or perhaps his grandsons. The passage of time made itself visible to him in the voices of those boys, and Lerako wondered for the first time how old Matshwenyego was. Without calling to anyone, Lerako unloaded the food he had brought with him—a bag of sorghum and a bag of mealie meal, some tinned pilchards and cooking oil, and a bag of tobacco. A dog, curious and fat, ambled over to him and sniffed at his ankles, then was bored and settled into its spot by the tree.

—Koko! Dumelang, Lerako called and waited.

Matshwenyego emerged from one of the huts, drying his hands on his trousers, squinting at him. His face split into a smile, revealing the great loss of his front teeth. He removed his hat from his head, kneading it in his hands. Lerako was queasy at the obsequious nature of that gesture, at Matshwenyego hurrying to him, who was younger, at Matshwenyego's knee bent for his benefit.

Matshwenyego pumped Lerako's hand in his.

—Lekgoa, it's been many years, Matshwenyego said.

—I have been away at school, Lerako said.

—All these years? Aren't you scared that all that learning will make you lose your mind?

Lerako laughed. He was feeling a little better already at the exuberance of Matshwenyego's welcome. A boy came out of the hut with two wooden stools and set them in the shade of a tree. Lerako followed Matshwenyego there, and just as they were getting comfortable, the boy returned with a tray of two cups, a large scarred kettle full of brewing black tea, and a cup of fresh cow's milk. Lerako shuddered slightly, remembering his first visit to the cattlepost, the whistle of his uncle's belt riding the air, the engorged teat, how for years afterward he could not drink fresh cow's milk. He covered the cup filled with black tea with his hand, so the boy didn't pour milk into it. Lerako sat back and watched the boy. There was something vital and animated about the boy, cocky; he had none of the deference of his father. He must have been about thirteen or fourteen. Did he go to school? Lerako wondered. It would be illegal, surely, to keep a boy like him out of school.

With the boy gone, Matshwenyego talked about the rains, the dryness of the boreholes, and the diminished quality of the pasture, how his boys had to take the cattle farther and farther away now for fresh green grass. He talked about the scarcity of good snuffing tobacco. They had almost been crippled by the foot and mouth outbreak of some years ago, but they were recovering well. A man never really collapses, Matshwenyego said, he just falls on his side.

Lerako studied Matshwenyego covertly. His hair had grayed at the edges and his face was a little more wrinkled, the thin ropes of his arms slackened somewhat, but he still looked the same. Had any time passed at all? In Gaborone, there were unprecedented rumors that a group of Basarwa would take the government to court. But his family cattlepost seemed untouched, impervious to the corruptions of time. It was unsettling, disorienting, like hiding behind as feeble a shelter as a finger while the hurricanes of change raged around you. Matshwenyego had fallen quiet and Lerako realized that he could no longer postpone it. He cleared his throat.

—I come with some words, Lerako said.

Matshwenyego folded his arms over his stomach and leaned in to listen.

—I am sure you have heard about my uncle's sickness.

—Yes, I had to go to Serowe, when was it? Three, four months ago? Some months had passed without him bringing any supplies and I thought, let me go see what happened. There, I laid my eyes on him. He wasn't himself. No. No. He was not himself at all. He did not even look like Rra-Esther. How is he?

—Owai, Lerako said. Go padile. He has left us.

—Ijo! Matshwenyego exclaimed, covering his mouth with his hands.

—We buried him a month ago.

Matshwenyego looked down in silence for a while, and Lerako was silent too. He could not know what the other man was thinking. Lerako himself was thinking again of the whistle of his uncle's belt riding the air toward Matshwenyego's back, where it had raised those angry welts, and he wondered whether, prompted by his uncle's death, Matshwenyego was thinking of the same. Lerako satisfied himself that, as for the task at hand, he had succeeded. He had been sent to deliver a message and he had delivered it. The heaviness of dread lightened now that he had completed his duty. He looked around at the bushes at the edges of the compound. Now he sat back and sniffed at the air and savored its freshness.

—In other words, Matshwenyego said eventually, in other words, you are our new White?

A sickly wave of dread swept over Lerako. He had been called this name before. Of course he had. By his family. Whom he knew, with whose teasing and mocking and flattery he was well acquainted. But from Matshwenyego, the name, he rejected it categorically. He did not want to be the new White. The name laid stark the configuration of the hierarchies of their world, into which they had been slotted by the accident of birth and history. He did not want to be imbued with that power. He did not want to be placed in that despised position. Lerako shifted his sneakers on the ground, making and unmaking patterns with his feet. When he raised his eyes, Matshwenyego confronted him with the directness of his gaze.

—Then it is you, who is our new White? he asked again.

Lerako was no extraordinary man, and neither was Matshwenyego. There was nothing mythological about either of them. They were, each of them, ordinary men, made of the same matter: of flesh and blood and bone and stardust; needing the same breath to live, living with the same knowledge that they would be buried in the earth, becoming one with it. Why, then, should he be a master to this man? There was a time, wasn't there, when his own people, the Batalaote, would have been in similar circumstances, a subjugated people. What was it, Lerako wondered, about humankind and this incessant, rapacious desire for superiority and dominion over others?

Matshwenyego cleared his throat, as though he wanted to say more, and something primal inside Lerako stirred with dread.

—The caretaking of the cattle has fallen to me, he said, quickly, because he was afraid of what there was to say.

FIFTEEN

He had started dreaming of his grandmother again. In some of the dreams, Nkuku Mma-Remmonye walked just ahead of him on a dusty footpath, wearing her church uniform and her little white starched hat. In that dream, he called to her: Nkuku! Nkuku! When she did not turn back, he called to her as though they were estranged: Mma-Remmonye, he called, Sekgele! Still she did not turn around, and in her relentless walk forward he began to be afraid that she would never again look upon him. He woke with a wounded heart then, in his university-subsidized house in Gaborone, and began his day quiet and withdrawn, not even playing the KTM Choir CD that was the usual soundtrack to his lesson planning in the mornings. He was subdued even after his two cups of Five Roses, and gave only terse answers to his partner's philosophical musings, and his brevity made her stop and look over at him with a keen expression he recognized. It was a look that he knew was a signal that some behavior of his needed dissecting, needed be talked about, needed unpacking. Her forthright manner was what had initially attracted him, reminding him of a girl he knew when he was just a boy in secondary school.

Other nights, he dreamt about his grandmother and uncle both, sitting out a too-hot afternoon under the mulberry tree in his grandmother's yard, talking earnestly to him. His excitement immediately tamped by the discovery that he could not hear what they were saying. He agonized over the dreams whenever he woke, convinced the key to understanding them lay just out of reach. By deploying all his knowledge upon them, he could decipher the vastness of his loneliness.

For months, he dreamt his dreams, for months the dreams followed him into the light of day.

Finally, he drove to Serowe, all the way to Mannathoko, to his mother, Dikeledi's, marital home.

He was received as a guest, in that house of ceramic dog figurines standing guard on the room divider; the "traditional corner" with its decor of wooden pestle and mortar, woven baskets, cured goat skin. His mother was gray haired, her face rounder and bare except for a trace of lipstick, traces of hair oil glimmered on her forehead. Before PP, Lerako felt as shy as a boy, and talked only about the matter of his grandmother's house, which had fallen into terrible ruin, which he could perhaps renovate and extend, turn into a home once again.

—Lerako, you have become a man, my son, Dikeledi said.

Yet Lerako did not feel like a man. He felt like a boy still, oblivious to the real substances of life. He asked to speak to his mother in private then, and at a table in her bright, well-lit kitchen he confessed the matter of the ceaseless dreams.

—I am not at all surprised, Dikeledi said, crossing her arms over her chest. The two of them were always so close. And your uncle, he always demanded, and we abided, and even now, years after we buried him, he is still demanding, and your grandmother is still right there beside him, allowing him to do whatever he wants.

—You have lost me, Lerako said.

He was a little impatient, looking at her, too detached to call her Mother, yet too polite to call her by her name.

He wanted to ask her, *Are you listening to yourself?*

—My son, I am just a person. I have nothing. I was not given the gift of sight, nor was I given the gift of wisdom. But, even though I am just a person, I know that sometimes the dead send a message to the living.

A shiver went through Lerako's spine.

—That's what you think is happening here? he asked.

—We would have to consult someone who has this wisdom, who can reveal exactly what this means. Maybe they are unhappy with you, or with us both. Maybe they are angry. Maybe they will need us to slaughter a goat, to appease them. Perhaps they feel we don't consult them or maybe they want us to honor them in some way.

—This does not make any sense, Lerako shouted. How can you believe any of this?

—Lerako, don't think about this with your mind of a professor. Not everything can be explained by your books, don't you know, my son? There are things that happen in the world that are beyond any explanation.

—But they were Christians, he said. He sounded to his own ears like a child, plaintive, needing reassurance.

—Nkuku and Uncle were both devout Christians, he said again. They believed in God, Jesus Christ.

—You know, even now I still don't go to church. And I was never really into the traditional ways. But what I know is that a lot of Christians, when all else fails, turn back to the Setswana way of doing things. It's always just there waiting for their return.

In his days of religion, Lerako had always yearned for a moment of arrival, when he would feel something click in his body and his mind and his heart, and fill him with absolute faith. He recalled that feeling now, seeing the conviction in Dikeledi's face. Here was the woman who had borne him, who was convinced of this story, that an animal might need to be consecrated and a ceremony performed for his dead grandmother and uncle. How could she be certain? His days of unknowing were inescapable, perennial, always ahead of him. He found he could not breathe and stood up, headed toward the door. Behind him, his mother was speaking. He walked outside, dazed, but alert, somehow, to the cluck of chickens in their coop, to the green and rotten stench of water stagnant in some ditch. Could they be out there still, somewhere? His grandmother and uncle? Was it possible that they had never left him? That they had seen him through his bereft days and his days of ordinary happiness? He was attentive now and saw the dust floating all around, and heard the voices of mothers calling to their precious children, all a part of the same world, and all a part of him. He was alert to the orange light of evening turning darker, there in the distance where the earth met the sky.

The First Virginity
of Gigi Kaisara

❈

She was a beloved girl, so she had accumulated many names. On
her birth certificate: Gagontswe Kaisara, two names that had little to do with her. The first she had been given by her father, a hand-
me-down, after an aunt of his who had never returned from domestic
work in Johannesburg; the second was a family heirloom, belonging
first to her great-grandfather, then to her grandfather, both of whom
had died before she was born, so she didn't even know them as she
lugged their name around. Also, on her birth and PSLE certificates: Penelope—her most despised name, a name given to her by
her mother for no reason other than its elegance and symmetry, its
appearance on the page. Only her teachers and classmates at the
private boarding school she attended in Gaborone used that name.
They chopped it up; they remixed it as they saw fit. *Penlop*, she answered to sometimes, *Penny, Pen, Pen-Pen, P.* To her father, she was
Nono, after some or other adorable thing she had cooed as a toddler,
something her father clung to through the ongoing fissures of their
relationship. Since the divorce, she refused to answer to Nono when
they spoke on the phone, insisting she would be fifteen this year, that

she had outgrown that childish babble, that her father should call her Sadi instead. Sadi was her home name, the name her mother called her, a diminutive she shared with half of the girls in Botalaote Ward, a name heralding the women they would grow into. She supposed it was sufficient, this sign of the immutable and unimaginative love her mother shared with the other mothers of Botalaote Ward.

At eight, she had spent hours with her forefingers stuck in her cheeks, a valiant effort to poke dimples into her face. What a waste those childish hours had been; her fingers were too feeble against the genetic material that had conspired to create her face. But no longer was she a child. She was rising fifteen and in possession of a new determination and a new taste for symbolism, such as: a winter break from school was a prime time for transformation, the bleakness and cloister of the season akin to a hibernation, which was basically what her school break would have been, had her mother not forced her to spend three weeks at the ploughing lands, insensitive to how her only daughter's skin would fare under the deceptive winter sun. Sadi had worked and worked and her skin had darkened and darkened, and now, though she and her mother were returned to Serowe, Sadi had only a week in which to attend to her complexion, and so she washed and exfoliated and brightened, all in an effort to molt and pupate and arrive at school sleek and self-possessed, novel and enigmatic, someone of her own invention.

She had been trying out a new name. *Gigi. Call me Gigi. I am Gigi.* In her notebooks: Gagontswe "Gigi" Kaisara. GG Kaisara. Scribbled in her copy of A *Midsummer Night's Dream*. Her *Tricolore Troisieme*, her *IGCSE Modern World History, 3rd edition*.

Another thing: she had just finished reading Steve Biko. Consequently she sat at her dressing table, a plastic bag open on her lap, full of the hair that she had just scissored off her head.

"I must to the barber's," she chuckled to her new image in the mirror. "I am mighty hairy about the face." She dusted the hair off her cheeks and her neck and her bare shoulders. Her face was big and naked and thrust into the world anew.

HER MOTHER was pissed.

"What did you do, Sadi?" she asked, her fatigue from that morning's shift at Namola Leuba seeming to lift off her.

The basis of her mother's anger, Sadi understood, lay in the money her mother had spent on Sadi's hair all these years. Hundreds. Thousands of pula, probably. On relaxers and conditioning treatments, trims and steams, braids and blowouts, cornrows.

Sadi tilted her head away from the mirror. She knitted her fingers under her chin and smiled sweetly, displaying her new face to her mother.

"Does it suit me?" she asked.

"Does it suit you? You are not supposed to cut your hair yourself, don't you know that? It is taboo."

It's taboo. It's not permitted. You are not supposed to. That is not the way of the Batalaote.

Younger, Sadi had believed every word her mother uttered, the words weighted with the alchemy of spells. Sadi had been terrified to walk with only one shoe on, lest she be swallowed into a clay pot. She had been afraid to push anything away with her foot lest her laziness show up as later-life barrenness. Many a time she had been coerced into public dancing so her mother's crops wouldn't fail. Now she saw that these superstitions were her mother's own talismans, with which she hoped to hold the disarray of the world at bay.

Sadi regarded her mother's face: the constellation of sun moles on its surface, eyebrows knitted together in concern, dark lips parted with their next reproach. A face so known to Sadi that it had been eroded of any and all mysteries.

"Why is it taboo to cut off my own hair?" Sadi asked. What she wanted from her mother was an answer upheld by reason rather than habit, rather than a lingering fear of tempting fate.

Her mother said, "I want you to gather up every single strand of your hair and throw it down the toilet. Every single strand. You hear me? I don't want any people lurking around to take your hair."

It had been three years since Sadi was plucked from her government school for her academic gifts and awarded a bursary to attend a private boarding school in the city. Her mother paid neither the tuition nor the boarding fees nor the small living allowance Penny received monthly. This trajectory of Sadi's life had been so inconceivable that her mother still insisted on a particular kind of vigilance, which included ensuring that no visitor could collect any vestiges of Sadi's body—not her nail cuttings, not her shorn hair, not the print of her feet in the yard.

"Sadi, your hair was so beautiful," her mother said mournfully. "Why did you do this?"

"Mama, have you read this?" Sadi held a book up. "Steve Biko said we are trying to be white women when we relax our hair."

"O-wo-o," her mother scoffed. "And is he going to marry you, that Steve Biko?"

"That's what my hair is for?" Sadi laughed. "To find me a husband? What if I don't want to get married?"

Her mother gave her *the* look. "What did you say?"

"Mama, Mum, Mummy." Sadi walked toward her mother. "Mumsy. Dimamzo."

She cupped her mother's face in her hands, watching the dawning of a smile on the older woman's face.

"I am just playing, Mummy," Sadi said. "I am going to get married and give you as many grandchildren as you want."

Her mother laughed.

"I am going to fill this house with grandchildren," Sadi said, flinging her arms wide. "So many babies. Babies everywhere. We won't know where to put them. We will be crushing them under our feet. There will be babies in that wardrobe, babies in the oven. Babies clinging to the ceiling, babies squirming under this bed. Babies e-very-where."

"Dear God, for whom I do so little," her mother said. "What kind of girl is this?"

"PENNY, what happened?" the other girls in the boardinghouse shrieked, the first week of August, as they all lugged their suitcases up the stairs to move into their rooms. *Gigi*, she thought, *call me Gigi*. But she did not say it out loud. They were not really her friends, these girls. She was not like them. She had not come from their world of exclusive kindergartens with years-long waiting lists. She had not attended the private primary schools the kindergartens had funneled the girls into, which had then funneled them into this private secondary school. The world they belonged to was rarefied and insular: last names recognizable from precolonial kingdoms and from the first class of legislators in 1965. Their parents were cabinet ministers, CEOs, diplomats, judges.

"What happened to you?" the girls asked.

Their attention was rare and Gigi was cornered in its brilliance. Their faces were stricken around her, mourning the loss of her hair more than she was. Gigi's fingers went into what remained of her hair. This was another new feeling, the springy, spongy texture as she patted it.

"I flushed it down the toilet," Sadi told them.

It was into a pit latrine that she had thrown her hair, but she didn't tell the girls that.

"It will grow back," the girls consoled her.

"Yeah," she said, though she didn't miss the rituals of sitting for hours at a time, the pungent, stinging relaxer crème, her legs shaking as her scalp started to sting.

Three weeks into the term, when her allowance had been paid, she took the Broadhurst Route 1 down to the Main Mall. At the table of a street vendor, she bought three pairs of gold-plated hoop earrings. Ten pula a pair. She slipped the earrings on and the vendor held a vanity mirror up to her. Gigi appraised herself honestly. Her face, framed by the earrings, was oval and dark and, regrettably, perpetually shiny. Her sebaceous glands were clearly overactive, releasing at every minute a flood of sebum that broke through layers of talcum powder and coated her face like the bottom of a frying pan. The shininess gave her a frazzled look, never cool and calm and collected. A crop of pimples bloomed on her forehead every few weeks and she mercilessly popped them whenever they ripened. There was nothing at all special about her large brown eyes. Her eyelashes could be longer and curlier. She wished her lips smaller, with a more discernible Cupid's bow. But the real bane of her existence was her nose, which she had inherited from her father's mother and was probably destined to pass to her own daughters one day. She regretted it, looking at herself in the mirror, how much bigger it seemed now that she had shaved her head. She tilted her head back and forth, posing for an invisible camera, finding ways to minimize her boulder of a nose.

"Thank you," she said to the vendor, and the woman put the mirror back onto the table. Gigi paid for six wooden bangles and slipped them onto her wrists immediately. She held her arms up, twisting the stack of bangles farther down.

THE EXTERIOR of the bank she walked by was covered in large panels of reflective blue-green glass, and strolling past toward the combi stop, Gigi gazed at herself, multiplied on the panels. Behind her, on the edge of every panel, a uniformed security guard watched her. The man tossed a black baton from one palm to the other. He was short and big bellied, like a toddler raised on a daily bowl of porridge and milk. In her reflection, she saw the man summon her with his forefinger.

She obeyed him.

The hand he extended to her in greeting was warm and damp with sweat and, too late, she realized what she had walked into.

"Did Uncle need help with something?" Sadi asked, referring to him in the plural.

"You are beautiful." The man smiled at her, still holding on to her hand. "You see, me, I prefer this. Short hair. No makeup. So simple. So clean. Not these Gaborone women who want us to buy them wigs and Revlon and Sheen Strate."

"Uncle," she said, "I am in form three."

"A girl in form three is a woman." He laughed and pumped her hand, and her new wooden bangles clank-clanked together.

"It's better that a real man teaches you before these little boys spoil you," the man said. "Hee, moroba, am I lying?"

His bent middle finger scratched the tender flesh of her palm.

Stupid bitch, Sadi thought bitterly, of herself. She had not yet rid herself completely of her habit of obedience, her ordinary trust in those older than her. She saw that she was defenseless against her lapses in vigilance, caused by all manner of things—such as the pleasures of slipping her bangles down her arms, such as the sight of her face framed by large hoop earrings.

Two middle-aged men in business suits emerged from the interior of the bank, laughing and shaking hands. In a just world, Sadi thought, the men would look toward her and, noticing her discomfort, rush to her rescue.

"Dumelang," she said loudly toward the men, in a way that, she hoped, would convey familiarity. The security guard let go of her hand and she ran off.

IN THE COMMUNAL SHOWERS of the boardinghouse, she ran scalding-hot water down her head and rammed her fingers through her foamy hair. She scoured her palm with a pumice stone. Her scalp throbbed and her body tingled as she dressed. Even after all that, through a supper of shepherd's pie and green salad, through evening study, through walking with her roommate, Ipelo, to the school tuckshop, the feeling of that finger scratching the meat of her palm flared alive at intervals. At lights-out, she lay very still under the covers and listened to Mrs. Brown coming down the corridor, opening doors and trilling, "Good night, girls." Same as every night. The second, truer life of the boardinghouse would begin as soon as Mrs. Brown left, desk lights switched back on so the girls could read their contraband copies of Jackie Collins and Danielle Steel. Some of the form five girls gathered in the upstairs living area at night to watch blue movies; some girls snuck into others' rooms for slivers of emergency gossip.

"Good night, girls," Mrs. Brown said.

"Good night, Mrs. Brown," Penny and Ipelo echoed.

Mrs. Brown switched off the overhead light and closed the door. The dark fell over the room like a shroud and, ensconced in it, Gigi felt the scratch of the man's finger inside her palm. She giggled. She heard the telling noises of her roommate's movements and through the cover of her sheets she saw the glow of Ipelo's desk light.

"What?" Ipelo asked.

Penny's roommate was a thin girl with a narrow, delicate face and almond-shaped eyes that met the world with guileless faith.

"What's funny?" Ipelo asked.

"Nothing," Penny said.

Ipelo switched off the lights.

Returned to the dark, Gigi imagined herself with the man. He would have a hairy torso, kinky little coils sprouting out of his chest. His face, close to hers, would smell warmly of tripe or some other glutinous animal innards.

Baby, oh baby, the man would say. He would invade her ear with the wetness of his tongue. He would enclose her breasts in his thick calloused hands.

Baby, oh baby, he would say. Except. He was old. He wouldn't say that.

He would probably say, *Moroba. Morobanyana wa me. Aah, sweetie! Aah, stirrer of my heart! Aaaaah!*

And she would say, *Oh yeah! Oh yeah! Oh yeah!* She would cradle his belly like a baby and lavish it with caresses.

She laughed out loud and Ipelo switched the light on again.

"Tell me what you are laughing at."

Penny sat up and told the story of her afternoon.

"Can you imagine me with that man?" Penny asked, laughing. "He was so old. Can you imagine his sweat all over me? Covering me? 'Oh yeah, baby, oh yeah, give it to me, yeah.'"

"That's disgusting," Ipelo whispered. She met with the Christian Union every Wednesday night. "That's someone's father."

"You don't know that," Penny said.

"Probably."

"He is the one who said all those things to me."

"Oh my God. Do you want to do that with him?"

"No. What? No."

"I am going to pray for you," Ipelo resolved.

BY MORNING, Gigi had decided that she would fall in love. She chose a boy in her drama class. Although he was in her year—he was in 3K while she was in 3L—she had never before taken a class with him. She had never even seen him at any of the swimming galas, the football matches, the softball games, the athletics days, the V-shows, the Tutti e Solos, the end-of-term discos. She gathered he was a day scholar. He was gangly, with unfairly clear skin and locs just out of that awkward stage. His daily uniform was a pair of black Levi's jeans, a white collared polo shirt, and black Converse All Stars. At the beginning of the term, in their first class together, they had been placed in the same group. Every double period of their drama class, the group sat in a little circle of chairs and brainstormed their mini productions and their sketches. But he never said anything. Whenever they had to choose roles for their sketches, he would choose the smallest possible role. A narrator, for example, who would step onto the stage and pronounce, "Three years later." On this Thursday, the day she had decided that she would fall in love, knowing that love could confer newness upon her, that it could slough from her her origins, which were unmistakably small and rural, an unheroic lineage of farmers and maids and diamond mine laborers, on that day she watched the boy burying his fingers into his hair and twisting methodically, moving from one loc to another. He must find it all stupid, Gigi thought. He must be one of those who had chosen the class because they thought it would be an easy A, a way to avoid Chemistry or Physics or the pedantic geography teacher who was notorious for instructing students to move their chairs exactly 3.52 centimeters away from the wall.

The boy's name was Tabona. Gigi dreamt of getting lost with him in the velvet curtains of the theater, emerging from their thick luxury with knowing eyes and a new deportment. During a break between the two periods of their drama class, she followed him outside to the fountain in the walkway. She watched his locs fall over his forehead as he bent down. She watched his pink tongue dart out to touch the upward trickle of water; in and out, in and out, before closing his lips over the spout. Gigi watched his Adam's apple ripple up and down his throat.

"I am Gigi," she said to him when he raised his head from the fountain.

"Aren't you Penny?" he asked.

"Oh, you know my name?"

"We are in the same group."

"Oh yeah," she said, as though she had only just that moment realized that. "Gigi is my other name. Call me Gigi."

NEITHER GIGI NOR TABONA had club or community service or sports commitments on Wednesday afternoons. They met in Geography 2, so close to the kitchen and dining hall that they could predict what her supper would be. Tabona talked about his uncle, with whom he was living while his parents were setting up a business in Mauritania.

He rhapsodized about the music he was obsessed with, but never the lyrics themselves, always some esoteric component that, he was convinced, finally brought the song together. Such as the timbre of the chuckle that faded a Toni Braxton song out or the adolescent-like break in a singer's voice. Gigi nodded and laughed at everything he said, impatient for the moment he would turn around to kiss her, the fever of his lips on her neck. When he did, weeks after they started hanging out, she dragged her hands into his hair, which was not sticky like she thought it would be but soft and dry, like an old cloth left in the sun too long.

Nights, in her room, she filled her thoughts with him. The weight of his arms, the heat of his skin, and nothing else. Even when she imagined herself on *Oprah*, pressing her hands to her chest as she extolled his virtues.

I worship him, she would say to Oprah.

I knew as soon as I saw him, she would say. *His eyes are my only anchors to this world*, and Oprah would nod knowingly, her eyes brimming with tears.

BY NOVEMBER, Gigi had saved P350 of her allowance. Tabona knew a motel in Mogoditshane that would cost P75 an hour.

Strangely, the board outside read PARADISE BUDGET MOTEL AND GARDENS. Strangely, it was a Chinese man who opened the gate for them, glancing only briefly, without reaction, at Tabona behind the wheel of his uncle's Mercedes. Strangely, there were no gardens, just a couple of widely spaced jacaranda trees in the yard and green netting providing shade in the parking lot, under which Tabona parked the car. The rooms were squat, gray, all connected to each other like train houses in Mogoditshane. Strangely, the woman at reception didn't say anything to them when they paid, but her whole face, her whole demeanor, seemed a knowing wink, and Gigi crossed her arms over her chest. They walked down the corridor to their room in silence, past wide-open windows and gauzy curtains fluttering in the air. Strangely, Tabona's hands seemed to shake as he slotted the key into their room door.

A TV was set up high across from the bed, which was made up in white linens and an orange coverlet. On the round table in the corner was a silver tray that held two glasses, two white mugs, two bottled waters. A gold-framed mirror hung on the wall.

Tabona walked into the bathroom. She heard him in there, his pee loud against the porcelain of the toilet bowl. He has his penis in his hand, she thought suddenly. She took her shoes off and slid her feet up and down the bristly brown carpeting. She lay on the bed and switched the TV on. On the Emmanuel TV channel, a row of congregants keeled over and crumpled onto the floor, kicking and screaming in ecstasy. Emerging from the bathroom, Tabona didn't go to her. He sat on the chair, fussing with the bottled water on the table. Gigi switched the TV off and sat up on the edge of the bed.

"We have to do it on the floor," she said.

"What? Why?"

"These sheets are white."

"So?"

"The towels are white too," she said. "And I am probably going to bleed."

"It doesn't matter," he said. "We paid."

"I can't," she said, thinking of her mother's hands. "I would be too embarrassed."

"The floor. How is that romantic?"

It was true that being inside the sheets might cast her into a romance, a fantasy, a deception. But she had the thought, just then, hearing him say the word, that what she really wanted was clarity. Gigi: clear of mind.

"Don't say romantic," she said. "We made a decision, right? To have sex. Let's just do it."

"If that's what you want," Tabona said.

"It is what I want."

"Fine."

"Fine."

GIGI'S LEGS were open. Her legs were up in the air. Her legs met on the small of Tabona's back. Pain crept from the insides of her thighs, slinked up to her knees. He is inside me, she thought. Pain radiated from her groin, intensifying as Tabona burrowed into her. He is actually inside me. The bristles of the carpet pierced through the coverlet into her back. Her arms lay awkward beside her hips. She lifted them and looked at her hands above the curve of Tabona's body. Cutting clear through the fog of pain was a pitiful canine yelping, emanating from Tabona's throat. It struck her as hysterical, as did the sweaty grimace of his face, his locs limp and stuck onto his forehead. She pressed her lips together to stop from laughing. Her eyes traveled to the window: the sluggish movements of the curtains. She listened with intention and this is what she heard: the overhead fan whirring torturously, as if it too were in pain; the receding slap-slap of the caretaker's flip-flops as she walked past the rooms; the breathless, harried fragment of a song the caretaker was singing, *Halleeeelujah, halleeee, halleeelujah*; the angry honking of cars out in the streets; the tired calling out of wares by vendors. She listened hard for other secrets of the world.

In another hour, she thought, she would walk out of the room a knowing woman. She would wait outside for Tabona to return the room key to the other knowing woman at the reception. She would climb into Tabona's uncle's Mercedes and Tabona would drop her off outside the boardinghouse and she would carry her knowing up the stairs to her room.

Tabona grunted and she rubbed her hands in his hair. She lowered his head, his lips down onto hers. His tongue pushed into her mouth. She moved her butt up, down, up, down, up, down. His humping grew frenzied, his yelping unintelligible.

"Oh yeah," she said, "oh yeah, oh yeah, oh yeah."

Tabona let loose an incomprehensible sound. At its culmination, he collapsed on top of her, breathing heavily. After, he retreated into the bathroom.

Gigi gathered the orange coverlet around her and stood in front of the mirror. She studied her face, its thin film of sweat, her lips parted in a slight smile. She studied her eyes. Later, just four years into the future, going by Sadi, broke and freshly dropped out of architecture school, she spent a winter living in the luxurious house of a man twenty years older than her. Nightly, she pretended she had never before had sex, whimpering I am scared or I am not ready whenever he approached. Nightly, she laughed to herself when she saw his growing reverence for her virtue. And even much later, older and more susceptible to her mother's superstitions, she went for years without sex, wanting to believe that her abstinence would exert some magic onto her life, turn it back on track. For her wedding, she chose white lace and believed fully in the purity it announced about her, her new body deserving its transcendence each time.

In room 5 of the Paradise Budget Motel and Gardens, she let the orange coverlet fall at her feet like a soundless waterfall. She swiveled back and forth, searching for the muscles that had ached just minutes prior. Her body was still her body: the same sly stretch marks on her hips, same 32AA breasts, same triangle of pubic hair, same birthmark on the inside of her right thigh. Tabona came to stand behind her. His hands were self-assured now, cocky as he cupped her breasts and kissed her neck.

"You are not going to tell anyone," she said.

"Why would you think that?"

"I am just saying," she said.

"I won't say anything," he said. "You are okay, right?"

"I am fine," she said with some impatience. "I am fine. I feel just fine."

ACKNOWLEDGMENTS

This book exists because of the generosity and support of many, to whom I owe endless gratitude. Thank you to my friends at Petlo Literary Arts—Barolong Seboni, Cheryl Ntumy, Sharon Tshipa—and to other Botswana writer friends—Wame Molefhe, Lauri Kubuitsile, Priscillar Matara—for your persistence and faith and devotion to Botswana literature. Thank you, too, to Drs. Leloba Molema and Mary Lederer for their early look at some of the work. I would like to thank my professors at the University of Mississippi—Tommy Franklin, Mary Miller, Kiese Laymon, Melissa Ginsberg, and Matt Bondurant—for everything you taught me. To my cohort—Matt Kessler, Ashley Mullins, and Sam Milligan—and dear MFA friends, particularly Elsa Nekola, Peter Wong, Amy Lam, and Maggie Woodward—your generosity and friendship were the best balms to my culture shock; because of you I will always recall life in Oxford, Mississippi, with fondness. Thank you to Adam Johnson, Elizabeth Tallent, and Chang-rae Lee at the Stegner Workshop for your incisive teachings and incredible stories. Many thanks to my brilliant (and sweet) cohort: Jamel Brinkley, Neha Chaudhary-Kamdar, Devyn Defoe, Sterling HolyWhiteMountain, and the rest of the Stegner Fellows for their generous readings. Eternal gratitude to Monica Sok, Ose Jackson, and Lydia Conklin for your kindness and your friendship. Thank you to the Kessler and Woodward families for all the Thanksgivings and Christmases. Many thanks to Ann Bradley and Virdell Hickman for your hospitality and many kindnesses. I am grateful for the generosity and community of The Ruby in San Francisco. Thank you to FEMRITE for my very first writer's residency in Kampala, and to Tin House, whose summer workshop allowed me the opportunity to work with the incredible Garth Greenwell. I have had the fortune to work with many incredible editors. Brigid Hughes and Megan Cummins at *A Public Space*, and Leslie Jamison, thank you for your tireless support and guidance; Eliza Borne at *Oxford American*; Rebecca Markovits at *American Short Fiction*; Karen Friedman and Patrick Ryan at *One Story*; Paul Reyes at *Virginia Quarterly Review*; Jamel Brinkley on behalf of *Ploughshares*: thank you all for taking a chance on my work. Thank you to my incredible editor at Viking, Laura Tisdel, and Jenn Houghton, for your tirelessness and your cheers. Furthermore, thank you to the entire team at Viking for your hard work and your support. I hope to meet you all one day to express my gratitude in person. I would not be writing these acknowledgments without the brilliance of my incredible agent, Julie Barer, and the hard work by Nicole Cunningham at The Book Group. Special thanks to my mother, Teko Botshameko Moeng, and my aunt, Bakgobi Ketwesepe, for your willingness to answer any random questions about how things used to be. Grateful, too, for the following authors and their books, whose work was informative in my understanding of certain customs and traditions: Gabriel M. Setiloane (*The Image of God Among the Sotho-Tswana*), Kgomotso Mogapi (*Ngwao ya Setswana*), and James Denbow and

ACKNOWLEDGMENTS

Phenyo C. Thebe (*Culture and Customs of Botswana*), as well as Jeff Ramsay and Fred Morton for their work.

Last, but not least, I owe a world of gratitude to my entire Moeng family, including friends who have become family, for the stories and the laughter, and for the patient support even when you did not fully understand what I was doing. Le kamoso, betsho.